The Murder Mystery

of

Mattie McDuffie

by

Jessica D. Reddick

Saved By Story

The Murder Mystery of Mattie McDuffie

Published by

Saved By Story Publishing, LLC
Prescott, AZ
www.SavedByStory.house

Copyright © 2024 by Jessica D. Reddick

Cover by Alyssa Noelle Coelho
Interior Design by Dawn Teagarden
Photo/Illustrations by Praneeth Madushanka

All rights reserved. No part of this book may be reproduced or transmitted in any form or by any means, electronic or mechanical, including photocopying, recording, or by an information storage and retrieval system without written permission of the publisher, except for the inclusions of brief quotations in review.

Disclaimer: The Publisher and the Author does not guarantee that anyone following the techniques, suggestions, tips, ideas or strategies will become successful. The advice and strategies contained herein may not be suitable for every situation. The Publisher and Author shall have neither liability nor responsibility to anyone with respect to any loss or damage caused, or alleged to be caused, directly or indirectly by the information in this book. Written permission has been obtained to share the identity of each real individual named in this book.

Any citations or a potential source of information from other organizations or websites given herein does not mean that the Author or Publisher endorses the information/content the website or organization provides or recommendations it may make. It is the readers' responsibility to do their own due diligence when researching information. Also, websites listed or referenced herein may have changed or disappeared from the time that this work was created and the time that it is read.

ISBN: Paperback: 978-1-961336-11-7

eBook: 978-1-961336-12-4

Printed in the United States of America

www.SavedByStory.house

"What truly touched my heart was witnessing the growth of the two main characters as the narrative enfolds. Their friendship, with all their delightful quirks, and the way they navigated the complexities of their reality breathes life into the story. This book transcends a mere mystery; it delves into the essence of family, friendship, and community. It is a meaningful read that will resonate with countless readers for years to come, reminding us all of the enduring power of connection and understanding."

Kathy Turner,
Retired, Avid Reader

"This novel offers a fresh historical, non-stereotypical view of middle class black families in the 1960's rarely seen in American literature. Well-developed characters face off with uncertainty and danger with their own unique gifts, and the suspense and surprises make it a page-turner that will engage all ages."

Ron Mulvihill, 66 Irish American, Filmmaker

"As an instructor in an inner-city school, I think this book would be of great benefit to middle school and high school students looking for a good mystery that explores many aspects of their own culture. The story remains rooted in its setting of the 1960s while still being intriguing and accessible to modern-day youth. It's engaging and so relatable to minority students, specifically their struggles and cultural differences."

Raymond Siaca Bey, Student, VSU Education Program
Teaching Assistant in English,
Richmond City Public Schools

"This book begins at a leisurely pace but quickly accelerates. The way the author brings the scenes to life really pulls you in. I especially liked the intense moments between family members; they felt so real and relatable. The ability to shift between 1963 to a moment in the past added a rich layer to the story. Jesika and Marina's bond stood out to me; their trust in each other as they chased the clues to solve the case was something I could easily appreciate. It's a complex journey that takes you deep into their world."

Jeannetta Y. Agorom, Singer/Songwriter

For Marina

Contents

Mattie

What happened here?

Mattie noticed something large strewn across the log where she and Jack had shared so many special moments— where he had just told her he loved her and kissed her more passionately than ever—before she was distracted.

It doesn't matter. I have to get back and finish that essay.

As she made her way back to the dismal trailer park, she thought about the persuasive writing project her history teacher had assigned and how hard it had been to deal with the other kids' childish reactions to the topic of civil rights.

Ugh, why don't I just speak up when they spew their cruel, racist jokes? The whole lesson is to stop judging people based on the color of their skin. And I just sit there! No more! I'm gonna speak my truth in this essay, and try to persuade those idiots for the last time.

She silently counted the months until she would be free of all of the immaturity and insanity, and start her own life.

At least I have Bethany. Oh! I should call her and tell her what happened with Jack tonight. She won't believe me.

As she approached the dirty trailer she called home, the familiar cacophony of her mother's angry screams and step-father's raging bellows slowed her.

I can't wait to get out of here!

At sixteen, she was a senior brimming with the dreams of college and adventure—and getting away from these awful humans. The chaos of her life seemed to unravel more every day like a tapestry of betrayal that had woven her existence, and it took all of her energy to hold onto the hope that she would be able to create something better for herself.

Knowing they could be at it for hours, she took a long deep breath and prepared to scurry to her room, hopefully unnoticed.

But when her hand reached the doorknob, she realized something was terribly wrong. In the dark of the night, she tried again.

What in the…?

Holding her hand up to the moonlight, she gasped.

Am I…?

Suddenly, a series of images and sounds flooded her memory, ending with the image of the object strewn across her favorite log and answering the question affirmatively.

Oh no! I have to find a way to tell someone what happened!

CHAPTER 1

The Year Everything Changed

*I*t all started a few months earlier in 1963 when my parents decided our family should leave Chicago and start a new life in sunny California. I was a straight A student, and leaving early wouldn't affect my grades at all, so I said goodbye to all my friends at Saint Thomas the Apostle Grade School and Sister Mary Louise and we hit the road.

My parents and I traveled by car on a five-day trip to San Diego, California, and at some point, I noticed that my father had a copy of the Negro Motorist Green Book.

"What's that?" I asked.

"A Negro mailman in New York City named Victor Hugo Green published this in 1936 to help Negro travelers avoid discrimination. It lists the businesses that Black people can safely patronize. If we needed a place to stay, a repair shop, a gas station, or a restaurant, it's in that book." With a subtle cue from my mother, Dad changed the subject. "You are going to love San Diego, Marina!"

He smiled at me in the rearview mirror and winked, and they both went on to talk about California's crystal blue beaches and the world-famous San Diego Zoo. "What do you think about that?"

"I can't wait to go, Dad!"

My mother talked about how she missed her mother and brother and couldn't wait to see them.

My parents didn't hold much back from me, but sometimes I wished they did. I suppose it made me smarter than an average child my age. I was always curious, drawn to the mysterious, and pumped with the desire to solve any type of mystery. Being the youngest of three and the only child in the car also meant that my parents included me in some of their conversations, as if I were an adult. We talked about the things that were happening in the world and about the difficulties that we faced as Black people. It was hard for me to imagine that some people would hate us for the color of our skin, but it was our reality.

My name is Marina Joy Massey. In case you're wondering, my mother named me Joy, because she said I was her bundle of joy.

CHAPTER 2

First Stop, Grandmother's House

When we arrived, I discovered my mother looked like a younger version of my grandmother, a slender dark-skinned woman who hugged me so tight I thought I would break and then quickly invited us in. As my eyes adjusted in the hallway of my grandmother's home, I discovered a lot of pictures of the family. My Uncle Lonny was skinny when he was little. I could see my mother's face in her father's. I was happy to find my grandmother both beautiful and funny and her old house smelling of greens, black-eyed peas, and cornbread.

"Child, don't ever stay away that long again. You know I love your letters, but you could have picked up the phone more often." It sounded funny hearing my mother being called a child.

"Oh, Mother, between the bills and my internship, we didn't have any extra money," Mother explained. Grandmother responded with a hug, and told us not to pay her no never mind.

As I watched them hug, I thought about the little I knew about my grandmother. She had moved to California several years before I was born. She'd married my grandfather young, but didn't know she was pregnant with my mother at the time. She'd always said it was lucky for the two of them that they loved each other so much that they couldn't wait to be married, that "God looks out for babies and fools, so He looked out for the two of us and our little bun in the oven too." Her father would probably have killed him if he'd known she was pregnant, but her mother didn't care because he came from a good family.

Because they had gotten married, her father allowed them to stay in the house. My grandmother had worked as a maid, and my grandfather had worked on a horse farm, and then they inherited her parents' farm when they passed away. Eventually, they sold the farm and moved the family to California, where she always wanted to live. My grandmother said all she ever dreamed about was moving to California. She was convinced that the woes of Black people could be washed away just by looking at the Pacific Ocean. With her modest savings, Grandmother helped my mother get through medical school and my Uncle Lonny through the academy because all he'd ever wanted to be was a police officer.

Grandmother grabbed my hand and softly asked if I wanted to stay in my mother's old room.

"Oh, yes," I happily replied.

I marveled as I walked into my mom's old room, full of her memories. From dolls to a high school yearbook, every item in her room held a story that I wished I knew. On the wall, there was a picture of a fat girl, about eight years old, that looked like it could be Mother, but I wasn't sure. Mom had lots of pictures of herself and her best friend, Nancy, who became a lawyer and lived in Los Angeles. I even saw pictures of my mother with old boyfriends, who looked funny. None were as good-looking as my dad.

I was washing up for dinner when I heard the doorbell and my mother yell, "It must be them!"

I nearly ran into my grandmother and the rest of my family at the front door. My mother's brother Lonny, his wife, and two children stood together smiling.

My mother threw her arms around Uncle Lonny's neck and hugged him, almost knocking him over.

"You missed me that much, Sis?" Uncle Lonny chuckled.

My mother merely grinned as she embraced his wife, Selma, and kissed her on the cheek. "It's so good to see you! This is my daughter, Marina." Mother put her hand on my shoulder and looked down at me with a proud grin. I couldn't stop smiling either. Seeing Mother so happy and being with family made me feel all warm inside.

"She looks just like you," Selma replied as she hugged and kissed Grandmother.

"Russell will be down in a second," Mother said as we all headed toward the dining room. "These are your cousins, Marina—Elisabeth and Brandon." Mother nodded her head in the direction of my cousins and beamed at the three of us.

"Hi," I said.

"Hi." Elisabeth smiled shyly at me.

"Sit next to me, Elisabeth." I eagerly patted the seat next to mine.

"Okay, Cousin." Elisabeth happily settled in next to me.

Other than a softly spoken hello, her brother Brandon remained quiet, except for asking when my brothers were coming home from military school. Mother answered that they would be home for summer break. The truth was that they were already here in California, but they had stopped visiting Grandmother because she never had anything good to say about our real father.

When the wonderful man I call Dad joined us, Grandma blessed the table. It wasn't your usual blessing. "I was on my knees praying to Our Lord." She looked around the table at each of us. "He told me that all of you would be sitting at my dinner table." Her eyes were gleaming with happiness as she concluded, "Thank you, Jesus, for bringing my family home safely."

The room resounded in an enthusiastic "Amen."

I wasn't hungry, but I didn't want to offend my grandmother by not eating all the food that she put on my plate. I looked at Elisabeth and whispered, "There's too much food on my plate."

"Yeah, Grandma likes to feed you until you explode," she whispered back, and we lowered our heads together giggling.

As a doctor, my mother didn't believe that we had to clean our plates and never put a lot of food on them to begin with. We could always ask for more.

"Lawd, child, what's wrong?" Grandmother chuckled while glancing down at my plate knowingly. "You don't have to eat all that food, baby. Your mama was a roly-poly when she was a little girl. I was always taking out her britches."

"You mean that fat girl in the picture was you, Mama?"

"Yes, that was me. We had to clean our plates, and so did my friends. We were certainly not allowed to waste our food; isn't that right, Lonny?"

Uncle Lonny nodded his head keenly with a mouth full of food.

My father wiped his mouth with a napkin and gave me a smile and wink as he pushed his plate away with a nice helping of food still on it.

"Dad, you aren't worried about those kids in Africa?" I asked.

"Nope, not today," he answered. "Just like my daughter, I'm more concerned about that peach cobbler that smells so delicious." He gave me a knowing smile, as if he could read the thoughts right out of my head, and I just laughed because he was right.

We sat at the dining room table that night and listened intently as my grandmother told stories about her children when they were young. I was especially amused when she talked about my mom's old friends.

We laughed so hard that evening, I hardly ate any of my food.

CHAPTER 3

Grandmother's Tree

I stayed at my grandmother's house for two days, helping her in the garden while my parents took care of all the moving in. Grandmother introduced me to her tree in the backyard that towered over her house. It was large, and its branches were majestic and its leaves a lush green. Its bark was like armor, so I scraped my knee trying to climb it with no success. That tree was a sculpture, a work of art, and I fell in love with it. Grandmother said that the tree was older than her, and it would be there long after she was gone if it didn't get cut down.

I hugged it and talked to it like it had its own voice and enjoyed the tire swing that I swung on way after dark. I spent so much time in that tree that Grandmother would yell out of the backdoor for me to come inside. "Child, come on into this house. That tree has had enough of your company!"

One night while swinging on that tree, I realized I didn't miss Chicago at all, especially the cold and the strict babysitter who never let me do one single thing. But I did love my mornings with my dad when Mom was doing her internship.

Every morning, he made pancakes, eggs, and bacon for me and said, "We sure do miss Mommy, don't we?"

I would nod my head with a mouth full of pancakes, "Yes, we do!"

We hardly ever saw my mother back then, but my father never complained. I could see how proud of her he was. She would fall asleep on the couch sometimes with a textbook in her hand, and he would say, "You want to tuck Mommy in?" I'd take the book out of her hands and put the blanket over her.

CHAPTER 4

Bollenbacher Street

The next morning, my parents came to pick me up, and I hugged my grandmother goodbye and told her I would see her soon.

On the way to our new home, I was full of questions. "What's the name of our new street?"

"Bollenbacher," my dad said.

"Bollenbacher Street," I repeated. "Are there a lot of kids?"

"Yes," my mother answered. "Our new neighborhood is called Emerald Hills."

"I like the sound of that, Emerald Hills," I whispered dreamily as I looked out of the window from the backseat of the car. Emerald Hills sounded like a magical place, as my mind conjured images from The Emerald City in *The Wizard of Oz*. Perhaps I would find an adventure of my own in Emerald Hills.

The sun was shining so brightly, the sky seemed bluer, and every inch of our new house was a perfect vision of a dream come true when we pulled up. When we finally parked in our new driveway, I jumped out of the car and ran to the sidewalk to look up and down my new block. I was impressed with our new neighborhood.

"Dad, can I walk down the street?"

"Sure, honey, go and explore, but stay on our block."

The lawns were perfect squares of evergreen grass meticulously cut and tended, and every house was a pastel shade of the rainbow. There were hardly any cars in the driveway, and I figured some of the parents were at work. I could tell that the people in this neighborhood took extra pride in their homes. Maybe that was the reason it had a name like Emerald Hills. As I looked around, I decided this was even better than the Emerald City in the Wizard of Oz and that I was the happiest girl in all of California.

As I walked further down the street, I could smell the scent of bacon and eggs floating on the breeze. I stopped for a minute and wondered if they were having grits too. My stomach started to growl, and I headed back to my new home. "What a big house!" I shouted as I walked up the driveway and immediately compared it to our old apartment in Chicago.

"Wait until you see the inside," Mom said, folding her arms proudly across her chest and leaning toward me, her eyes wide. "It has three bedrooms and two bathrooms."

"Marina, let's go look at your room." My mother smiled at me with a gleam in her eye when we walked into the house. I followed her into my bedroom and saw how beautiful it was. I was delighted. My room had white curtains with beautiful, colorful butterflies on them. My bed was French Provincial, white and gold, with a matching dresser and end table. The best part of my new room was a picture of two Black children with a Black guardian angel standing over them. I stared at that picture on the wall for a long time. I had always seen it depicted with White people, never with Black people, and asked my mother where she had gotten it. She told me her friend drew it for her.

"Mom, this is the prettiest room in the whole house. I love it!"

I jumped on my bed and put my hands behind my head with a smile on my face that was the size of Texas.

"Nothing but the best for you, pumpkin," she replied. She always called me pumpkin when she was spoiling me. The rest of our home was actually decorated just as beautifully as my room, as my parents took great care and pride in making our home look nice.

Even though I loved our new place, I missed my grandmother, the tree, and her garden, so I dialed her number and she answered on the second ring.

"Hello." I was so glad to hear a warm voice answer.

"It's me, Grandmother. How are you doing?"

"Just fine, baby."

"How's the tree?" I asked.

"The tree is still standing." She laughed.

"Can you come over for dinner? I want you to see my new room."

"I'm sorry, baby, I've got a doctor's appointment. But you can tell me about your room right now." Her tone was sweet and comforting.

As I began to describe my room, my grandmother cut me off. "It sounds really nice, sugar. Tell your father to come over and pick me up next Saturday around 4:30 p.m."

"Okay, Grandmother, I'll see you then." On the way outside, I yelled, "Grandmother wants Dad to pick her up at 4:30 on Saturday!"

"Okay, Marina!" my father yelled back, smiling mischievously.

CHAPTER 5

Dinner with Grandmother

Turns out my father and mother had already invited her over for dinner that night as a surprise for me.

I giggled when she laid in my bed with her hands behind her head just like I did when I first saw it.

"I think I'll stay in this room when I spend the night. It is lovely," she agreed.

Over dinner, my grandmother talked about how proud she was of her children and grandchildren. She kissed my mother on her forehead, and exclaimed, "Ava, you're a doctor—a doctor!"

Grandmother had a way with words and could tell you a story in a way that made you feel like you were right there watching it all happen. I filled my ears and thoughts with everything she shared with us as she told us how hard it was in her day and how hard White folks made it for Black people. She called Martin Luther King our champion as he carried the spirit of our ancestors on his back.

"Martin has got White and Black people marching in the street together," she said. "He's the bravest man in the world, and he will lay down his own life for us, and so will others. Mark my words!" She declared this with such fierce certainty that it gave me the chills!

"Oh, Mama, we don't know that for sure," my mother offered with a cautionary tone.

"I know," Grandmother agreed, raising an eyebrow at Mother, while slowly nodding her head. "But it's a new day, baby." She looked at me and smiled. "My great-grandchildren will have it better than my children because God will make it so." I looked into Grandmother's eyes and saw two deep brown pools of emotions and a lifetime of wisdom and something else that made me pause. Although she was joyful, there was also a sadness in her eyes. A sadness that I would sometimes see in my mother's and father's eyes. Grandmother had been born January 1, 1901, thirty-six years after slavery was officially abolished in 1865. She had seen a lot of progressive changes for Negroes in her lifetime, but she had also seen a lot of cruelty against them too.

CHAPTER 6

Our Catholic President

The next day, my grandmother called the house to tell me that she wanted to go see President John Fitzgerald Kennedy in person on June 6th. Grandmother was brimming with excitement about our new Catholic president.

"Marina," she went on passionately, "I want to be standing on 54th and El Cajon when he passes by in his motorcade!"

"Can I go with you?" I asked, imagining how much fun it would be to travel with Grandmother and see our beloved president in person.

"If it's okay with your parents, you sure can. I'm going to take the bus if your parents can't take off from work. Come rain or shine, I am going to see Kennedy that day!"

Luckily for me, not only did I go, but Dad drove us there. It was a proud day for Grandmother, my father, and me.

CHAPTER 7

A New Friend

It was only three days later that I met my Jesika. I was in the front yard of my house, watching a busy family of ants harvesting food with my magnifying glass, when I noticed this girl standing on her small front porch and staring at me. She had on a plaid green uniform with a white shirt and black and white patent leather oxfords, and I quickly identified it as a Catholic uniform.

As I looked closer, I noticed she had something hanging out of her nose. I couldn't make out what it was, so my curiosity propelled me across the street.

"Hi." I offered a friendly wave. "What's that in your nose?"

"It's my Vicks inhaler," she replied, switching the inhaler to her other nostril. "I can't stand my nose being stopped up, and it seems like I always got a cold." She shrugged her shoulders and sniffed. "It's so I can breathe at night." She sighed and smiled at me. "My name is Jesika Denise Beckford. What's yours?"

"Marina Joy Massey. We moved from Chicago."

"I saw the moving truck when your family was moving in, but I didn't see you," Jesika said.

"I've been over to my grandma's house. What Catholic School do you go to?" I asked, pointing to her uniform.

"St. Rita's," she replied. "How old are you?"

"I'm twelve," I answered. "How old are you?"

"I'm twelve. I'll be thirteen in October. I had nephritis, it's a kidney disease. I was in the hospital for half a year, so I had to repeat the first grade," she explained.

"Oh, that stinks." I nodded sympathetically. I didn't want her to feel bad, but I couldn't resist the sudden urge to pull that Vicks inhaler out of her nose. I reached right over and plucked it out of her nostril.

"Hey! What did you do that for?" she exclaimed.

"It was bugging me. You look silly with that thing hanging out your nose!" I chuckled, handing it over to her.

"I suppose I do, but it helps me breathe." She reinserted the inhaler into her nose with a frown.

"Can you come over and play with Barbies?" I offered, hoping that she wanted to play.

"Nope, I would rather ride my bike."

"I can get my bike out of the garage," I compromised.

As Jesika and I rode around the neighborhood, she introduced me to most of the kids. I met Douglas, Vicky, Marie, Irene and all her siblings, Diane, and Sherry, and Bobbie, who lived right next to me. For some odd reason, she wanted me to meet this girl named Deidra Bladelock. We laid our bikes down in her driveway and walked up to the front door.

Jesika knocked on the door, and a girl in a T-shirt and blue shorts opened it. She had lots of freckles and looked like she was about three years older.

"Who is it?" she asked as a look of irritation crossed her face.

Jesika started, "Hi, Deidra, this is my new friend, Marina. She just moved up the street."

The girl looked at me, paused, and said, "Who gives a rat's ass!" Then she slammed the door in our faces. I knew then and there that Deidra and I weren't going to be friends.

We were walking our bikes up the block and around the corner when we came to a white house with black shutters. Jesika pointed at it and said, "There's a kid named Gerald who lives there." Her face became grave. "You'll want to stay away from him."

At that very moment, Gerald came out of the house and walked onto his driveway while staring us down.

"Hey, ugly!" he shouted at Jesika.

"Your mama!" she shouted back and jumped back onto her bike. "Marina, it's time to get out of Dodge!" she exclaimed anxiously over her shoulder.

CHAPTER 8

The Kraut

Startled by the panic I heard in her voice, I quickly jumped on my bike and followed her lead, and we took off pedaling away from Gerald's house. Just as we were turning the corner, I felt something hard graze the top of my head. I looked back just in time to see Gerald picking up another rock to throw at us.

"Faster, Jesika, faster!" I pedaled as fast as I could around the corner.

When we got back in front of Jesika's house, I jumped off my bike and put my kickstand down.

"Are you crazy, Jesika?" I was bent over trying to catch my breath.

"No, we were on our bikes. He can't catch us on our bikes." She laughed, her face flushed from our fast getaway. Jesika pointed her finger at the beige and brown house near hers. "See that house next to mine?" She squinted her eyes in the direction.

"Yes," I replied. "What about it?"

"Germans live there," Jesika whispered darkly and then suddenly exclaimed, "Krauts! You know, Nazis!"

I looked at the house and imagined a bunch of men wearing stiff green uniforms, loading their guns in preparation to kill all their Black neighbors. My eyes widened in horror as Jesika shared that her father almost got into a fight with the German man who lived in the house next door when he called her mother a nigger.

"My mom always watered the grass in her bare feet, and one day, she decided to water a brown patch of grass in *his* yard to improve its appearance. Nice, right?" I nodded in agreement. "Well, he pulled up in his driveway and told her to keep her nigger feet off his grass." Jesika shook her head. "My father was in the garage and overheard that nonsense and came running out of the garage, yelling, 'What the hell did you call my wife?' The German man repeated what he had called her several times. It infuriated my father to the point of rage!" Jesika shook her head again woefully. "He was like a rabbit dog," she said, gritting her teeth and growling for effect.

I started to laugh, realizing she meant a dog with rabies.

"Good thing my mom stopped the whole ordeal and cradled my father's face in her hands. She said, 'Calm down, Wade. It's not worth it. Let's go back into the house.' My mom has a voice that could soothe a savage beast. If it wasn't for her, he would have killed that old man."

My last few years in Chicago, I'd noticed that when Black people moved into the neighborhood, the White people moved out, so I found the German man and his wife mysterious, and I would often watch their house with my binoculars from Sherrie and Bonnie McCarthy's front porch. I thought maybe he was in Hitler's Army. He was certainly old enough. But they kept to themselves and went to work every day just like my parents did. I wanted to find out their last name. Since he didn't like Black people, perhaps he spoke with somebody White in the neighborhood.

One day, I mentioned a bit of information to Jesika to see if it would spark an idea, "My father told me that Bollenbacher was a German name derived from the German province of Bollenbach. He said that it even had a coat of arms."

Jesika just gazed beyond me. She would do that quite often. Jesika would be talking to me good-naturedly and then suddenly just looked away into an invisible abyss, her eyes glazing over as though certain thoughts took her halfway to another place while the other half sat there talking with me. Her expression went completely blank for a moment before she softly answered, "Hitler tortured the Jews and put them in death camps. He was a horrible man."

"How do you know this?" I wondered.

"I watch *Combat* after school." She slid her inhaler back into her nose as she spoke. "You know, the one starring Vic Morrow. He's Sergeant Saunders, and Rick Jason is Lt. Hanley." She saluted me and I saluted her back and we laughed at how silly we looked.

She continued, "If the Germans had won the war we would have been all walking around going, '*Sieg heil! Sieg heil!*'"

"Yes, I know, he wanted to take over the world," I responded.

She got off of her bike and started marching with her hand extended in the air like a German soldier.

Then she marched straight up to my face and shouted, "Sieg heil, mein führer!"

I shook my head, laughing at her dramatic impression.

Jesika stopped mid-march suddenly. "Do you want to ride to the end of the block with me?"

"No, all of this riding around is making me tired." I was also worried that there were more crazy kids that she wanted to introduce me to.

"But I forgot to show you my canyon," she pleaded and pushed her lower lip out.

"Oh, okay." Relieved that it would be just the two of us, I was glad for her company even if it meant riding around some more on our bikes.

CHAPTER 9

Jesika's Canyon

Once we were on our bikes, Jesika started peddling so fast, I could barely keep up with her.

"Look at it, Marina. Doesn't it look wonderful?"

We stopped our bikes at the metal barrier leading into the canyon.

"Yes, it's beautiful," I replied. I gazed out at the grassy canyon with its mysterious dips and ditches. I knew it had to be filled with a plethora of wildlife, and it felt like a great place for adventure. "We have woods in Chicago, but I don't remember ever going in them. I've seen lots of deer, though." I said.

"It's got cactus, jackrabbits, lizards, poisonous rattlesnakes and tarantulas." Jesika's gaze met mine. "Some of the older kids like to kill tarantulas. When I see them dead, I bury them." She looked down at her shoes sadly.

"How do you know that rattlesnakes are poisonous?" I inquired.

She turned to face me with a serious look on her face. "My father warned me about rattlesnakes. If you get bitten, you better get to the hospital quickly or you're a goner. The first time I saw a tarantula, it scared the crap out of me. When I walk to school, the canyon seems to make a lot of noise, and I'm constantly looking behind me!" She was quiet for a bit and then added, shaking her head warily, "My dad never told me what to do if I ran into a rattlesnake. A kid at school told me to just stand still."

Listening to Jesika talk about how her dad told her about rattlesnakes made me think about how my parents were always teaching me things too.

"You know, my parents taught me how to read at the age of three. Instead of telling me fairy tales, they told me stories about slavery and what contributions Black people have made in America, and the history of World War One and Two. They told me recently that America might enter another war called Vietnam, and they also made me read articles out of the newspaper. I hate that," I moaned with a frown.

"That sounds like homework. It must be boring." Jesika looked at me sideways, then shook her head at me.

I chuckled softly at her dramatic response. You would think I'd just told her I was being tied to a chair and forced to read dictionaries from the look on her face.

"Well, I do love to read. I just don't get to watch that much TV," I admitted, smiling. I didn't like being the object of anyone's pity, and from the expression on Jesika's face, mine was the most pitiful existence of mankind.

"Yeah, my father calls it the idiot box." Jesika sighed. "Sometimes he punishes us by not letting us watch it. What a drag! I *really* like watching TV. It's my favorite pastime. I think life would be boring without television or music."

We were still facing the canyon and the wind blew loose strands of her pony tail towards her pretty face.

"Do you want to see the hill we climb up before and after school?" Jesika asked.

"No, I don't want to get bitten by a rattler or a tarantula," I said nervously.

"Don't worry, we'll stay on the trails." She smiled reassuringly.

"Okay," I reluctantly agreed and we entered her canyon and rode to the top of the hill. "What's the street down at the bottom of the hill?" I wondered out loud.

"Oh, that's Market Street. We'll have to cross it."

When we stopped, I marveled at the landscape and scenery. "Do you do this Monday through Friday?"

"Don't forget Sunday," she added, smiling smugly. "Let's go to my house and watch Johnny Downs."

"Okay!" I wondered who Johnny Downs was but did not want to let Jesika know just how little television I watched. My curiosity always got the final say in these sorts of things, so my pride never stood a chance. "Who's Johnny Downs?" I queried.

Jesika's response was less rueful. "You don't know who Johnny Downs is? He shows cartoons like Gigantor and Popeye, but my favorite segment is the Magic Key." She looked at me with an expression close to disappointment. "It's hard to believe that you don't know pogo-stick-on-top-of-a-milk-bottle Johnny Downs! What planet have you been living on? Mars?"

When she pulled her inhaler out of her nose and put the cap on it, I decided I really liked Jesika.

We went into her house, and when we entered the den, her brother Jayden and her sister Sariah were already sitting on the couch. I was about to sit down when her sister Sariah told me to sit on the floor because there wasn't enough room, even though there would have been plenty if she wasn't all stretched out on the couch.

"Take your feet off the couch," Jesika yelled at Sariah.

"No, you and your friend can sit on the floor!" Her round face scrunched into a mean scowl. Sariah had dusty, reddish-brown, straight hair. She was short, cute and chubby. Unfortunately, she was also a bully.

When Jesika told Sariah to shut up and move, Sariah balled her fist up and put it in Jesika's face threateningly. So, we both ended up on the floor. Neither Jesika nor I had any intentions of dethroning her from the couch.

Her three-year-old brother, Jayden, was sweet and soft-spoken, and cradling one of their baby dolls.

"He likes dolls, and he likes cars," Jesika explained. "He draws these highways in the dirt outside. Want to see?"

The Magic Show wouldn't start for another hour, so she took me to see Jayden's roadways in the backyard.

"Wow! He could probably draw maps!" I was impressed with the intricate little roads that her three-year-old brother had created.

"Yes, my mother thinks he's a genius." She nodded proudly as we looked at Jayden's little road city.

"Does your sister do anything special?" I wondered.

"Nope, but she could be a boxer." Jesika pursed her lips sarcastically, and we both laughed.

"Why is she such a bully?" I kept my voice low. Lord forbid that little girl might overhear me and come to shut me up.

"I think she was just born that way." Jesika said soberly, looking down at the grass as we sat on the two steps facing the backyard with our backs to the sliding glass door.

Out of all the kids I met that day, I liked Jesika the best. She was odd, but I liked the way she told stories; she made me feel like I was right there in that moment with her. I could see that we would be best friends forever. And I didn't know it yet, but she had an antenna straight to heaven.

"So," I asked. "Do you want to meet my parents?" I wanted my parents to meet my new friend.

"I — I don't know." Jesika looked uneasy. "I think so …" Shrugging her shoulders, her voice drifted off.

"Don't be shy. They won't bite you." I nudged her softly and tried to make her laugh. "They're harmless, I promise."

"Okay."

She followed me to my house and waited for me to put my bike in my garage. Reluctantly, she followed me into my house and into my living room. My mom came out of the bedroom when she heard us enter the house and looked at me expectantly when she saw that I had a guest.

"Mom, this is my new friend, Jesika Denise Beckford. She lives across the street. Jesika goes to Catholic school too." I pointed from my mom to Jesika, "Jesika, this is my mom, Mrs. Ava Massey."

"Nice to meet you, Mrs. Massey." Jesika's voice was so low, you could barely make out her words.

"Jesika, what Catholic school do you go to?" Mom asked with a welcoming smile.

"St. Rita, ma'am." Jesika glanced up at my mother and gave a tentative smile of her own.

"It would have been nice if Marina could have attended the same school." She looked at me and seemed to relax. "Saint Joseph downtown is more convenient for Marina to go to." Mom nodded, smoothing her dress unconsciously. "Her father works downtown at San Diego High."

"I'm familiar with Saint Joseph, Mrs. Massey. It's an all-girl Catholic school," Jesika nodded, meeting mother's warm gaze and smiling back

"Yes, it sure is. Well, it's been nice meeting you, Jesika," Mother said. "I'm getting ready to start dinner. Marina, be sure to tidy up your room when your company leaves."

"It was very nice meeting you, Mrs. Massey," Jesika replied.

"Let's go to my room, Jesika." I grabbed her hand.

"Wow! Your room is nice. I wish my room looked like this. My sister and I share one bed and my little brother is in the other. My mom's always yelling at us to keep it clean." Jesika's eyes moved swiftly all over my bedroom. She ran her hand across my comforter as if she were trying to determine what kind of fabric it was.

"My mother has that same problem with my brothers," I scoffed. "Wait until you meet them. They're a pain in my neck. It's like a vacation when they're not here."

"Don't you miss them?" she wondered.

"Yeah, but only for a short while," I admitted.

"How do they like being away at school?" Jesika had moved over to my dollhouse and was admiring the furniture inside.

"They like it just fine. Get to play silly war games. They come home for Christmas, Thanksgiving, spring break, and all the major holidays. They'll be home for three months in the summer." I shrugged lamely.

"I can't stay long. I gotta check on my little brother and sister." Jesika sighed.

"I saw them in your front yard. Just tell them to come over here." I was not ready to say goodbye.

Jesika's face lit up hopefully and then she frowned. "I'm supposed to stay in the house when my mother isn't home. She'll be home around 4:00 p.m."

I walked with Jesika back to her house. Sariah had drawn a hopscotch on the driveway and was trying to teach Jayden how to play. But her little brother looked funny because he wasn't coordinated, and he kept falling over.

"Come on, Sariah! We have to go inside the house before Mom gets home," Jesika said sternly.

"You don't tell me what to do!" Sariah snapped with her hands on her hips.

"Okay, just come on! Mom will be here any minute," Jesika huffed, and Sariah and Jayden finally went into the house. "I better get in the house and change out of my uniform," Jesika said to me. "Do you want to meet my mother?" she asked.

"Maybe tomorrow. I have to get home for dinner," I replied as I waved goodbye and headed home.

Jesika nodded and gave me one of her big smiles, put her inhaler back in her nose, and went inside. I went home, contentedly thinking of what an amazing day I just had, glad that I had met a wonderful new friend.

CHAPTER 10

Dinner with Our Neighbors

I knew it wouldn't be long before my mother invited Jesika's family over for dinner. Knowing that whenever my mother invited people over for dinner, we dressed in our best clothes, I called Jesika that morning, "Wear your Sunday best."

"What for? It's just dinner." She didn't sound like her usual, bubbly self.

Jesika showed up in a green dress, white ruffled socks, black patent leather shoes, and a black satin jacket with a red dragon on the back. Her father had just returned from Japan with one for each of the kids.

"Look at our jackets, Marina! They have dragons on their back!" Sariah turned around and showed me the dragon. "Aren't they cool?"

Jesika's mother was dressed in a black cocktail dress and just as beautiful as my mother, only younger. The two women embraced and my father offered Mr. Beckford a seat at the table.

Jayden walked into the dining room and said, "Good evening, everyone." He walked straight to my father and introduced himself, while holding a little truck in his left hand. "My name is Jayden Wade Beckford. How are you today, sir?" He had the most adorable smile on his little face.

"I'm fine, thank you, little man," Dad replied, smiling down at Jayden, reaching out to shake his extended hand. Jayden then promptly turned around and shook my mother's hand too. My mother was so impressed by his manners, she picked him up, kissed him on the cheek, and sat him right next to her.

"What a polite young man you are."

Jayden smiled. "My daddy wouldn't let me bring my doll over. I got my truck."

We all heard it, but no one made a comment. Jesika's father put his hand on his forehead, as if embarrassed. And Sariah looked back at him with an expression that said, "You shoulda let him bring his doll." Everyone was quiet, and for a minute, Jesika looked like she wished she could disappear.

Breaking the silence, my mother asked Jayden how old he was.

Jayden replied very frankly, "I'm three."

"You're a smart young man too," Mom said.

Rita smiled warmly at Mother and then at the table. "Everything looks yummy."

Conversation slowly picked up again, and the adults began to talk about the movie, *Paris Blues*.

"Mom, can we watch it with you?" I asked.

"No, honey," she said. "It's a movie for adults."

"What's it about?" Rita asked.

My mother answered, "It's about American jazz musicians living in Paris, France. Both men are content with living and working in Paris, when they meet two American tourists, Lillian and Connie, and fall in love. Ram wants to develop his music career, and Eddie wants to be far away from the racism in America. The pair must choose between artist integrity or love."

"I can't wait to see it!" Rita declared. "What time does it come on?"

"About 7:30 p.m.," my mother replied. "Rita, where are you and Wade from? It seems as though everyone I meet is a transplant from somewhere else."

"We're from Chattanooga, Tennessee. Wade and I met in high school," Rita replied. "It wasn't long after that he joined the navy. We moved around a lot, but I didn't mind. It was nice to get away from my birthplace. We moved from Tennessee to Chicago to Connecticut to Las Vegas, Nevada, Oakland to San Diego, California."

"We're from Chicago," Mom said when Rita paused. "San Diego is by far the nicest place that we ever lived."

Wade interrupted. "I had heard from a friend that California was a great place to live. When I found out from my Commanding Office that I would be stationed in San Diego, I couldn't wait to get home and tell Rita all about it. The submarine I'm on is docked over in Point Loma."

"What's it like living on a submarine for several months?" my father wondered.

"Man, it is cramped!" Wade exclaimed.

"What do you do for the navy?" my father asked.

"I'm a cook for the Chief. He has a gourmet palate, so I had to learn how to cook lobster tails and cordon bleu with white wine sauce. His steaks had to be cooked to a perfect medium rare. He got rid of the last cook, who just couldn't get it right. As a country boy, all I knew was cornbread, black-eyed peas, fried chicken, greens, and tasty buttermilk biscuits, but I figured it out."

After dinner, my mother served hot apple pie and homemade vanilla ice cream, followed by cocktails for the movie. The cocktails were my cue to take my friends outside and play.

Sariah wanted to climb the treehouse, but the side rails weren't up around the fort.

"I'm going to the top," she yelled as she began ascending the tree.

"Sariah! It's too dangerous to be up there without the side rails!" I yelled up at her, but she kept climbing. Jayden ran into the house and cried, "Sariah is going to get hurt! She's climbing the treehouse!"

Mr. Beckford ran out of the house and snatched her down before she could get halfway up.

"I ought to wear your little ass out! Hard head makes for a soft behind," he said and then he slapped her on the bottom.

"I'm sorry, Daddy," Sariah sobbed.

I could tell Mrs. Beckford was embarrassed by his behavior, and so were my parents.

"Wade, she's alright," Mrs. Beckford insisted. "Let's go back in and watch the movie."

After they went back into the house, I asked Jesika if she wanted to listen to the movie.

"That's no fun. We can't even see the picture," Jesika whined.

"It'll be like someone is reading to you," I suggested with a solicitous grin.

"Okay, but I'd rather play tag," she said, shrugged her shoulders, and smiled back at me.

We grabbed two patio chairs and placed them as close to the window as we could without being seen. Hearing it was like reading it, only better.

I nudged Jesika and whispered, "See, isn't this great?"

Jesika paused, "Yes, this is great," but then she started to tell me about the Swing and how she met the Hobo. The movie quickly faded into the background while she shared the story.

CHAPTER 11

The Hobo and the Swing

"Before we lived in our house, we lived in navy apartments. The location was called Frontier. The navy had given each family a notice to vacate because they leased the property and the navy decided not to renew it. Families were moving out one section at a time, and some of them were torn down, and others were left standing with no doors, windows, or roofs. And there was only one abandoned swing on the playground. It reminded me of a ghost town, only more modern."

"Sounds spooky," I interjected.

"Yes! But every Sunday after mass, you could find me on that swing. I would pump my legs and point my feet to the sky. With the wind in my face and pigtails behind me, it felt like my face could kiss the clouds. I was flying, and it was fun."

"Ooooh, flying. That sounds thrilling!" She had activated my imagination for sure.

"Right? Well, one time, I found this kid with one missing tooth on my swing. Annoyed, I sat on the ground and waited patiently for him to let me have a turn. Before he got off the swing, he said, 'I bet you can't do this! Watch!' And he began pumping his legs forcefully, shifting his body forward. He got so high, I was afraid for him and yelled, 'Hey! What are you doing? You're going to kill yourself!'"

I leaned forward, wishing I could see exactly what she was seeing in her mind.

"Before I knew it, he had made a complete circle. I couldn't believe my eyes for a second. I thought he had a guardian angel for sure. He jumped off the swing and said, 'Let me see you do that!'"

"Maybe he was in a circus," I interrupted.

"No, I think he just practiced," she replied. "But then he said, 'Let me see you do that!' twice, and I said, 'I can do it.' I sat on that swing with my head down, kicking the dirt underneath my feet. I felt scared, and he teased me, saying I was just a dumb girl. Can you believe it?"

"Gah! Sounds like a jerk!" I affirmed.

"When he left, I was determined to do what he did. It was no longer about fun; it was a serious challenge. Eventually, I gave up. I didn't want to swing any more. But then, I noticed a smell. I got off the swing and began to follow the smell. It took me over to one of the abandoned navy houses. I walked through the doorway and sitting on the dirt floor was a hobo heating up a can of baked beans in the fire. I asked him what he was doing, and he said he was making dinner and asked if I'd join him. I agreed and walked over and sat down, and he put some of the beans on a tin plate for me and asked my name. Since he was a stranger, I told him I was Denise, and he introduced himself as Fred. Seeing his clothes in a bundle, I asked him if he was a hobo, and he confirmed he was. He told me he likes to travel by freight train, even though people are only supposed to ride on passenger trains, and he works different jobs and sleeps outside."

"Sounds like a crazy life." I could hardly imagine it.

"Yeah, he said he loves San Diego because the night sky is like his blanket. And then when I asked if he had a family, he said that he once had a wife and two children and that the children were grown. I asked him if he missed them, and he said yes. His face showed sadness, so I didn't ask him any more questions about his family. But I wanted to. He asked me if I wanted more beans, and I said yes. For some reason, they tasted good. It started to get dark, so I told him I had to go home. I thanked him for sharing his beans and told him that they were the best beans I'd ever eaten. Then I went back to swing and sat thinking about the boy who did the complete circle. I began to pump my legs and the harder I pumped my legs, the louder my heart beat. I got really high, but I couldn't keep it up because I was afraid. So I swung for fun and then I went home."

"I'm so glad. You could have hurt yourself, Jesika!" I scolded my new friend.

"Well, that following Sunday morning after mass, I went to swing." She smiled mischievously. "'I can do it,' I said to myself. I began to swing at a steady pace back and forth, then faster. I pumped my legs as hard as I could, and the next thing I knew I was parallel to the bar that the swings were attached to."

"Oh, my God, Jesika, that could have been fatal!" I shrieked.

"I was upside down and then over. It was fast, and I had done it! I jumped off the swing screaming, 'I did it! I did it!' There was no one there to see me go over the bar that day, Marina, but I did it."

"I believe you, Jesika," I assured her.

She smiled, "My victory was my own."

"Wow! Do you think you could do it again now?" I wondered.

"No, that was once in a lifetime."

"That takes guts. Did you ever see the hobo again?"

"Yes, I saw him again as I was walking to the corner store with my mother, where he handed me a tootsie roll pop with chocolate in the middle and kept walking. I was so excited, but my mother took it and threw it in the trash. And I never saw him again."

Sariah came stomping over to us. "You guys are boring! I'm telling Mom on you!" She put her hands on her hips and stuck her tongue out at us.

"Ah, you're just mad cause Daddy spanked you." Jesika stuck her tongue out at Sariah.

After listening to the movie for a while, Jesika said she wanted to live in Paris. The movie was a good love story, with Black people in it. And Louis Armstrong made a guest appearance in the bar where Eddie and Ram played. When he started to play, we started dancing, and Sariah and Jayden joined.

Jesika's parents really liked my mother and father, and they stayed another hour and a half while we played hide-and-go-seek outside. Eventually, Mr. Beckford came out of the house and told Jesika that it was time to go. Dinner was a success.

After they left, I heard my parents talking about Jesika's parents.

Mom started, "Not all is well in the Beckford household. I think Rita wants Wade to get out of the navy. I can imagine that it gets really lonely."

"How do you know?" His voice was skeptical.

"I know ... because she told me how she felt."

"She's employed, isn't she?" my father asked.

"Yes, she works as a nurse's aide at Paradise Valley Hospital, over in National City. I'm sure he sends money home. That poor baby, Jayden. You saw the look on Wade's face?"

"Ah, there you go," my father sighed.

"What?" Mother frowned. "Wade can only see that he might grow up to be a sissy. What you see is what you get in those two. Don't get me wrong, I like them both."

Father remained silent in response to her frankness.

"He'll never focus on the fact that he has a gifted child," said Mother.

"You don't know that," Father rebuffed.

"He's very intelligent for his age," Mom replied. "I've seen it too many times before, Russell." It was my mother's turn to sigh.

"So, whenever you're around him, you'll be the encouraging source in his life." Father chuckled.

"You mean, as long as we continue to live across the street," Mother replied. "We are two very busy people. I have a hard enough time trying to keep up with my own two sons."

Hearing my parents' conversation made me sad for Jayden.

CHAPTER 12

A Dangerous Sport

Jesika and I became inseparable; we were like Siamese twins. I would spend the night over at her house, and she would spend the night at mine. We even walked to St. Rita's for Sunday mass together. One of our favorite games to play in the neighborhood was kickball. My father made plates by cutting some old linoleum that was in our kitchen before we moved in. We made a rule that you couldn't hit anyone in the face or back of the head. It was an automatic three points gain run for the other team if you broke this rule.

One day, Douglas was pitching for Jesika's team and Sariah was up. She kicked that ball so hard, it hit Douglas square in the face and knocked him over. Douglas was so mad, he ran over to her on second base and pushed her down, but Sariah came up swinging. Jesika and I had to break up the fight. We made them shake hands and then we started playing all over again.

Jesika was up to kick. She kicked the ball over everyone's head. The bases were loaded and she brought everyone home. That home run gave their team four points. History was made that day. I'll never forget how happy we all were at the end of that game because even after that, our team won.

CHAPTER 13

Billy's Army

My brothers, Lewis and Billy, came home from military school for summer break. They were fourteen and sixteen years old, and so they got everyone's attention when they came home. In fact, even though Billy hated military school and its military gear, tents, fake wood rifles, and bayonets, he enlisted every kid in the neighborhood, it seemed, into his mock army. Even kids two blocks over would stop playing dodgeball, hide-and-go-seek, and even kickball to be pretend soldiers with Billy. I hated it.

And Jesika was always on his side because she had a crush. She thought he was cute.

Sariah favored Lewis.

"Come on, Jesika, let's do something different," I would plead. "I know, let's play with our Barbies!"

Jesika wouldn't even look at me sometimes, as she would get that dreamy look and a silly grin on her face while staring over at Billy and reply, "No, I want to join the army."

Eventually, they had everyone in green camouflage pants. Some of the kids asked for pretend machine guns for their birthdays all because of my brothers. Whenever a new kid would bring their cap gun or their cowboy guns, Billy would belt out orders, "You got five minutes to find something green to put on if you want to join this man's army! And get rid of those cap guns!" Billy and Lewis issued fake military weapons. Even Gerald from around the corner wanted to enlist.

It was fun for a while until they became so serious that it wasn't fun anymore.

One day while we were all outside and the pretend soldiers were getting yelled at by Billy during one of his training exercises, Gerald called my brother, Billy, "a stupid dipstick." Gerald was apparently tired of taking orders from my two loudmouthed brothers, and my brother Billy got so mad that he kicked Gerald in the crotch. His older brother, Harold, came over to our house, and called my brother Billy out. He tried to apologize to Gerald, but Gerald was in too much pain for Harold to just leave without what he felt was a proper retribution. Lewis wasn't going to let Billy fight alone. Next thing I knew, the fight had started.

Jesika and I were yelling, "Stop it!"

We had to hold Sariah back because she wanted to help Lewis. The fight was broken up by Irene's mother, Mrs. Chaplin. She was a short, stocky woman who was usually cheery and funny, but she didn't think twice about taking on Gerald's brother or my brothers. When my dad and mom came home, Mrs. Chaplin was right there to give them the lowdown.

They stayed on restriction for one week. My mother was so angry. Billy's reputation went from a nice, clean-cut young man to "You don't mess with that boy, he's crazy." Douglas told every kid that wasn't there that they had missed the fight of the century. It would take a couple of days before the excitement from the fight died down because Gerald's brother Harold threatened Billy and Lewis. He said if he ever saw them in the street, he would kick their butts again.

CHAPTER 14

Bazooka Gum Disaster

My brother Lewis, the nicer one, befriended the most mischievous of boys, with the exception of Gerald. They were inseparable comrades who shared a love of baseball cards.

It was a beautiful afternoon, and the boys were gathered in Carl's front yard on the grass, armed with their stack of prized baseball cards. Each boy proudly displayed their collections, filled with legendary players like Willie Mays, Sandy Koufax, Frank Robinson, Camilo Pascual, Hank Aaron, Mickey Mantle, and Roy Campenella, along with many other notable baseball players. I observed their exchange, bored out of my mind. I had no exciting activities to occupy myself with. In fact, I had nothing to do at all while they began trading cards. But I noticed Lewis had this mischievous grin on his face. Glancing at me, he demanded that I find something else to do.

"No!" I shouted back. "It's a free country and I can stand wherever I want to."

"Fellas, just ignore her," Lewis responded flippantly.

"She's not bothering me." Douglas smiled.

With a strategic plan in mind, Lewis proposed a game of "The Dozens" to distract his friends. I knew he was up to no good. The rules were simple: While passing the baseball, they would engage in playful and witty comebacks. "And fellas, No your-mama-so-fat-jokes." I knew that rule would be broken because those were the funniest. It was a perfect opportunity for Lewis to strike.

Round and round, the boys exchanged clever insults, trying to outdo each other. Carl's inability to catch the ball without tripping over his own two feet didn't help him. Mark retaliated by teasing Jerod about his lucky hat, claiming that it had more holes than a block of Swiss cheese. Lewis came back by saying to Albert that his first base hit was fueled by his gas: "It stunk!"

Then Jerod broke the rule, "Your mama is so fat that they were going to bury her in the dugout."

"That's low," Douglas replied.

Carl targeted Douglas, "Your mama is so fat that when God said, 'Let there be light,' He asked your mama to move out the way."

"Okay, okay!" Lewis said. "I thought we weren't going to tell 'your mama' jokes because they incite violence."

Laughter ensued and I rolled my eyes.

Meanwhile, Lewis slyly maneuvered through the trading chaos, subtly swapping less valuable cards for their best ones. He managed to snatch Koufax from Mark, Hank from Albert, and even Willie Mays from Carl. The other boys were so engrossed in their verbal banter that they didn't notice Lewis's card heist.

Just as the boys resumed trading, Lewis began slowly blowing his breath into his Bazooka gum into a rather large bubble. It was so large, it pulled their attention away from trading. He blew the right amount of air into the bubble skillfully.

"Wow!" Douglas said. "That bubble could be in the Guinness Book of Record."

It covered Lewis's face. Lewis froze, stopped blowing, and his face turned red just before that gigantic bubble exploded all over his face and head. The sight was both hilarious and gross.

Lewis, covered with sticky, pink gum all over his face and Afro. The boys and I burst into laughter.

"That's what you get!" I remarked, choking with laughter.

Lewis rubbed the back of his hand across his eyes only to make the situation worse.

"Wow, you're a sight for sore eyes," Albert said, dripping with sarcasm. "What kind of disease do you have? I don't want to catch it."

Our laughter turned to pandemonium.

Douglas gave him a scornful look, realizing he had lost his favorite baseball card. "Now, you have only a face a mother could love."

As the laughter subsided, Albert, with his mischievous grin, quipped, "Hey Lewis, I guess you finally found a way to stick it to your friends."

Jesika came out of the house and stumbled across the scene.

"What's so funny?" she asked, smiling from ear to ear. She looked at Lewis's face and said, "We should have a bubble gum blowing contest!"

Lewis bellowed a loud, "NO!" and Jesika shrugged a smile. Intrigued by their baseball cards, she dashed back into her house and raced to her room, determined to join the fun but with her cherished saint cards. St. Teresa of Avila, St. Rita, and St. Christina the Astonishing were her favorites.

She plopped down next to Douglas, whose prize was Tommy Davis and placed her Saint Theresa of Avila next to it. I was embarrassed as confusion and amusement swept across the boys' faces.

Douglas blurted, "What's that, Jesika? Are you some kind of weirdo?"

Ignoring his jibe, Jesika proudly replied, "Well, Douglas, I thought we were trading cards, so I brought my Saint Teresa. She's the patron saint of sufferers, you know. Anyway," she frowned at Lewis who looked like he was suffering quite a bit, and I couldn't hold my laughter back.

A baffled Douglas shook his head and said, "Come on, Jesika! We're in the middle of trading baseball cards. This is serious business." He grabbed the Saint Teresa of Avila card and flung it past her.

Disheartened, Jesika picked up her beloved card, her head down, and ran back to the house, and I ran after her. In her haste, she bumped into her mother, who noticed her distress.

"What's wrong, Jesika?"

Tears welled up in Jesika's eyes as she explained, "My friends were making fun of me, calling me weirdo." Her mother's eyebrows arched in surprise as she responded, "Well, what did you do, sweetheart?"

Sniffling, Jesika replied, "They were trading baseball cards, and I wanted to trade my cards. So, I brought my Saint Teresa of Avila card, but they didn't understand. They hurt my feelings, Mom!"

Her mother chuckled softly and said, "Oh, Jesika, that's because they were trading regular baseball cards, not saint cards! You did something a little silly."

Jesika wiped away her tears and asked, "But Mom, why didn't they understand? Marina didn't laugh, Mom."

"Honey, that's because she knows who you are. And I gave birth to you …" Her mother kneeled down, looking into Jesika's eyes, and said, "Sometimes people have different interests, and that's okay. It's important to find friends who appreciate you for who you are. And let's be honest, trading saint cards in a baseball card exchange is pretty unique!"

Jesika's tears transformed into a giggle, and she hugged her mother tightly. Understanding dawned upon her, as she realized that the boys may have misunderstood her intentions, but it didn't mean they were being mean-spirited. They were simply caught up in their own playful world of baseball card trading. With her spirits lifted, she returned to our friends, who welcomed her back with all her quirkiness.

CHAPTER 15

An Unfinished Fallout Shelter

Whenever I visited Jesika's house, I was intrigued by the fallout shelter in her backyard. It seemed out of place in our neighborhood where no one else had one. Jesika even had a copy of the Fallout Shelter Handbook.

"We don't have one," I reiterated, wrinkling my brow at her emphatically.

Jesika explained to me that her father had purchased their house from a lieutenant commander who worried about the bomb destroying the West Coast.

"Then why does it have two large pipes sticking out of the ground?" I asked.

"That's so you can breathe," Jesika explained.

"That doesn't make sense. You would be breathing in radiation," I said wryly, shaking my head in disbelief.

"My dad says that the lieutenant didn't finish it. Maybe he ran out of money. It doesn't look anything like the picture in front of the handbook." She shrugged. "Do you want to see the inside?" Her eyebrows raised expectantly.

"Oh, yes," I replied excitedly. Finally, my curiosity would be satisfied.

Jesika grabbed a flashlight and we climbed down the metal ladder. There was a narrow hallway that led to a room with a drain in the middle of the floor.

"There's not a lot of room down here," I said, looking around the tiny space.

"Yeah, it's just enough space for a family of four," Jesika explained, looking around the small room that we stood in.

"Oh. Do you think your father will finish it?" I wondered.

"Nope, I don't think so." She shook her head.

We sat on a bench, looking through the handbook with the flashlight, and realized that there was much more to a fallout shelter than the lieutenant had built.

"You know about the bomb? Right?" Jesika asked, her voice filled with concern.

"Of course," I replied.

"My friend, Silvia, told me during a drill that no one would survive a 50-megaton bomb," Jesika said matter-of-factly. She didn't have her Vicks Inhaler today, and I could tell that her nose was getting a little stuffy.

"Yeah, you know she's right!" I mused. "My father is a history teacher, and he told me that grown-ups worry about it too. He says an atomic bomb can wipe out whole cities. Have you ever heard about a movie called *Them*?"

"No. What was it about?" Jesika asked excitedly, her eyes meeting mine.

"It was one of the first science-fiction thrillers to issue a warning about nuclear testing and the radioactivity of atomic bomb creation. My mother said the 1954 film was unique in its concept. The basic plot begins with the FBI investigating a series of deaths. Their investigation leads them to a storm drain underneath the city of Los Angeles where they hope to locate and destroy the ants that had mutated into giant man-eating ants due to atomic radiation."

"It sounds like a movie we could see on *Moonalisa*." Jesika's wide eyes betrayed an unusual glint of fear.

"Moona who?" I asked.

"She's the host of Science Fiction Theater," Jesika replied, looking down at the ground. "But I try not to think about the bomb."

We both fell into a heavy silence for a minute, the handbook now closed on the bench between us.

"Yeah, I know. It's awful to think that Russia could launch a bomb, resulting in our complete annihilation from the face of the earth, and maybe we would launch one in retaliation before theirs hit us. The whole notion is scary as hellfire." I shook my head, trying to dislodge the awful images from my mind.

"No more human existence, and anyone left on earth breathing in radiation would become mutants," Jesika said. "It's all so scary, Marina. Why can't the people in charge just get rid of them? We don't need them."

"I don't know, Jesika." It wasn't something I'd thought about. "Maybe the whole world has just gone mad," I replied, not knowing what to say. "Speaking of madness, I saw Fidel Castro on the television the other day. He went to visit Moscow and became friends with the Russian government. What's even worse is that nuclear missiles have arrived in Cuba, which is not that far from Florida."

It was Jesika's turn to shake her head. "I read in the newspaper that the Catholic Church excommunicated Castro because he expelled 139 Catholic priests from Cuba. I guess he was raised Catholic, but as an adult, he no longer practices."

I nodded soberly. "In my second-grade class at St. Thomas the Apostle in Chicago, there was a girl that peed on herself every time the sirens went off. It would make my teacher so mad. I just felt so sorry for her."

Jesika's expression was sympathetic as she replied, "Yeah, it's just a drill, no need to be scared. I know that Our Lord,

Our Blessed Lady, and Saint Michael the Archangel worked overtime to prevent the Russians from using the bomb. Do you know how many times the Blessed Virgin Mary has appeared to different people?" Jesika asked expectantly.

"Nope," I said, "How many?"

Her brown eyes lit up and there was a wondrous smile on her face as she softly explained, "Well, there was Juan Diego in 1531 at Tepeyac near Mexico City, where she appeared four times. Then Catherine Laboure in 1830 at Rue du Bac, Paris, France, where she appeared three times. Melanie Calvat and Maximum Giraud, in 1846, in Salette, France. Bernadette Soubirous in Lourdes, France, on Thursday, February 11, 1858, when she appeared eighteen times that day. Joseph and Eugene Barbadette, in 1871 ..." She recited a few more and then took a deep breath. "I saw the movie, *The Miracle of Our Lady of Fatima.* She made the sun dance in the sky and told Bernadette that her two cousins would die and go to heaven, and they did. Of course, there were the five children from the Voisin and Degeimbre families, Beauraing, Belgium, where she appeared thirty-three times between late November 1932 and January 1933. And finally, Mariette Beco, on January 15, 1933, in Banneux, Belgium; she was called the Virgin of the Poor and appeared eight times in one day."

"How do you remember all these details?" I was floored.

"I memorized it, silly." She nudged me playfully. "She left more messages with children than she did with adults. I guess she thinks we're better listeners. I know my father doesn't listen." She rolled her eyes.

"What were some of the messages?" I was intrigued.

"When I watched the movie, *The Miracle of Fatima,* I felt she was warning us. She asked us to pray the rosary for peace in the human heart, and to stay strong in the face of war. She said to live in peace with one another, and then the world will be at peace. She said that Jesus, her son, was sad, because we hurt each other. He wants us all to live in Heaven with him when our souls leave our bodies. We need to love one another, and through love we can do anything. You could even cure another human being just like he did. It seems like it's very simple, but we make it difficult." Jesika's expression was earnest, and her eyes held the wisdom of an elder.

I felt sorrow in my heart for mankind at that moment because I knew that people were having such a hard time just accepting one another, let alone loving one another. I realized that I wasn't paying attention during any of those Catholic movies they showed during the school year. I always ended up falling asleep because they were so boring to me. It was then that I decided to pray with my heart.

Jesika patted my hand as if to comfort me and smiled softly. We sat there quietly for a few seconds.

Suddenly, Jesika changed direction. "You know, this bomb shelter got us into big trouble, and it put us to work. Every Saturday and Sunday, we had to move these large rocks from around the bomb shelter to the other side of the house. After the rocks were removed, there was a big mound of sand around it. Then we had to shovel the sand and put it into buckets and carry it around to the other side of the house. I know how the Flintstones felt at the rock quarry," she joked, referring to the silly cartoon we watched Saturday mornings. "At least we got a lunch break. My mother gave us sandwiches and watermelon. My little brother would get so tired, he would fall asleep with the peanut butter and jelly sandwich hanging out of his mouth, and my mother would say, 'Wade Clinton Beckford, you can't work them children like they're on a farm.' And he'd answer back, 'A little hard work isn't going to hurt them.'"

I shook my head sympathetically at Jesika's story. She had so many similar stories that involved her father being a very harsh and strict disciplinarian. I could tell that it was a source of pain for her, but like everything else she shared with me, she always told the stories so candidly.

My grandmother once told me that suffering can create character and strength in people. And listening to Jesika, I knew that what Grandmother said had to be true because Jesika was one of the best people I had ever met. I wished with all my heart whenever I heard Jesika's stories about her father that he would be just a little nicer to his children, especially Jesika.

A lover of Nancy Drew mysteries, I was excited to share my favorite book, *The Hidden Staircase* with Jesika. But then I remembered she hated Nancy Drew. Said she found Nancy Drew to be boring.

Her father made her go to the library and pick out five books during the summer and insisted that one of them was a Hardy Boys or a Nancy Drew book. She said that Nancy Drew wasn't interesting to her, and Hardy Boys were even worse. She liked books like *The Adventures of Huckleberry Finn, The Adventures of Tom Sawyer,* and *Robinson Crusoe.*

But I was hooked on Nancy Drew and all things mysterious. In fact, I fancied carrying around my sleuth kit in a brown canvas bag my brother Lewis had given to me. I was excited when I got the kit with a large magnifying glass, a flashlight, small plastic binoculars, a notebook with a cheap pen, and powder to lift fingerprints! I added tweezers, pencils, and expensive binoculars that my father had given to me.

CHAPTER 16

Spying on Mr. Mueller

On the weekends, I would spend time pondering about the Krauts that lived next door to Jesika. I even started watching *Combat* on television with my father and two brothers. I wanted to know more about my German neighbors. What a curious pair they were.

Mr. McCarthy came outside one Saturday afternoon while I was sitting on his steps, watching the Germans' house with my binoculars. His steps had a better view than mine.

"They're going to do something any minute," I said under my breath.

Just then, Mr. McCarthy stepped outside his door and looked down at me over the top of his black, horn-rimmed glasses that appeared to be sitting just at the tip of his nose.

"Hello, Marina."

I looked up at him and smiled sheepishly. "Hi, Mr. McCarthy." I'd been caught.

"You know… it's not nice to spy on people." Mr. McCarthy raised his eyebrows at me and pushed his glasses a little closer to his face.

I sighed, a little exasperated that I needed to stop spying to give Mr. McCarthy an explanation. "Yes, I know. I'm just curious about them. He called Mrs. Beckford the 'N' word." I raised my own eyebrows at Mr. McCarthy, expecting that he would now understand the need to keep an eye on such a person.

Instead, he frowned and scratched his head. "I'm sorry he did that." I nodded as Mr. McCarthy sat next to me on the porch and looked at me appraisingly. "Is there any other reason that you are spying?" His expression was serious but not condescending like some grownups.

I put my binoculars on my lap, "Well, one day I was skating down the sidewalk, and one of my skates hit a small rock, and I fell into his grass. He came running out of his house yelling, 'Get off my grass, and stay out of my yard!' He could see that I was hurt, and he didn't even bother to help me up. So, I got up, and I put my hands on my hips. I looked him straight in the eyes, and said, 'July 31, 1936, Jesse Owns, the fastest human being, captured four gold medals and became the hero of the Olympics.' Then I stuck my tongue out at him and took off down the street." I couldn't help but to jut my chin out proudly as I told McCarthy how I stood up to that mean man.

"Boy, you're a brave little girl. Did that make you feel better, Marina?" he asked.

"Yes, it did," I said. "Do you know their last name?" I asked, taking advantage of the conversation to further my investigation.

Mr. McCarthy looked down at me, his glasses at the tip of his nose again, "His last name is Mueller."

"He's not a very nice man," I said.

Mr. McCarthy nodded his head in agreement, "Mr. Mueller was from a different time. He was in World War II. Fought in Africa under General Johannes Erwin Eugen Rommel's command in 1941."

"He did?" I was shocked. "I know it was a battle between our allies and Germany."

Mr. McCarthy nodded, "He was twenty-five years old and fought with his comrades to hold onto Tobruk. It remained in Germany's hands until 1942."

"Well, we defeated the Axis Power in 1945. We won, and he's a sore loser." I said, resisting the urge to fold my arms over my chest.

"I suppose he is." Mr. McCarthy smirked. "I have never met anyone who has been in a war, and come out of it the same way that they went in. Can I tell you a secret, Marina? I'm a conscientious objector. Do you know what that means?" he asked, his tone lower and much more serious than before.

"Yes," I said. "It means you don't believe in killing anyone. You don't believe in war."

"Correct! How did you get so smart?" He grinned at me, visibly impressed.

"My parents," I responded, smiling back.

Mr. McCarthy stood up and looked across the street for a few seconds at the Mueller house, frowning sadly. Then he shook his head slowly and looked down at me. "Don't you waste this beautiful day staring at people's houses, Marina. Days like today were made for bike riding and playing."

I nodded, but it was clear that unless he asked me to leave, I planned to stay put on his porch. He nodded back and went into his house.

I heard everything Mr. McCarthy told me, but I had no sympathy for Mr. Mueller.

CHAPTER 17

The Heartless Murder of Mr. Muggins

It was a typical summer break. Arguing over who would be team captain and who should be invited to a sleepover, and intense debates about who was the fastest runner on the block. Every parent felt responsible for each other's children. The people on Bollenbacher Street were very tight knit, and I liked feeling like I had a big, extended family. Most of the time we got along fine and had mounds of fun. Whenever something big happened, Irene and her siblings got the blame for it. There were six of them, so if it wasn't one of them, it was usually Gerald.

One sunny summer day, Jesika was riding her bike when she saw Bonnie and Sherrie standing over Mr. Muggins, their pet cat, and crying.

Jesika pedaled as fast as she could to my driveway, sprang off her bike and ran into my house, excitedly yelling my name.

"What happened?" I asked as I marked my spot in the Nancy Drew book that I was reading and placed it on the kitchen table. I looked up expectantly at my best friend who was huffing and puffing like a steam engine. If she wasn't so serious, I would have laughed.

"You have to come outside and see this," she said through gasps for air. "Bonnie's cat… Grab your kit!" she yelled, shaking her head in disbelief.

I grabbed my kit, and we ran outside. It was horrible.

Some kid in the neighborhood had poured gasoline on the cat and set him on fire. Poor Mr. Muggins was almost unrecognizable. His gray fur was singed and mottled with blood and pink skin. His eyes were burned shut. The burned cat's body was so stiff and lifeless. The smell made my stomach turn. I pulled out my magnifying glass.

"Let me look, Marina," Jesika said in almost a whisper. I handed her the magnifying glass. She looked at Mr. Muggins with the glass and handed it back to me quickly. "What a horrible way to die. It looks like he ran around first." She looked sympathetically at Bonnie.

Bonnie sniffled, grabbed her sister's hand, and started walking slowly home. The two girls were distraught.

Sariah was across the street, jumping rope in the driveway, when she noticed us hovering over something with my magnifying glass.

"What are you guys doing with the magnifying glass?" she asked, dragging her jump rope behind her.

"We are investigating, Sariah." Jesika sounded slightly annoyed with her little sister. "This cat has been deliberately set on fire." She pointed at Mr. Muggins.

"Yuck, it's funky! Can I look at it?" Sariah held her hand out expectantly for the magnifying glass. I handed it to her so that she could take a closer look

"Okay, that's enough. We have got to find the killer." I snatched the magnifying glass back and put it in my bag. My face was set in a determined glower. I had to get to the bottom of this horrible crime.

Jesika nodded her head knowingly but smirked at me, probably because I sounded so official. Somehow, she knew I was already forming the questions to ask around the neighborhood. She had an uncanny way of knowing what I was thinking sometimes.

Irene's brother, Carlton, had gotten blamed for the crime. Bonnie, who was the oldest, was sure he had done it but had no proof. I felt so bad for the two of them. Their mom had just gotten the cat for them. Jesika and I went to Carlton's house and rang the doorbell. Irene answered the door.

"Hi," she said sullenly, "I can't play."

I shifted my bag to my other shoulder and tried to stand as tall as I could. "We're on official business, Irene. We want to ask Carlton a few questions."

Irene looked at me and Jesika over appraisingly before opening the door wider for us to enter. "Come on in. He's in the backyard watering the grass."

We found Carlton with the hose in a gopher hole, trying to get the gopher to come out. The gopher caught Jesika's attention. "There he is, Carlton!" she yelled, pointing in the direction that she had seen the small animal. "Now he's over there." Jesika kept pointing to each hole in the ground. "That gopher is watching us." She crossed her arms over her chest, amused at the sly gopher. I didn't know how to ask Carlton so, I just blurted it out. "Carlton, did you pour gasoline on Bonnie and Sherrie's cat?" My hand was on my hip, and I was looking intensely at Carlton.

"Yeah, why did you burn up their cat?" Jesika mused, still looking at the gopher.

Carlton shook his head in annoyance but said nothing. I got impatient. I didn't plan on spending my afternoon watching Carlton water his grass.

"Did you set the cat on fire!?" I stomped my foot on the mushy lawn.

Carlton looked at me with wide eyes. "No!"

"Where were you an hour ago?" I demanded.

"I was around the corner at my friend Martin's house. Go ask him!" he replied, fuming.

We rode our bikes around the corner to verify his story. His friend Martin said that they had been playing together, when his mom called and said that he had to come home to water the grass. He had an alibi, but Bonnie was sure that Carlton had done it.

"If he didn't do it, Marina, who did?" Jesika asked while putting her inhaler into her nose. Then she giggled, "That gopher sure is smart."

I laughed and agreed. Carlton was probably going to be in his backyard, going at it with that gopher all day.

"Let's go back and look at the crime scene. I think the cat was trying to run home when it dropped dead." We began looking around in the area closest to the cat and found nothing. I handed Jesika a magnifying glass so that we could look on the ground for clues. We were so busy looking at the ground that before we knew it, we had walked around the corner and across the street.

I gasped when I saw matches next to the hedges that surround Gerald's driveway. "Look!"

"Matches." Jesika pointed to the open garage door. "And there's the gas can."

We knocked on the door, and Gerald answered, "I can't let anyone in. My mother and father aren't home."

"Oh, we aren't here to play. Can we come in for a few minutes?" I asked pleasantly.

We walked in, and Gerald asked me if I wanted some Kool-Aid, with this big, dumb grin on his face.

Jesika elbowed me softly and whispered, "I think he likes you, yuck! He didn't ask me if I wanted some."

I suppressed a giggle and elbowed her back.

"What about me?" Jesika snapped. "I would like some!"

"No! Ugly girls don't get any," Gerald said scornfully.

"Who are you calling ugly?" Jesika raised her eyebrow at Gerald and turned her head sideways. "You're a stinking cat killer! You nappy-headed buzzard, you're going to burn in hell. Just like that poor cat did!" Jesika shouted.

I don't think that's what she really meant to say but she was so upset that those were the words she chose at that moment. Gerald's face looked guarded as he looked down at the green carpet in his living room.

Now, I was wondering if Jesika would be able to keep her cool in a real investigation. I was getting a glimpse at how we would be in a real case, but I had figured out my next step.

I rolled my eyes at Jesika and shook my head in disgust and exclaimed, "I… hate cats!"

Gerald's face lit up. "So do I." He was smiling at me, apparently glad that we had something in common. "Every time I get a chance, I try to get rid of them. I burn their little asses up!" He was gloating.

He had admitted to the crime, and Jesika was my witness.

I looked at Gerald and declared, "I hafta to turn you in."

"Who are you going to turn me into, the police?" His laugh was almost a sneer. "They don't care about that stupid cat."

I didn't like the sound of his laugh. Gerald sounded crazy. I guess Jesika thought so too, as she moved slowly toward the front door.

I couldn't believe how nonchalant he was about killing a living thing.

"No, first, we're going to let Bonnie and Sherrie's parents know, and then they're going to talk to your parents." I rolled my eyes at him in disgust.

"You're going to squeal on me?" Gerald started balling up his fist.

Jesika was already at the front door with her hand on the doorknob.

"My parents ain't never home. My big brother takes care of me while they're at work, and he doesn't care what I do! Get outta my house, before I punch you in the face. Squealer!"

I balled my fist up to defend myself, ready to knock Gerald into the middle of next week if he approached me. But I had no intention of fighting Gerald. I was doing a victory dance inside. We had solved the case! Now we had to get the heck out of there.

I assured Gerald that we would keep it our little secret. Before Gerald could respond, his big brother came out of his bedroom and looked at all of us incredulously.

"What's all this noise out here? I'm trying to get some sleep! Gerald, go out in the backyard and play, and you two go home. Boy! You know, you ain't supposed to have company!"

We ran for the door. He didn't have to tell us twice! Jesika and I could hear his big brother yelling at Gerald even after we had closed the front door and began walking away.

"That boy is nuts!" Jesika declared.

I chimed in, "Yeah, he is crazy, loonier than a Looney Toon."

Jesika laughed and added, "My dad always says you're not supposed to mess with crazy people or cross-eyed-fools."

We giggled, relieved to be out of Gerald's house.

"Marina, were you really going to fight him?" Jesika's expression was serious.

I shrugged, "Most of the time you should try to be calm, cool, and collected. A true detective must defend herself. I wasn't afraid of anything, not even that crazy boy. Shoot, I have two brothers who taught me how to defend myself."

As we ran over to Bonnie and Sherrie's house to tell them that Gerald had killed their cat, their father pulled up in their driveway, and we told him the entire story. He thanked us for being great detectives. He was just going to get them another kitten.

Jesika volunteered to bury the cat. I wondered why he didn't go and talk with Gerald's parents. Maybe because he wanted to avoid any interaction with Gerald's parents. My mother would always say "crazy can run in a family." Perhaps in Gerald's case, it was true.

CHAPTER 18

Pishoung

It was Friday, and I was spending the weekend at Jesika's house because my parents were going out of town, and Billy and Lewis were going camping with some friends of the family. I loved it at her house. There was never a dull moment. I loved her mother and Pishoung, a young man who was renting a room at Jesika's house and was treated as part of their family.

He had a strong Filipino accent, and he always made me laugh. He often asked us to teach him how to dance. He played Chubby Checker's *Let's Twist Again* over and over, and he knew how to twist. He wanted to learn the cha-cha, but he had two left feet, so we taught him how to do the Jerk and the Mashed Potato. He looked so silly doing the Mashed Potato.

Pishoung was in the navy, and he worked on the 32nd Street Naval Base at night. He talked about his wife, mother, sister, and brothers. He told us funny stories about them. He would come to Mrs. Davis's house, our babysitter, and get Jesika, her sister, and her brother and act as if he were breaking them out of jail. Sometimes they would be sitting right up there with me, hating every minute of it. They hated being at Mrs. Davis's house because she wouldn't let them watch *Combat*. Imagine that! I didn't mind either way. I didn't like *Combat* as much as they did.

My brothers were so excited about camping, they were all packed up and ready to go. They were so stupid, going up there with their military gear to put on military camouflage, paint their faces, and run around the woods. They were hoping

Sammy's older brother wasn't going to be there. Sidney was a pot-smoking, hippy-dippy stoner who would make fun of their haircuts and uniforms while he said stupid things like, "Marijuana is wholesome, and everyone needs to trip out sometime. Why be part of the killer establishment?" When he said that, my brother Billy would blow his top. He'd get so mad, that's all he talked about when he got home—unusual ways he could torture Sammy's brother.

"What's Mary-Juana?" Jesika asked.

I was pleased to inform her, "It's like tobacco, only it's supposed to make you feel good. My brother told me it's like being drunk, only you don't fall or pass out. I asked if he had tried marijuana and he said, 'No way, I'm a good soldier.'"

Once they were gone, it was time for us to have some fun.

Jesika was the kind of kid that would wake you up if you fell asleep during a scary movie. She woke me up during *Godzilla*. How could she be afraid of *Godzilla*, a big dinosaur, for crying out loud? As we watched movies and talked, I heard her say things like *Frankenstein* was blasphemous. According to her, the idea that man would try and make another man from dead spare parts was just plain scary and an abomination. She also mentioned she didn't believe in original sin.

"How could an innocent baby just be born and be a stamped sinner?"

I laughed because I agreed that the concept was quite ridiculous if you thought about it.

But she went further with the strangest questions: "What was the difference between Adam and Eve's bodies?"

"Is this a riddle?" I wondered.

She shook her head, her eyes gleaming mischievously. "No, I'm serious." She gave me plenty of time to answer, but I couldn't think of anything. "You give up?" she asked, smiling.

"They had no navels because they weren't born—they were made by God. And not out of dead spare parts," she concluded, rolling her eyes.

I shook my head. Sometimes Jesika could be downright timid, and other times she was fearless. She told me once that your friends were people that you picked to be your family. "Your real relatives… they just get on your nerves."

I absolutely agreed. We were like sisters, two peas in a pod.

CHAPTER 19

Our Sunday Best

*I*t was Sunday morning, and it was hard waking up at 7:00 a.m. to get ready for mass, even after a good night's sleep in my own bed. I looked up and saw Jesika standing in the doorway. It was comical that we spoke the same words at the same time, "What are you wearing to mass?"

I chose a baby blue, flowered-print dress that was unique because it looked like patent leather. It went perfect with my baby blue shoes, belt, and white socks. I picked out a white headband to keep my hair off my face. I would be going over to Jesika's house to get ready and ride to mass with her family, as my mother and father both had early morning commitments doing volunteer work at the nearby food bank. They rarely missed mass, but because it was to help others, and the food bank really needed extra hands, Mom decided that the Lord wouldn't disapprove.

"I'm going to wear my light green skirt and my white, sleeveless blouse because it is too hot to wear anything else." Jesika fanned herself. I nodded in agreement and she started with the checklist, "You have everything you need? Underwear?"

"Check," I said.

"Toothbrush?"

"Check."

"Sneakers?"

"Check!"

"Play clothes?"

"Check."

"Sleuth Kit?"

"Check."

"Sunday church outfit."

"Check!"

For breakfast, we ate cornflakes with thinly sliced bananas on them. As I ate, I ran my hand absentmindedly down the soft shoulder strap of my sleuth kit that hung on the back of my chair. I had daydreams so often about solving a case, but I never really thought it would happen. I drifted off in thought as Jesika and I sat there munching on our cereal. She seemed to know when I was having these moments and never felt the need to interrupt my thoughts with busy chatter. We spoke each other's language even in silence, Jesika and me.

Getting to church took no time at all because we talked all the way about different things. The minute we walked in church, we dipped our fingers into the holy water, and Jesika changed the way she always did. During Lent, I would catch her looking at the stations of the cross near the ceiling, as if to say, "You're the son of God. You didn't have to go through the torture." She became very focused, almost zombie-like during mass. Meanwhile, my mind often strayed as I put myself into a Nancy Drew or a Hardy Boys mystery as one of their crime-solving friends, always upstaging Nancy and the Hardy Boys, of course.

Jesika's friend Silvia started waving frantically trying to get her attention during mass, but she didn't even see her, so I nudged her, so she would notice. Jesika blinked and waved blandly at Silvia with a soft smile but remained consumed with the service.

CHAPTER 20

The Dead Girl

On the way back from church, the sun was bright and harsh. It was so hot that I needed something cool to drink.

"Faster we get home, the faster I can get something to drink," I pleaded.

"Wait!" Jesika pointed to a pair of go-go boots sticking out of the sewer opening. "Yuck, there's a pair of pantyhose in one of the boots." She wrinkled her nose, taking the pantyhose out of the shoe and stuffing them down in the sewer. I was shocked when she sat down on the curb and put the boots on her feet.

"These boots look practically brand new!" Jesika was looking down at her feet, admiring the stylish boots.

I must admit they were very nice go-go boots, but they belonged to someone else.

"You don't want to put them on your feet, Jesika. The person wearing them could have the cooties. Besides, there was a pair of pantyhose in them!"

"Stop tripping." She shook her head at me, her eyes still admiring the boots as she pointed her toes and extended her legs as if she were modeling them. "Besides, my mother would never buy me a pair of boots like this."

I sat quietly next to her while she ran her hands up and down the dirty white boots that fit her perfectly. As I watched, a putrid smell wafted toward us on the breeze.

"Gross! Do you smell that?"

"It sure ain't these boots," she laughed. "What do you think it is?"

I shook my head. I couldn't describe what I was smelling, as I hadn't smelled anything like it before. It was so horrible.

"Where do you think it's coming from?" Jesika finally turned her gaze from the beloved boots and looked at me. Her sense of smell wasn't always keen when she'd had her inhaler in her nose.

"Maybe it's down the hill?" I replied, my nose wrinkled in disgust.

"It could be a dead dog," Jesika replied, her head tilted to the side as she studied my face. She bit her lip and looked down at her newly acquired prized possessions and sighed as she grabbed her shoes and we headed down the hill. The trail led us through the patch of canyon we walked all the time.

The smell hung in the air, filling our nostrils until it became intolerable. We both put our hands over our nose and mouth.

My instinct was to follow that smell, but Jesika became apprehensive, "We don't know what this smell is." She looked at me wide-eyed, her mouth covered by her shirt. Maybe she was sensing something bad, but I was just plain curious.

The smell got stronger as we veered off the main trail, getting closer to dense bushes and two large trees. Suddenly, Jesika let out a bloodcurdling scream.

About ten feet from where we stood, a dead body was sprawled over a large, decaying tree trunk.

I felt lightheaded, and my heart pounded out of my chest. Jesika and I both passed out.

When I awoke, we were both lying on the hard, dry ground. I poked Jesika several times, and she woke up, hysterical, shaken, and speechless. She pulled herself up, looked at the dead body, and took off running and didn't stop.

I watched my friend run up the big hill with the speed of Mighty Mouse. It was almost comical. She looked like the Road Runner racing through the canyon like that. I knew then that her precious canyon wouldn't ever be the same for her.

I called for her to stop, but she just kept on running, leaving me alone with a dead girl's body.

I grabbed Jesika's black, patent leather shoes and walked over to the body to get a closer look.

The girl had an ugly bruise with a large cut at her temple where insects crawled. The expression of horror on her ashen, lifeless face was like something from a horror movie. She had hoop earrings in her ears and a mood ring on right ring finger. Her jean shorts were down around her ankles. I thought maybe someone came up from behind her while she was sitting on the fallen tree trunk.

I wished Jesika hadn't run away. I needed to bounce ideas off her. Our two brains would be better than one, but I did the best I could to take in all of the details. There was a significant amount of space between the trees and the decayed tree trunk that body laid upon. There were also two cigarette butts on the ground.

Deciding I had to find a neighbor that would let me use the phone to call the police, I ran up the hill to the house on the left, closest to the trail. I felt uneasiness in my stomach as I rang the doorbell. No one answered. I ran across the street, and a gray-haired lady answered the door. I told her that I had found the body of a teenage girl in the canyon.

"Oh, my word, come on in," she said in her southern accent and grabbed the phone to call the police. I stood there while she talked to an operator, worrying about Jesika and what she was telling her mother. I was sure she was home by now with how fast she was running. The lady told them as much as I told her and hung up the phone.

"The police will be here in no time," she said as she placed the phone on the receiver. "What an ordeal. You must have been frightened!"

"Yes, my friend and I actually fainted. We had just come from eight o'clock mass," I replied, looking down at the beige shag carpet in the stuffy living room.

"Oh, you poor dear." She frowned and then headed toward the kitchen "My name is Mildred. What's your name?"

"Marina," I answered, taking a seat at the small Formica dining table when she motioned for me to do so.

"Would you like some milk and cookies while we wait?"

"No, thank you, Miss Mildred. I couldn't eat anything right now." I was still thirsty, so I asked for some cherry Kool-Aid.

"Sorry, I don't drink Kool-Aid, sweetie, but I have iced tea." She smiled at me and grabbed two glasses from the cupboard. "Where's your friend? You didn't leave her with the dead body, did you?"

"Oh, no, ma'am. When we woke, Jesika ran home."

Mildred placed the glass of iced tea in front of me on the table and patted my shoulder softly, her face sympathetic. "Unfortunately, I would have reacted the same way. Oh, that poor girl's parents. I wouldn't want to be the one to give them the shocking news."

Mildred seemed nice, but I wanted her to stop talking, so I could think. My mind had so much information—the boots Jesika had found, the stockings found inside the boots, and yes, the cigarette butts near her body. The bruise near her temple had me puzzled. *How did she get that?* The information seemed to be closing in on me. *Where would I start? Maybe the killer had hit her and then strangled the girl with her own stocking and then placed them in the sewer opening. But then why would she have stockings on with her shorts?* I was a logical thinker. *Could it be that the killer was in a hurry and placed the boots and stockings in the sewer?* Jesika had the dead girl's boots on her feet. I wondered how she would react when I told her.

The police finally arrived, and Mildred didn't wait for them to knock on the door. We walked outside to meet them.

"My name is Officer Benson, and this is Officer Johnston."

Mildred nodded toward me, "This is the little girl that found a body. Let her tell you her story."

"What's your name, little miss?" Officer Benson held a pen and pad in his hand and was looking down at me expectantly.

"My name is Marina."

"What is your last name?"

"Massey. My friend Jesika and I found a dead teenage girl." I suddenly wished that I hadn't left my sleuth kit at home. I would have been able to check out the body more closely if it were with me.

"How do you spell Jesika?"

"J-e-s-i-k-a," I spelled my best friend's name.

"Last name?"

"Beckford."

"What time was it?" the officer asked.

"We walked to an 8 a.m. mass at Saint Rita's. It was over at 9 a.m. It takes approximately twenty minutes to get here from there, so it was about 9:30 a.m., give or take a few minutes."

"Where is your friend now?"

"She ran home." I grimaced as the officer wrote the information in his notepad.

"How do you feel?" Officer Johnston asked.

"I'm okay." I shrugged.

"Can you show us where you found the body?"

"Yes!" I was excited and relieved they weren't going to take me home.

CHAPTER 21

A Real Crime SCene

We walked down the trail, the smell of the decomposing body invading our nostrils as we neared it. The officers grabbed their handkerchiefs from their pockets and placed them over their mouths as they slowly approached the crime scene.

Officer Johnston put a hand on my shoulder and told me to stay back. He then turned around and headed back up the trail to where their car was parked. I watched him as he walked up and then back down the trail with yellow tape and masks in his hand. He handed me a mask to cover my nose and mouth.

"Thank you," I began as I secured the mask around my face. "The girl was strangled, and the murderer snuck up on her from behind the tree." I looked at Officer Johnston expectantly.

Officer Benson looked at me with an obvious sense of irritation. "We'll let the coroner decide all that!" he growled as he began taping off the area with the yellow tape.

Hmmm, I said to myself. I hoped that he was making notes of the red bruise on her neck and temple, position of her hands and body. I got down on my knees and noticed underneath her right foot was an indentation on the ground.

"Do you realize—" I couldn't get the rest of the words out of my mouth before Benson cut me off.

"Shhhhh," he frowned down at me. "I'm trying to focus!"

Just then, we heard a siren, and two men in an unmarked car pulled up to the curve. They weren't police officers. They were homicide detectives, and one of them was my Uncle Lonny. The other detective went behind the trees immediately, as if he knew something. How could I forget about Uncle Lonny? All my prayers had been answered.

"Uncle Lonny!" I screamed, running to my uncle's side.

"You know this girl?" Johnston asked.

"Yes, she's my niece." I could tell that Uncle Lonny was surprised to see me and it was a nice, safe feeling when he gave me one of his big bear hugs.

"Fancy meeting you here, Uncle," I said.

"Are you okay?" he asked. He was looking me over as if he expected me to be injured. "Where is your friend, Jesika?" He smiled.

"She ran home," I replied.

"No stomach for police work, huh?" I could tell he had been briefed.

"You know, you can go home right now," he winked and smiled softly down at me.

"Uncle, can I stay, please?"

As grim and unsettling as the murder of a teenage girl was, this was my first shot at an important case, and I didn't want to miss the opportunity.

"Sure, you can," he answered. "I'll give you a ride home when we're done here," my uncle said, nodding at me reassuringly.

"Okay," I said excitedly. I was going to be able to discuss the case with him. The other police at the crime scene wouldn't let me talk.

My uncle was the best detective in the world, and I knew he would uncover something I didn't know about the crime.

People were starting to gather from the surrounding neighborhood. Officers from several other squad cars arrived to keep the crowd at bay. A photographer arrived to take pictures, an ambulance pulled up, and the medical examiner was on the scene. Channels 6, 8, and 10 news reporters, along with their cameramen, tried to come down. There was also a reporter from the *San Diego Union* newspaper, who was quickly stopped. My uncle didn't want our names on the evening news or in the paper. Boy, did news travel fast.

I watched my uncle take out his gloves and place them on his hands and get to work. The way he worked was methodical and meticulous. He found two different sets of footprints including mine, and bagged a hair on the tree, cigarette butts, and her shorts. I watched him and the other detective talk about what he had found behind the trees. I assumed they were footprints from the killer. Officer Johnston placed a marker at the top of her head on the ground and markers near her hips and at her feet, and then put powder around her body to outline the exact placement of her body. Finally, the two men from the medical examiner's office picked up the young girl's body and placed it gently into a black bag and zipped it up. Then they placed the black plastic bag onto a stretcher and carried it up the hill.

I told my uncle some of what I knew, but purposely held back the information about the boots, until I could get more information from him.

"I'm concerned about your friend, Jesika," he said.

"Aw, she's all right," I assured him. "Uncle, can I help with this case?" I needed to know, and I didn't give him a chance to answer. "You know the girl struggled. There was an indentation on the ground under her feet."

"Very good eye," he commented. "Her shoes are missing. Where do you think they went?"

"I don't know," I said, trying not to give myself away. I wanted to talk to Jesika first. But then he asked me about the shoes I had in my hand, and I quickly lied, saying that Jesika had taken them off because they hurt her feet.

He looked perplexed, "She ran home without her shoes?"

"Uncle, I'm sure Jesika didn't feel a thing, she was running so fast." We both laughed.

On the way back to Jesika's house, my uncle told me that dead bodies always have a story to tell, and they would find out more once the body was transported to the Medical Examiner's Office.

"What will happen once her body is there?"

"The medical examiner is responsible for determining the cause and manner of her death. It's required by law that the examiner investigate because she died in a suspicious manner, and we don't know her identity."

Realizing that I didn't know as much as I thought I did, I felt privileged to learn from the experts.

We pulled in front of Jesika's house, and he followed me inside to speak to her mother. Jesika's mother was in the kitchen washing dishes.

"Hello," she said, turning from the sink and wiping her hands on her apron.

"Mrs. Beckford, this is my uncle, Detective Lonny Talbert."

"The girls found the body of a dead girl," my uncle started.

"Oh my God, Marina, where is Jesika?"

CHAPTER 22

Fear and Angels

I spoke up quickly, "She was so scared, she ran home."

She shook her head. "I've been home all day, and I haven't seen her since you and she left for mass this morning."

"I know where she is—down in the bomb shelter. Uncle, would it be all right if I talked with her first?"

"Yes," he agreed.

"I can get you some iced tea, Detective."

"That would be great," he answered as he sat down in the living room to wait.

I opened the sliding glass door and walked over to the opening of the bomb shelter.

"Jesika!" I yelled down.

"What do you want?" she answered back.

Her mother appeared behind me and called down to her, "It's okay, baby, you're going to be alright."

"Jesika, there's nothing for you to fear. The girl has been dead for a couple of days now."

"But what if the murderer comes looking for the two of us?"

I smiled, thinking she had the making of a good PI.

"If that was the case, at any time, he could have done something while we were passed out in the dirt." I hoped that made her feel better, but I couldn't tell. "You know, Jesika, Archangel Saint Michael's up here and he wants you to come up."

"How can he be up there if he is down here with me? He's my protection!" she exclaimed with conviction.

"You know, he wouldn't want us to hide because he told me that he doesn't want you to be afraid. He always has our backs," I encouraged.

"I saw her…. her face. Who would do such a horrible thing?"

"Let me talk to her, Marina," her mom said as she lowered herself into the shelter, and I listened to their conversation.

"I'm not going to let anything happen to you, okay? It would be over my dead body," her mom said tenderly.

"Mom, don't say that," I heard Jesika say.

"Well, I mean it," her mom said.

I beamed when I saw Jesika climb up and stick her head out of the bomb shelter and smile, with her mother right behind her.

"Marina, I'm going to help solve the case!" she exclaimed as she climbed out.

"Wait one minute, you two. I don't want you to be involved!" her mom interjected.

"But Mom, we are involved!" Jesika retorted.

"You know what I mean, Jesika. Marina, let your uncle handle this! It's one thing to solve a cat murder, but this… this is for the adults."

"I heard you guys found a dead girl's body." We all turned to see Sariah stepping out of the house. "Tell me what it looks like. Please, please tell me."

"Later, Sariah," I said.

"I bet the two of you are hungry. It's been a long day. Sariah, are you hungry?" Mrs. Beckford changed the conversation. "Hamburgers and french fries from Jack in the Box?"

"Yeah!" we screamed as we all stepped back into the house.

My uncle was still sitting in the living room, ready to ask Jesika the same questions he'd asked me in the car. I was so happy she didn't have the boots on her feet.

That night, we sat eating our Jack in the Box, waiting for the local six o'clock news on Channel 6. It was breaking news. The Reporter didn't give much information, except for the girl's age, height and weight, eye and hair color, and the fact that she was White.

"If you have any more information regarding the teenage girl, please call 619-555-0155," finished the reporter.

For a minute, I thought that they would mention our names, but they didn't.

A few hours later, Jesika and I went to bed but stayed up talking about the case.

Jesika's fear had mysteriously gone away, and I wanted to know how.

"Saint Michael talked to me in the bomb shelter. He said that we would be getting medals, and to make the sign of the cross when we feel the fear. It's through God that he can be everywhere at one time."

I should have known it would be Saint Michael, but I realized I didn't know much about him.

"Who is Saint Michael? I know he's an Angel, but what's his job?"

"He's an archangel, and he lives in heaven with God, the Almighty. He's more like a superhero to me, and he has a great sense of humor. All angels have the gift of unwavering faith, and his job is to protect and defend our immortal souls. And, oh yeah, he protects us from bad people."

"Well, speaking of bad people…" I was eager to get back to the original conversation, "we need to talk about boots and stockings."

CHAPTER 23

Withholding Evidence

"**Y**ou know, Marina," she said, "ain't nobody going to find those stockings now. They're probably all the way down in the sewer."

In our minds, it became imperative that we go back and see if we could get the stockings, as we both concluded that the murderer had used them to kill the victim.

Jesika wanted to give the stockings and boots to Uncle Lonny, and I wondered if they could lift fingerprints from nylon, or better yet, maybe there was some skin on the stockings. I told Jesika that we needed to hold on to our evidence. Uncle Lonny was the professional, and I wanted to know what he knew before we did anything else. Jesika was apprehensive, but I was stubborn, and she finally agreed.

The next morning, we woke up to the aroma of bacon and eggs that Pishoung had made. We got dressed and were ready to head out the door to look over the crime scene once again and check the sewer for the stockings. Pishoung asked us if we were hungry. We both said, no, trying to get out the door without a lot of information.

"Are you two going somewhere?" Pishoung asked.

"Oh, we're going to play in the canyon," I said, knowing he hadn't heard about the dead girl.

If he had known, he would have wanted to take us and hang around, but this investigation was ours to solve, with the help of my uncle of course.

I grabbed my sleuth kit, and we left.

Walking as fast as our legs could carry us, we reached the end of Bollenbacher and entered the canyon. From the dead end, it took about ten minutes to get to the top of the hill that leads down to Market Street.

"Wait a minute, Jesika," I said before descending. I reached into my sleuth bag, and handed Jesika the plastic binoculars, and I took the expensive ones. "What can you see from here?"

"You can see everything, the yellow crime scene tape—"

I interrupted, "No, just look at the surrounding areas."

She continued, "You can see Market Street, the factories to the left and right, railroad tracks, the trailer park, the rooftops of the houses that line Naranja Street…"

"I bet she's from that trailer park," Jesika said.

"Why do you think she lives in the trailer park?" I asked.

"I've walked through that trailer park with Sariah on the way home, and the kids in there are meanies. They chased us out one day."

I thought about the dead girl's jean shorts, halter top, hooped earrings, and the mood ring on her left hand. We ran down the hill and made our way across to Market Street, passing the factory and the parking lot. We decided to walk down 54th Street and make a right turn at the railroad tracks.

In no time, we were at the crime scene. We entered eagerly but carefully, so we didn't disturb anything. I noticed the markers that were placed where her head and feet had been. I remembered where my uncle had bagged her shorts, two cigarette butts, and the black hair he'd found on the tree. The perimeter of the crime scene had been extended past the trail, the three trees, and the bushes, up the incline to the curve.

"Let's look at the footprints first." Jesika pointed her binoculars to the ground. "There are so many footprints.

There's our footprints," she said, "there are some sneaker prints and some that might be a flip-flop."

As she spoke, I wondered if Jesika and I had ruined the crime scene by finding the body. I knew my uncle had noticed that the boot prints didn't follow the path to where the body was found, but he never said anything to me.

"Let's go, Marina!" Jesika wanted to go to the trailer park and ask some questions. We exited the crime scene and saw a kid on his bike near the curve.

"Hey, you guys aren't supposed to be down there!" he yelled. "Don't you know how to read? The yellow tape says: crime scene, stay out!"

"Aren't you Marty Jennings?" Jesika asked and then turned to me. "He goes to my school."

"I knew the dead girl," he said.

"Liar!" Jesika challenged. "What's her name?"

"Her name is Mattie McDuffie, and I don't care if you believe me or not."

"Did you report this to the police?" I asked.

"No! We weren't home when they came to our house. My mother didn't want to get involved. She says the people that live in the trailer park bring nothing but trouble." He scuffed the ground with his shoe. "You want to come over to my house and play?"

"Yeah," I said, eager to get more information, but Jesika looked back at me like she didn't want to go.

CHAPTER 24

Mr. O'Kelly and the In-between

His house was in the middle of the block on Carver Street, and once we got inside, he asked us if we wanted to play with his tops. We agreed and went into his bedroom. A typical boy, his room was messy from top to bottom.

"How can you find anything here?" I wondered as he reached up and pulled shoe boxes from the top of the closet.

Jesika looked around, her mouth half-hanging open. "My mother would beat my butt if my room looked like this…"

"Pick one," he said.

"I got this one," Jesika said after taking a good look at her options.

It didn't matter to me, so I stuck my hand in the box and blindly pulled out a blue and white top.

"You got the best one," he smiled.

I handed it to Jesika, and she gave me hers.

On the way to the backyard patio door, Jesika and I froze when we heard the hoarse voice from one of the rooms.

"Marty, come here."

"Who's that?" we asked.

"That my grandfather," Marty answered.

"Aren't you going to see what he wants?" I asked when Marty kept walking.

"No, my mother takes care of him. He's got cancer, and he's dying. He was supposed to die eight months ago, but he's still here."

His voice was sad, and I started to wonder about this boy.

"Where did your mother go?" I probed in my regular voice and then whispered to Jesika, "Maybe we should go, Jesika. Something's wrong with that boy."

"Yes, his grandfather is dying of cancer." Jesika remarked, "How would you act?"

"I would be sad and confused." I thought of my grandmother.

"My mother just went to the store. She'll be right back," Marty offered. "Don't worry, she never leaves for a long time."

"Maybe he just wants some water." Jesika said, as she turned to follow the voice.

We entered a blue room with two windows on the wall on each side of the bed and two brown nightstands. There was a picture of Jesus and Mary on the wall above him. On the nightstand was a pitcher of water and a rosary and a beautiful bronze statue of St. Michael.

Saint Michael seemed to be everywhere, just like Jesika said.

Marty's grandfather was lying in the bed, his face thin and chalky, and his hair looking like they hadn't combed it in weeks. Jesika leaned over to ask him if he wanted water, and he whispered, "Yes, please."

She picked up the pitcher and poured water into the glass, and I helped her raise his head as she held it in front of his chin. He drank the water slowly through a straw.

"Thank you," he said. He was so weak, his eyes closed when we lowered his head back.

Jesika asked, "Is he dead?"

"No, he's just sleeping. Let him rest now." Marty smiled sadly and turned to leave the room.

As we turned to follow him, Marty's grandfather sat up and said, "Mattie is here with me."

Both of us nearly shrieked and froze, as we looked at each other and then back at him and then around the room.

"She won't return, not tonight," the old man declared.

"He's always talking about the dead girl," Marty said matter-of-factly.

In disbelief, I asked, "Did you see the news the other night? Did your grandfather?"

"How is he going to watch the news, for crying out loud! No!" he exclaimed.

Jesika whispered, "His grandfather is *how* he knows the dead girl's name. His grandfather told him," she said with certainty.

Marty overheard and confirmed it. "You're right. Now can we go play with tops?"

"We can't stay long. We're going over to the trailer park. Does your mother know Mattie personally?"

"No, no one in our family has met Mattie. My mom was feeding Grandfather some soup when he said that Mattie shouldn't leave the trailer park. Then later, he said, 'Jack, don't leave her in the canyon alone. Jack, don't leave!'"

"When did he say this?" I probed.

"It was late Tuesday night during his sleep."

"I'm asking because I don't know what to believe."

Jesika whispered to me, "Marty's grandfather is… in-between."

"What do you mean, he's… in-between?" I pressed.

"You know, one foot is still here, and one foot on the other side," she answered.

"Okay, I get it. . . I guess we can play for a little bit."

Marty and Jesika were in the midst of a heated competition when his mom got home and offered to make lunch for him and us, once she discovered we were there.

"Mom, this is Jesika and Marina," Marty said, still focused on the game.

"Nice to meet you… Mrs.?" I extend my hand.

"Mrs. Jennings," she responded." "Do you girls live nearby?"

"No, we live in Emerald Hills. I go to St. Rita's with Marty," Jesika says.

"Mom, Grandfather needed some water, and they gave it to him."

"How sweet of you two. You are welcome here anytime," his mom said.

"Did you know—?" I started but Marty cut me off.

"Grandpa was talking again."

"Did you know Mattie?" I asked quickly.

Ignoring my question, she asked, "What did Grandpa say now?"

"He said Mattie was in the room."

Marty shook his head.

"Girls, Grandpa says lots of things," she giggled.

"Mama, tell my friends what Grandpa said the other night," Marty prompted.

"Well, he sat straight up in the bed and said, 'Jack, don't leave Mattie! Don't leave her alone!'"

But then Mrs. Jennings said something peculiar about her father having been born with a caul on his face.

"What's a caul?" Jesika asked.

I had heard my grandmother use the term before, and asked my mother what it meant, so I explained, "A caul or a veil is a thin, filmy membrane of the amniotic sac, which covers a newborn after birth. It looks like a shimmery coating on the face and head. It's harmless and can be removed by a doctor or a midwife. My nana told my mother that it meant the child was going to be psychic, accomplish wonderful things, or bring good luck to its parents."

"Aren't you a smart one?" Mrs. Jennings exclaimed.

"My mother is a doctor, ma'am." I retorted.

"Would you girls like some iced tea with your sandwich?"

"No thank you, Mrs. Jennings, we have somewhere to be," I responded.

"Mom, they're going to the trailer park to question those people."

I sighed, upset that Marty dropped the dime on us.

"Who do you girls think you are—homicide detectives?" His mother commented. "You two girls better be careful over there. The people there have arrest records. Besides, my mama always told me to mind my own biscuits, or you won't get any gravy." She giggled again.

Jesika whispered, "His mama's touched in the head."

I responded with a smile, and we left.

Marty followed us outside, "You want me… to come with you?"

"No, we'll take it from here."

"I can make sure you don't get hurt," he insisted.

"Okay," we said, knowing three was better than two *and* he was White.

CHAPTER 25

Words Don't Mean a Thing

The three of us headed toward 54th Street and took the entrance to the trailer park closest to Naranja Street. We didn't know whose trailer to pick first, so we started walking toward a young man standing outside his trailer, smoking a cigarette. He took a puff and stared in our direction.

"That's Jack," Jesika said as she grabbed my hand.

Jesika seemed nervous, and Marty was anxious.

"How do you know?" he asked.

"It's a feeling," she answered.

Before I could say anything, the young man said, "I'm not buying anything you're selling."

"We're not selling anything, mister, " Marty responded.

"Do you know Mattie McDuffie?" I asked.

"Yeah, I know Mattie." His tone was strained. "What's it to you? I haven't seen her in several days. Sometimes she disappears. She's probably at her best friend's house."

"Mattie's body was found Sunday morning, over in a canyon off Naranja Street," I said matter-of-factly.

"Mattie's body?" His pitch and volume increased. "How do you know that? Who found her?"

"We did!" I responded.

His face turned red as his body slid down the side of the trailer and onto his knees. "No, it's not Mattie! It can't be! I saw her Tuesday night," he said looking up at us. "What did she have on?" He became so emotional he couldn't talk.

When we began to describe her clothes, he grabbed his head and started to cry.

I knew right then and there that he didn't kill Mattie, but I had to ask him where he went after he left her that night. He said that he and Mattie had argued because he wanted her to go to a party, but she didn't like his friends.

"I'm… so… stupid," he stammered.

I asked him his name and wrote Jack Higgins in my notebook when he gave it to me. Marty's grandfather was right on the money.

Jack told me that he met her at 9:30 p.m. on Tuesday night. They kissed for a while and then argued about whether she would go with him, and he wasn't really sure about the time he left her. He thought that it might have been 10:30 or 11:00 p.m.

"I shouldn't have left her, but my temper got the best of me." Pounding on his forehead, he pointed to the back of the trailer park. "She lives on the left side of the street, closest to the other entrance. She hasn't been there for a while. Her mother kicked her out. It's a long story," he said. "I guess she was upset with me too."

Jesika spoke softly, "I'm sorry, Jack. I can see you loved her."

Marty put his hand on Jack's shoulder.

I asked him what trailer the party was located in, and he said it was three trailers away and we'd passed it on the way in.

"Thank you, Jack. I'm sorry. I'm sure we'll talk again soon," I said before we turned to leave.

I knocked on the door of the trailer where they had the party, and a boy came to the door.

"What do you little niggers want?" he spat when he opened it.

Marty bristled. "They ain't no little niggers. They're my friends, and don't you call them that. They have names… you stupid ass!"

"Calm down, Marty," I reached for his arm and smiled when I saw that Jesika was impressed with Marty's quick response. "Do you know Jack?" I said.

"What's it to you?"

"Did he attend a party here?" I asked.

"Yeah, he was here!"

"What's your name?" I asked.

"Puddin' Tame. If you ask me again, I'll tell ya the same…"

"You're an ignorant peckerwood, aren't you?" Jesika blurted.

I cut my eyes to signal her that this wasn't time.

"Now you little Black ankle biter get off my porch!"

"Don't have a cow. We're leaving!" Jesika said. "He ain't nothing but a peckerwood," she said loudly. The word nigger ignited Jesika's temper, and she looked back at the boy with furious eyes and yelled, "You're a Mr. Potato Head, Mr. Potato Head!"

"Jesika, calm down!" I raised my voice.

"We aren't going to get any more information out of him." I motioned for her to follow my lead.

"I'm sorry, Marina. I'll be cool next time," she said as we walked to the next mobile home.

Jesika decided it was her turn to ask the questions, so we walked onto the porch, and she knocked on the door.

"I have a bad feeling about this," Marty mumbled. "I'm going to head home."

CHAPTER 26

A Bad First Impression

Maybe we should have been scared too, but we weren't. We were waving goodbye to Marty when the door opened and Mattie's mother stood before us with a beer in her hand. She was dressed in a red and white flowery smock that wasn't at all flattering.

"Ma'am, I'm Jesika and this Marina, and we're the two girls that found Mattie's body."

"Mattie's dead?" Something about Mrs. Harriet McDuffie's expression and tone suggested she already knew. She didn't open the door, but through the crack, we watched her walk away and drop onto her couch and then let ourselves in.

"Yes," Jesika said, her voice calm and sympathetic. "Ma'am, we just want to offer our condolences. We're sorry for your loss."

Jesika put her arms out to hug the woman but stopped when Mattie's mother's face became sour and twisted.

"Girl, put your arms down!" she scowled.

Jesika's arms dropped, and her face fell.

"Mattie was nothing but trouble, bad news! And that good … for … nothing boyfriend of hers, Jack! He was always hanging around. He's the one she loved! She cared nothing about me. She only cared about her boyfriend and her hotty-totty best friend, Bethany. 'Bethany gets all As, and is graduating early from high school, and she's going to college!

Bethany is this, Bethany's that, Bethany got that!' I was sick and tired of hearing about Bethany!"

She took another swig of beer, and neither of us dared speak.

"I asked her to drop out of school to help me pay the rent, and you know what that little heifer told me? She wanted to finish high school. I didn't finish high school, and I turned out just fine!" She stood up and pointed her finger at us. "I have taken care of her all her life, and she couldn't help out her poor old mama!"

Shocked by Harriett's complete lack of compassion for her daughter whose reputation was kind and sweet, Jesika could no longer hold her tongue.

"All her life? She was only seventeen!" she shrieked.

"Well, I told her she couldn't stay here if she couldn't help pay the rent. Her good-for-nothing-stepfather took her side. I threw his butt out too!"

The conversation between Jesika and Mrs. McDuffie was awkward. Mattie's mother's face was contorted, and Jesika folded her arms and stood beside me.

Jesika composed herself and started again, "Ma'am, do you know anyone who would want to harm your daughter?"

"No! I didn't get into her business," she insisted.

"Do you know where Bethany lives?" I interjected.

"I don't know her complete address. She lives near Skyline Drive. That's all I know." I made a note of the street as she continued, "Somewhere near Mable E. O'Farrell Jr. High School."

"Mrs. McDuffie, where were you on the night your daughter was killed?" I asked gently.

"I was here asleep. My neighbor, Kathy, came over and woke me up to have a couple of beers. Go over and ask her— she'll tell ya."

Her story seemed disconnected. One moment, she was asleep and the next, her neighbor came over and they were drinking beer. After Kathy left, her husband had come over that night, begging her to let him back in the house. So, he spent the night with her and left in the morning.

Jesika whispered, "Her story sounds real fishy— real fishy."

"I'm not entirely sure that Harriet shouldn't be considered a suspect," I said to Jesika, and she agreed. We had no real conclusive evidence at this time.

"Do you have your husband's new address?" I tried a different direction.

"No! And I don't give a shit!" she screamed.

I lowered my voice. "Ma'am, did the police ask you any questions about Mattie's murder?"

"No! I'm sorry, I didn't answer the door." Her tone was sarcastic. "I saw them pull up. It's nothing but sad news when the police come to your house anyway." She belched, then she sat back on the couch. Suddenly, tears swelled up in her eyes and one tear dropped to her chest.

"I'm truly sorry for you, Mrs. McDuffie," Jesika said as we turned to leave.

As soon as the door closed behind us, Jesika said, "Man, she's cold! I couldn't imagine a mother not caring about her own child."

"I just feel sorry for the woman. Let's go and see if Kathy will collaborate on her story," I suggested.

We walked over to the next trailer and knocked on the door. Kathy came to the door. She had a small frame and reddish-brown hair. Holding a cigarette in her right hand, she puffed smoke in our faces. Both of us started coughing. When she offered us some water, we said no thank you.

"Ma'am can we ask you a few questions?" I asked.

"It depends on what it is," she responded dryly.

"It's about Mattie McDuffie," I answered.

"Did something happen to Mattie?" she questioned.

"Yes, ma'am. She was found in the canyon not too far away from here."

"What happened to her?" she asked, taking another drag.

"She was strangled to death."

"Oh, no, not Mattie!"

She opened the door and we walked in. She sat in her rocking chair and began to rock back and forth.

"I can't believe this. This didn't happen," she said.

"Ma'am, we found the body."

"Does Jack know? Harriet? Oh, dear, I could not be the one to tell her. Oh, no!"

"Yes, ma'am, he does know, and so does Harriet. We just spoke to both of them. He was really upset."

"Ma'am, that's why we're here, to ask you a few questions." Jesika's voice was soft and kind.

"Poor babies, I just knew the two of them would get married someday." Kathy sighed sadly.

"Ma'am, where were you on Tuesday night?" I asked.

"It was about 10:30 p.m., and I couldn't sleep. So, I grabbed the six-pack of beer in my fridge and took it over to Mattie's house. Harriet was asleep, I woke her up by knocking hard. We talked and laughed about Harriet's husband. She kicked him out of the house earlier. The doorbell rang and it was him. So, I took one of the beers, so that they could have some alone time. Poor Harriet, she must be beside herself."

"Thank you for your cooperation, ma'am."

"When did they start to hire midgets to work for the San Diego Police Department?" She laughed and then she started crying again.

"Don't you worry, ma'am. We're going to get to the bottom of this," I promised.

"I doubt that." She shook her head. "I can't believe I'm talking to kids. My first name is Catherine, and my last name is Perry. Kathy is my nickname."

I wrote her name in my notebook, and we left.

Marty was on the corner when we walked out of her house. "I thought you were going home?" I said.

"Nope, I was worried about you guys. If you didn't come out of there in another second, I was going to call the police."

We laughed because we knew no one around there answered their door when the police knocked.

"You two are really, really brave, or really stupid," Marty mused.

Jesika punched his arm softly. "Thanks, Marty, for defending our honor." Then her expression turned serious. "Everyone has an alibi around here."

"Yeah, something smells a little fishy," I agreed.

"You guys are going to get yourselves in deep trouble if you keep snooping around this trailer park," Marty warned.

CHAPTER 27

The Wrong Thing to Say

Just then, my uncle's car came around the corner, and we watched him park it in front of the McDuffies' trailer.

"I have some questions for the two of you." He looked between me and Jesika. "I'll give you a ride home."

"Uncle, Mrs. Harriet McDuffie is at home now. You should interview her first." I tried to tell him, but he ignored me and headed toward Jack's trailer first.

"You two can wait in the car with your friend," he said without turning his head.

Jesika and I got into the car, but Marty hung back.

"I can't go home with you guys," he said. "I'll just get in trouble. My mom will put me on restriction for a month. And I'd go crazy in the house for a month."

We waved goodbye again just as my uncle returned with Jack, who had volunteered to go downtown. He put him in the back seat with us, and then we watched him walk to another trailer. He knocked on the door of the boy we had spoken to who answered the door again.

"I thought I told you little niggers to stop knocking on my door!" the boy shouted before he saw who was on the other side of the door.

My uncle twitched at the term before he responded calmly, "I'm Detective Talbert. I'd like to ask you a few questions."

"When did they let niggers be detectives in the San Diego Police Department?" he taunted.

Uncle Lonny's temper got the best of him, and he yanked the boy off the porch, put his face in the ground, and handcuffed him behind his back. "You didn't have to go downtown. This could have been really simple, but you had to be stupid."

Jesika and I jumped out and hopped in the front seat quickly. He shoved the boy in the back seat with Jack and slammed the door. My Uncle Lonny was mad. I had never seen him so angry.

"Isn't this cozy?" the boy said to Jack.

"Shut up, Larry!" Jack snapped back.

Jesika looked at me and whispered, "That was a big mistake!"

My uncle was silent all the way to the police station, and so were we. He had us wait in the car until he returned with another officer. He took Jack in first, and the other police officer came and got the other boy. They placed the boys in two different interrogation rooms, and my uncle let Jesika and me watch Jack's through the interrogation mirror.

He sat across the table from Jack, and the other homicide detective stood up against the wall and asked him point blank, "Did you murder Mattie?"

"No! I didn't! I love her with all my heart…" Jack told my uncle that he had been going with Mattie since ninth grade. They had planned to marry after high school, and they were thinking about attending a college together. He said that she was smarter than him and had convinced him that with her help they could both graduate with degrees. "You know she wants to be a nurse." He paused. "Mattie was a sweet girl, with rotten parents."

"Larry said you left the party for forty minutes. That's suspicious, don't you think?" my uncle pressed.

"You better stop tripping and check her mother." Jack's face showed his concern. "I know Harriet was jealous of her own daughter!" He went on to say that her mother was a miserable, old, fat bitch, and her stepfather was a drunk. And he told the detective the same things he had told us. His story didn't change, and neither did his emotional response.

Jesika said, "I think he's right about Mattie's mother being jealous."

"Did you know that her mother kicked her out of the house?" my uncle asked.

"Yeah, everybody knew. I was so pissed off about it, I went over there to talk to her mother. She told me to mind my own business."

The detective asked him what kind of shoes Mattie had on when they met, and he told him pink flip-flops.

"Did you by chance take Mattie's flip-flops? There were no flip-flops at the crime scene," the detective pushed.

"Why would I do that? You can't pin this on me!" he shouted. "I loved Mattie. I'll take a polygraph test, if you don't believe me."

"That's not necessary," my uncle started. "Just give me the name of one other person that attended the party."

They released the two boys because they didn't have enough evidence to hold them. Uncle had asked Jack if he had any idea where Mattie's stepfather was living, and he said he thought he had moved in with his brother. They were going to question him next.

Mattie's mother was brought to the precinct for more questioning, but Mattie's stepfather verified her mother's alibi, and so did Kathy. Uncle exited the door and told us that we could use the phone at the front desk to call our families and let them know when we would be home.

Jesika spoke with Pishoung and told him that she had met up with my uncle, the detective, and that we were downtown at the police department and got to watch the interrogation.

"Do you need me to post bail?" He was laughing so hard, she couldn't get a word in until he stopped. "Get home before your mother does."

CHAPTER 28

The Interrogation Begins

We had been gone all day, so we were both exhausted and starving. It was 5:30 p.m. when we got in the car, and Uncle Lonny started another interrogation. "Okay, is there something you two want to tell me?"

"Yes, Uncle, but please don't get mad," I pleaded.

"That depends on what it is, Marina."

"Well, Jesika found a pair of practically brand new boots in the sewer with some stockings in them. This happened right before we found the body." I noticed I was talking really fast as my heart sped up.

"Slow down, and take your time," he said.

"We didn't know the boots or the stockings might be evidence. I told her not to put those boots on her feet, but she put them on anyway."

"Mattie had on a pink flip-flop, not boots," he pressed.

"We know!" Jesika and I shouted at the same time.

It had occurred to me that we had completely forgotten about the stockings, the very reason that we decided to revisit the crime scene.

"You told me a bold face lie, Marina. A good investigator would never impede an investigation. We work together!"

"I'm sorry," I said, my head down. I had never been scolded by my uncle.

"You had Jesika's patent leather shoes in your hand!" he exclaimed. We saw the footprint on the ground that led away from the crime scene. Don't keep valuable information from me, Marina, ever again!"

If Marty hadn't shown up, we would have stayed focused. But on the other hand, if he hadn't shown up, we wouldn't know Mattie's name. I realized that we'd both slipped up because we didn't remember to get the stockings.

Jesika told him where the stockings were located, and he changed course. He got off I-94 South and merged onto the Euclid Street exit, and we took Euclid all the way to Naranja Street. It was still light outside, so it was easy for us to point to the sewer opening. Uncle got out of the car and, leaving the door still open, put on one glove and pulled out the stockings. I began to survey the area from the car, my eyes looking toward the house next to the trail. I had a hunch about the house, but I had no idea who lived there.

"Uncle, did you talk with anybody at that house over there?" I pointed.

"Yes, Marina. Nigel Glasgow lives in that house. He is a twenty-six year-old White male. He works during the day and takes night classes over at San Diego State. He's got a solid alibi. He stayed late to speak with his teacher. Then later he went to the bar to drink with some classmates. Everyone I spoke to said he was there."

He put the stockings in a bag and got back in the car.

"I also had a hunch that Mattie lived in the trailer park..." My uncle recalled that Mrs. Rutherford's was the first trailer he went to that night. Upon showing her Mattie's picture, she did not provide him with Mattie's name, but instead gave him the name of another girl, Claudia, and took him to the young girl's home. Claudia's father, a large man with a deep voice, was angry about being woken out of his sleep and jerked open the door. When he looked at the picture, his large hands began to shake.

It was then I realized that we had Mattie's name before my uncle did. Communication was lacking on both sides, but I didn't say anything.

"The only person we did not question was Bethany because she lived too far away…"

He also told us that Mattie's mother was reluctant to identify the body because she just couldn't bear to see her daughter that way. So, the stepfather identified it.

"Harriet didn't want to see her daughter because she didn't care," Jesika said.

"I'm sorry to say, but I think you're right," my uncle agreed as he pulled up in the driveway and parked the car.

Jesika tried to exit the car in a hurry, but Uncle Lonny stopped her.

"Wait, young lady, I have something for you." He handed Jesika a small box that had two gold Saint Michael medallions in it. "One is for you."

"It's the medallion! It's the medallion!" She exclaimed that it was a sign from Saint Michael. "Thank you, Uncle Lonny." She exited the car and ran across the street with the box that had my medal too.

"I guess I'll get my medal later," I said smiling.

We entered my house.

"Is that you, Lonny?" My mom greeted him with a big hug and kissed me on the forehead.

"Marina looks more like you every day," he said.

"How did the two of you meet up?" Mother asked.

"I was doing some investigative work off 54th Street," Uncle Lonny started.

Mother looked at me sternly. "Marina, what were you and Jesika doing all the way over there?"

"Jesika has a friend that lives over there, Mom. His name is Marty."

"Sis, did you hear about the dead girl found off Naranja Street?" Lonny continued. "The girls found the body."

"No!" Mother exclaimed. "Russell and I didn't watch any television up at Big Bear. The news is too depressing," she said.

She wrapped her arms around my neck. "Lonny, are they safe?"

Lonny hugged my mother and me, and said that he would make sure that we stay safe.

"I would have called you, but Marina told me that you were on a weekend getaway. I didn't want to spoil your trip."

"Lonny, you could have called me."

"Sis, what could you have done?"

"Mom, we weren't hurt in any way… I'm okay. It scared Jesika. She ran all the way home."

He told my mother the whole story. As I watched my mom's face, I thought that I might have to stay in the house for a month. Instead she gave me the same warning Jesika's mom had given me.

When I walked my uncle outside, he reminded me that he needed the boots because they might be evidence.

"Are you mad, Uncle?" I asked.

"Marina, we need to work together, you know."

"I'm sorry," I said. "We should have given them to you sooner."

Uncle got in the car, and I ran across the street to get my medallion and the boots. I rang the doorbell, and Jesika jerked open the door.

"I knew it was you." She put my St. Michael medallion around my neck. "I'm sorry I ran off with yours."

"It's okay." I hugged her.

"I really like your uncle. He's nice."

"Yeah, I like him too. And he needs those boots."

She looked sad before she went to the other room to retrieve them.

"I'll see you tomorrow." I grabbed the boots from her and hurried back across the street. After handing him the boots, I hugged him goodbye.

When I walked in the house, my mother was on the phone with Jesika's mother, asking her about Jesika. I guessed they were talking about today's events. Then I heard my mother say that she had three more days off, and she wanted to return the favor. She had made plans for a fun day at The Plunge and said that Jesika and her sister and brother could spend the night too. I knew it was impolite to eavesdrop, but I was glad I did.

CHAPTER 29

Answers at The Plunge

On Tuesday morning, Jesika and her sister and little brother came over to the house early. Mom fixed scrambled eggs, pancakes, and sausages for breakfast. Sariah ate enough for all of us, and Jayden only ate his pancakes while Jesika and I cleaned our plates.

My dad ate breakfast with us since he had a late morning at work. He was a teacher at San Diego High school. Normally, he would have the whole summer off, but he decided he would teach summer school. He told us some funny stories about his students, and I could tell he was a great teacher. He knew every one of them by name, could tell you how intelligent they were, and how they behaved. The student that behaved the worst would get lectured, but I knew him to be a big softy.

"We're going to The Plunge today!" Mother declared.

We started screaming and jumping up and down in excitement..

I knew she was taking us to our favorite place in Mission Beach because she knew me. I knew it was her way of distracting me. It was okay because I loved swimming. The other kids had their own experience. Sariah wasn't afraid of water and didn't mind going under. Jayden didn't like water and would only get in if my mother got in with him. Jesika didn't know how to swim, but she liked going to the pool.

When I tried to teach her how to swim, she choked me around the neck because she couldn't feel the bottom of the pool. I gave up after that.

I felt sorry for her when she apologized and told me her father had thrown her in deep water, expecting her to automatically swim, when she was younger. Because she was afraid of water, she panicked and started to drown. She recalled her father pulling her out of the pool and coughing up water. She said her life flashed in front of her eyes. I think she was just exaggerating.

We couldn't help talking about the case a little bit, but we didn't want my mother to overhear us. So, we huddled in the corner while she played with Jayden and Sariah in the pool.

When I got home, I told Jesika, "I'm calling my uncle," my voice laced with impatience.

"What new information do you think you're going to get out of him? We already know everything he has to say. You remember looking at Mattie's corpse lying on the ground with a dark bruise on her temple. Unless you want to ask him how the killer bashed her skull in and then arranged her body like a twisted doll…"

I shuddered as Jesika painted the scene, "He must have looked into her eyes when he hit her, but she didn't die right away. She was still gasping for air, so he strangled her with his bare hands."

Jesika's words pierced my mind like a sharp knife. I couldn't find any evidence to contradict the grim scenario she painted—a vivid picture of horror that unfolded there— although it hurt to imagine.

To ease the tension, we started talking about events that led up to Mattie's tragic end.

"What we do know is that she had her shorts off, so she and Jack were doing more than just kissing." Jesika sounded very confident.

"They weren't off. They were around her ankles," I corrected her.

"That's what I meant, they were doing the horizontal mambo." Jesika smirked.

"You mean they were having sex? Yeah, maybe. Good point," I said.

"After they argued, she wasn't herself," Jesika said. "I can see the whole thing. She said that his friends aren't friends, and he shouldn't hang around them. They go back and forth. Mattie tells him he is better off without them. He tells her that she's been hanging around Bethany too long, and she is starting to act just like her. Then he gave her the choice to go back with him or not, and she said no.

So, he trudged up the hill back over to the trailer park and left her sitting in her underwear on the tree stump crying. There was a man in the brush who saw that she was by herself. He had his chance, and he took it."

The look on Jesika's face was fixed and distant. When she finally came out of her trance, she said, "Marina, What do you call a killer that kills for no rhyme or reason?"

"He's a serial killer!" I answered, thinking that she was onto something.

"Oh, no!" Jesika responded.

"The boots that you found. If they don't belong to Mattie, who do they belong to? What if they belong to another girl, and we haven't found her body yet?"

It was true that the boots and the stockings were just there, and that was odd to both of us.

"I'm sure they lifted fingerprints from them, and possibly the stockings."

I recalled Uncle Lonny had taken both our fingerprints down at the police department. He had made it seem like a learning exercise, but I was on to him. He wanted to make sure all the prints were identified. Jesika, looking at me with glazed eyes, cocked her head to the side in deep thought.

"You know that the truth is bound to come out sooner or later. Besides, Mattie wants us to find her killer."

I was just about to ask Jesika how she knew that when my mom's voice startled us. "What are you two girls whispering about over there?"

"Nothing!" We replied at the same time.

It was no longer a race to solve a murder, but to catch a serial killer.

"You girls seemed pretty occupied by something at the pool. Is it the case your uncle's working on?" my mom asked on our way home.

"No, Mom," I responded.

"You know, Marina and Jesika, you will be teenagers and then adults with your own children, so enjoy your childhood while you can."

We took a shower and washed the chlorine out of our hair, and then we went outside to play. When she saw us, Irene ran up the sidewalk to my porch.

"Where have you guys been? Did you guys hear about the dead body of a girl that police found in the canyon?"

"Where have you been? We found her!" Jesika chimed.

"Uh-un, that's not what the news said." Irene shook her head.

"My uncle wouldn't let them release our names," I answered.

"Aren't you guys scared that a killer might be looking for you?" she gasped.

"Nope!" we answered, but we both were.

"Well, I would be locked up in my house, under police protection," Irene declared.

CHAPTER 30

Footprints and Fingerprints

We didn't feel like talking about the murder anymore, so Jesika suggested we play a game of kickball. Jesika was one team captain, and I was the other. Jesika picked Irene, and I picked Sariah, and before we knew it, every kid on the block picked sides. We played until it got dark.

Then it was time to call Uncle Lonny. I grabbed the phone and took it in my room, and we sat on the bed.

"Why is the phone cord so long?" Jesika asked.

"You can thank my brothers for that! They talk to their girlfriends in their room, in the bathroom, and on the porch, just so they can have some privacy. I don't care about listening to them talk to their girlfriends. It grosses me out."

The phone rang, and I was lucky that Uncle wasn't in the field.

"Marina, how are you?" he asked. "How are my little junior detectives?"

"Good, Uncle."

"I'm glad you called," he started.

"What's new in this case?" I couldn't wait.

"I have no suspects now and no new leads. Been going through our fingerprint database, and it's tedious work, and Detective Bramston is helping me. Jesika's fingerprints are on the boots, but none belong to Mattie. There were traces of Mattie's skin on the stockings, and Detective Bramston and I found footprints from the curb, going down the hill and between the bushes. They stopped behind the tree. Maybe the killer had a medium-sized shoe print and loafers because footsteps that are coming down the hill are the same ones behind the tree stump. We also searched the area looking for the flip-flops. We even accessed the sewer to see if the flip-flops were there, but they weren't."

I stared wide-eyed at Jesika as I listened.

"It was confirmed by the medical examiner that Mattie was killed Tuesday around 11:30 p.m. due to suffocation. Strangled. He said that there was a bruise at her temple, and she had been hit with a blunt object first and strangled afterwards."

Since the boots didn't belong to Mattie, I thought maybe there was another victim the boots belonged to.

"Uncle, maybe those fingerprints belong to another girl that is missing."

"You could be right, Marina." No one had called in a missing person report. "This murderer might as well have been a phantom," he said reluctantly.

"What about her stepfather?" I asked.

He said that he had a good and solid alibi.

"What about her mother?" I was grasping at straws.

"No, Marina; her mother is not a suspect."

"I know. That was dumb," I replied, sorry I'd said it.

"I know you want to find the killer, and so do I, before he kills again. I think we may have a serial killer on our hands, and no conclusive evidence. At least, the evidence isn't a part of this crime scene."

I knew my uncle was holding back information.

"What are we going to do now?" I asked.

He said that the chief of police was going to be on Channel 6 news at 6 p.m., and they were going to release Mattie's name. Hopefully, someone would call with more information.

"Okay, Uncle, I'll talk with you tomorrow."

"Wait, Marina! How did you find out Mattie's name again?" he inquired.

"From Marty's grandfather. You should go and talk with his mother, Mrs. Aileen Jennings," I suggested. "They live at 5234 Carver Street. Remember, I told you about Marty's grandfather, Mr. O'Kelly."

"Oh, I remember now," he said. It only confirmed my suspicion that he had dismissed it.

"Marina, I would like it if you and Jesika would stay close to home for your own good."

"But Uncle, what about the case?"

"Goodnight, don't let the bedbugs bite!" he said before he hung up the phone.

Jesika was anxious to hear what he had told me. "What did he say?"

"He said the evidence that we have isn't a part of this crime scene…" I could see the disappointment on her face as I told her everything. "He also thinks that the murderer is a serial killer, and that he's still out there looking for his next victim."

"Well, he didn't tell you anything we haven't figured out ourselves."

"He doesn't want us to be involved anymore. It's too dangerous." I grimaced.

"We're officially off the case?"

"Yeah," I replied.

We sat quiet for a few minutes, not saying anything. I couldn't help but think about my uncle, whose voice seemed out of sorts. He camouflaged it by trying to sound upbeat when he hung up. As I wondered what was up with him, it occurred to me that he was the only Negro detective in the San Diego

Police Department. I thought there might be something going on downtown that he didn't tell me about. I remembered the story of the other detective that had been demoted and was now walking a beat downtown.

My mother had told me about my uncle when he was promoted to detective. It was a real-life example of how Black people had to prove worthiness, ignore racism, stay strong, and prove that they could be as good as Whites applying for the same position. When he was promoted to detective, someone had put an altered picture of Frank Carter, San Diego Police Department's first Negro officer, depicting him as "ape-like" on my Uncle's locker.

She said that he snatched it off his locker, folded it up, and put it in his pocket when he saw some White officers standing around waiting for him to react. When he showed up at her front door later that day, he was crying like a baby. And when he showed her the picture, she cried. He told her that he was gonna carry that picture in his pocket to remind him that he could never get too comfortable. Frank Carter became my uncle's strength and inspiration that day.

I knew that Negroes had to work twice as hard to prove they were good at their job, as my parents talked about this with me and my brothers all the time. Our report card was such a big deal, and my parents had very high expectations for me and my brothers. We couldn't get anything below a C.

"What's wrong, Marina?" Jesika asked as she followed me back to the living room.

"Nothing," I said.

I really wanted to talk with my father, but he wasn't home from work yet. When I found my mother in the kitchen, fixing us chili dogs and fries—my favorites—I decided to talk to her.

"What if Uncle doesn't solve the case, Mom?"

"It's an unsolved case, honey, and there are plenty of them. Don't worry about your uncle. He's good at his job." She put her hands on my face. "What did I tell you?"

"I know… you don't want me to think about his cases."

"Right," she confirmed.

I asked her if it would be okay for us to sleep in the tree house in the backyard.

"Now, that is an excellent idea. Ask one of your brothers to pitch a tent outside with you."

Of course, my brothers ignored me.

It was a large tree house with plenty of room, and my dad had put a window on the roof, so that we could look up at the stars. I loved it, and so did Jesika and Sariah. It also had a bucket that had a toilet seat over it. He had put that there so my brothers wouldn't have to come down in the middle of the night. It even had a pulley with a basket attached, so we could pull stuff up, and that's what my mother used to send our dinner up to us. For the rest of the night, we told ghost stories and laughed about the kids and parents in the neighborhood.

CHAPTER 31

The Funky Zoo

One Saturday afternoon, Jesika's mom took us to the zoo. Sariah didn't want to go.

"Animals at the zoo stink! They smell!" she said, scrunching her face up in disgust.

I had never been, so I was anxious to go. I hoped she wasn't going to spoil it for us. It turned out Jesika wasn't excited about the zoo either. To her, all the animals looked kind of sad. She was certain they remembered the jungle.

"What if you had to live out your life in a cage? You'd be sad too."

When we got home, we found Carlton sitting on Jesika's front porch eating out of a carton of their ice cream with his hands. Mrs. Beckford was surprised, but she wasn't angry. On the other hand, Jesika and Sariah were as mad as wet hens.

"Mom, he went into our freezer!" Mrs. Beckford didn't respond. "Mom!" Jesika said a little louder, "Aren't you gonna beat his butt?"

"No," she said softly as she walked past him. "Carlton, are you enjoying that ice cream?"

"Yes," he said with his head down. I was laughing so hard, I could barely walk up the steps.

"That boy is brazen!" I quipped.

"What if *we* went into *your* garage and got *your* ice cream out of *your* freezer?" Jesika asked, spitting her words toward Carlton.

"Yeah! What if? We'd hafta take on your whole family!" Sariah said, smacking him in the back of the head as she walked into the house. She was right. If you fought one of them, you had to fight all six of them.

CHAPTER 32

The Dream

In the tree house that evening, we talked about neighborhood gossip.

First, we questioned why Irene's brother, Tommy, called Georgia "hairy" every time she rode her bike down the street. Whenever her mother was outside watering the grass, she would yell back, "Don't you call my daughter hairy!"

"Maybe it's cuz she's part chimpanzee," Sariah suggested, and we laughed.

All the boys on the block made fun of Douglas because his mother rang for him to come into the house.

There were a lot of things that were said about the adults on the block.

Irene's father, an officer in the army, had left her mother with six kids.

Some time back, it had been rumored that Georgia's mother was seeing the husband of the neighbor that lived directly across the street from them.

"A year later," Jesika filled us in, "his wife found out and shot him dead. And went to prison for it. My mom says that's the reason Georgia's mom became a Jehovah's Witness."

"My mom likes to talk to the Jehovah's Witnesses," I said. "We listen in sometimes. I think she just likes arguing with them."

"Why would your mom even talk to them?" Jesika wanted to know. "We're Catholics."

"My mother is not going to turn away anyone that wants to talk about God. She says God works in mysterious ways and can show it through different people."

The conversation moved to Deidra Bladelock's parents, who lived across from the dead end of our block and were always in the middle of the street arguing.

"My mother goes on and on about how bad it looks and says they need to take their business inside."

I felt bad for Deidra. Sometimes, I would see her sitting on the porch looking like she had lost her best friend. She was older than Jesika and me, so we didn't see much of her.

"Deidra always looks so angry," Jesika mused.

"That's because she has so many freckles," Sariah explained.

"Yeah, you could play connect the dots, there's so many," Jesika added. We all burst out laughing at once.

Sometimes I wondered what was said about my parents. They gave cocktail parties, but they were very selective about who they invited from the neighborhood. They always invited Jesika's parents. Even though my mother was older, they got along just fine. But once I overheard Jesika's father telling Rita that he thought we were uppity Black folk. Her mother was embarrassed and changed the subject.

I decided to ask Jesika why he thought that way. She said it was because he grew up on a farm and was just an old country boy. "He doesn't know any better."

That made sense to me.

As we fell into a quiet silence, I thought about how my mother found Jesika's mother charming and funny at the same time. She would always say, "Well, I declare." Or "I-yi-yi-yi-yi."

Whenever Jesika's mother walked into a party at our house, you'd think she was a movie star. She would come through the front door as if someone was snapping pictures of her. "I'm here, I'm here!" she would announce to anyone listening. My mother always complimented her on the way she was dressed, even though she had a different eye for fashion.

Jesika broke the quiet by asking me about my real father, and I told her all I knew.

"I don't know that much about him. He was an officer in the marines, and he was in the Korean War. He wasn't the same when it was over. My mother divorced him when I turned three. My brothers remember more than I do and never have anything good to say about him. When my mother remarried, we took my stepfather's last name. He's the only father I've ever known."

After a few moments of silence, I continued, "When I was five, my brother told me that our father had died of a drug overdose. He said when they got home from school, Billy found my dad on the floor with a needle stuck in his arm. He was supposed to be watching me. They found me in my father's closet crying and called 911. Chicago police arrived, and the ambulance took his body away. He told me I cried all day long. To make me stop, they took me to an ice cream soda shop. He said I kept saying, 'More,' after every ice cream soda. I remember getting really sick. Maybe that's why I don't eat much ice cream now."

"Where was your mom?" Jesika asked.

"I don't know. I don't remember." I said, as another heavy silence fell between us.

Full of chili cheese dogs and Kool-Aid, Sariah was the first to drift off to sleep and was snoring like an old man. Jesika was next. I laid awake with one thing on my mind: Mattie.

Nancy Drew was the one who inspired me to even want to try and solve a case. I should probably give my Uncle Lonny some credit too. But Nancy… She was fearless. I was scared, and I felt like we'd never solve this case. Maybe this case was just plain over our heads. I got angry again thinking about my uncle deciding we couldn't help him anymore. I understood, but I felt as if I knew Mattie and that she was calling out for justice.

Drifting off, as my eyes shut, I was suddenly surrounded by darkness. I could hear noises, but I couldn't see anything. I thought I was in the middle of the street and bent down to touch the asphalt to be sure. I saw Bonnie and Sherry's cat, and I reached to pick it up, but it hissed at me and scratched my hand.

Then I heard a voice that said, "Don't be afraid. You're on the right track."

As I turned toward the voice, a cold, White hand reached for mine, leading me. Once we got to the dead end, we started floating across the canyon to the hill. Her cold hand let go of mine, and I started running down the big hill. The faster I ran, the longer the hill got. Finally, I reached the bottom.

The yellow crime scene tape was in the shape of an arrow. Marty's grandpa was on one side of the arrow, and Jesika was on the other. They were pointing toward the trees and telling me to hurry up. I ran over toward Mattie and Jack, but I was stopped by the yellow tape. I finally got free of it.

The gate that Jesika had shown me at the top of the hill kept opening and closing, and I looked toward it for a moment. I saw Mattie's mother at the top of the hill just watching and whistling. She wasn't doing anything to help her daughter. I frantically pointed to Mattie, and her mother's whistling got louder and louder. I saw Mattie and Jack arguing, their mouths moving fast—super fast. They didn't see me, even though I was trying to get their attention. I couldn't see the killer's face, but I knew he was there, prowling like a cat about to pounce.

Then Mattie was sobbing and pulling up her shorts. She didn't hear him or see him. I yelled for Jack to stay, but he left anyway. Mattie was starting to sit down on a tree stump, and I yelled to let her know the killer was there. I saw the bruise on her head, and it was huge. I started yelling again…

"Wake up, wake up!" Jesika was shaking me. "Marina, wake up!"

I woke up trying to catch my breath, mid-scream.

Sariah woke up confused, "Wha-wha-what … what's wrong?"

"Uh… sorry. I guess I was screaming…"

"You weren't screaming. You were growling in your sleep, Marina. I had to wake you up. You were scaring me."

I heard my father at the back door, calling my name, "Marina? Are you okay? Is everything alright, girls?"

"Yes, Dad, I'm fine," I hollered to reassure him.

"Marina just had a bad dream, Mr. Massey," Sariah added.

"You girls wanna come inside?"

"No, Dad, I'm okay!"

"I do!" Jesika said.

"I just had a nightmare, Jesika. I didn't mean to scare you," I said sharply. I felt bad because this wasn't typical of me.

"Are you sure you're okay, Marina?" she questioned.

"Yes! I'm okay. Stop asking me!"

"Well, if you start growling again, I'm going in the house."

"Okay, just don't ask me if I'm alright again."

I tried to play it off by closing my eyes and pretending to be asleep. Soon, I drifted off again.

CHAPTER 33

Impromptu Talent Show

Irene woke us up. "Time to get up, sleepyheads." We could hear her climbing the ladder.

She had brought the Supremes album over so we could dance and sing to it. Every girl in the neighborhood wanted to be a Supreme. Sometimes we would fight over who was going to be the lead singer, Diana Ross. Jesika was a good Diana Ross. She had all of her expressions and gestures down pat. Sometimes Jayden would be the fourth Supreme. Mom loved to watch us perform. When my brothers would bark like dogs and throw shoes at us, Mom would make them go outside and cut the grass in the front and the backyard for teasing us. The Supremes always brought fun and excitement.

We all washed up, and my mom fixed breakfast. We couldn't finish eating fast enough.

Mom put the 33 on the stereo and took a front row seat on the couch to watch us. We went through the entire Supremes album, singing it word for word, taking turns being Diana Ross. Even Jayden got in on the act.

"Let's sing something else," Jesika suggested.

"What?" I replied.

"I got a surprise," she said. "I'll be right back." She ran out the front door and across the street. When she returned, she told my mom and me and everyone else to sit on the couch. She put on a 45 and started singing "Goldfinger." Irene started laughing, and so did Sariah. Jayden was clapping.

"Shhh," my mother said. "Listen!"

To our surprise, Jesika was getting down. In the middle of the song, she made a hand gesture to, "For a golden girl, know when he kisses her, it is a kiss of death from Mr. Goldfinger." At the end of the theme song, she belted out, "He loves gold, he loves only gold."

We all stood up and clapped. My mother and I thought Jesika was very talented. Mom asked Irene to go get Tommy, so he could dance to JB's "Out of Sight." Oh, man, it was on then! Everyone was up dancing. Even my brothers came into the living room to join in. They thought Tommy was the coolest ever because his imitation of James Brown was perfect.

While we all knew how to have fun, the real talents were Irene and her brother, Tommy. She could play the piano, and he could make suitcases sound like drums and trash can tops sound like cymbals. So, after a while, we decided to go to their house, and we danced and sang all day long, until someone had to go home.

It was already 4:30 in the afternoon, and my mother had made us hoagies for dinner. Jesika and I wanted to go and eat dinner in the tree house, so I put our hoagies in the basket, and Jesika pulled it up.

"Please tell me more about the dream," she said as she took a bite out of her sandwich.

"It was just strange. I don't really want to talk about it."

"You know, Marina," she said, as she took a gulp of her Kool-Aid and started choking. I hit her on her back, and we laughed. Undeterred, she went on, "My mother says that you can face your worst fears through dreams and work out all your problems. You can do anything in a dream. I know it is true, because I can fly in my dreams. And we can solve this mystery too."

"It was just strange," I gave in. "I was running down the hill in slow motion. You and Marty's grandpa were holding onto the yellow crime scene tape and pointing. Telling me to hurry! Mattie and Jack were talking at a fast speed. Mattie's mother whistled, but she wouldn't help. It was just plain eerie!"

"You mean their mouths were moving fast like the people in a karate movie."

"Yeah, you could describe it that way."

"Dreams can show you things that in real life you can't see, Marina."

"There you go again! How extraordinary!" I responded, annoyed.

"I'm just trying to help!" Jesika hurled back. "Solve your own damn mystery instead of wasting my whole summer."

She was so mad, she got up and headed toward the ladder to leave.

"I'm sorry, Jesika. Come back. Please come back!"

Jesika had stopped and was staring at something I couldn't see.

"You won't believe who's here," she said. "It's Marty."

"Hey!" Marty hollered as he began climbing up. "I've got something really important to tell you guys." It must have been important for Marty to ride his bike all the way over to my house. "My grandfather told me that the two colored girls must be careful. It wasn't in his sleep this time. He was looking right at me. Can you guys come over to my house?"

"Yeah," we both said.

"I've written it all down, but I was so excited that I forgot my notepad. Some detective I am," he snickered.

Jesika went to get her bike out of the garage while I told my mother that we were going to play over at Marty's house.

She told me to be home before dark. Marty assured her that if it got too late, his mother would bring us home.

"Are you sure, Marty? Because I don't want them to ride their bikes from your house after dark."

"I'm sure, Mrs. Massey. Can they have supper too? We're having chili."

"Mmmm, I love chili!" Jesika walked through the living room out of breath.

"Marina, call me when you get to Marty's house," Mom said and hugged us as we left.

Before we took off, Marty had several questions about the tree house, and I felt compelled to answer all of them. He wanted to know about the wood, the nails, and how long it took to build. He liked the design, because it resembled a fort—but on a smaller scale.

"A girl with a treehouse. That's cool," he finished.

Jesika got jealous and told him that she had a bomb shelter in her backyard.

"What? A bomb shelter! Show me!" I guess he didn't believe her. So, we ran across the street, so he could see her bomb shelter.

He looked down and confirmed, "It's a bomb shelter alright." His comment was not as enthusiastic as she thought it would be.

"Let's ride!" he cheered.

I was really starting to like this boy, but not the way Jesika liked him.

We decided to ride our bikes through the canyon because it was quicker.

CHAPTER 34

Mr. O'Kelly's Warning

"**L**ook!" Jesika said, "It's a full moon!"

We looked up at the huge moon for a couple of minutes. It seemed to be following us as we rode. We rode down the hill, which took skill. If you weren't careful, you could end up over your handlebars with your face in the dirt. We cut across Market Street and up the sidewalk, passed the trailer park, and then rode in the street and on the sidewalk, straight to Marty's house. His mother was sitting in the living room watching television and laughing when we arrived.

We made our presence known by saying, "Hello." She waved in response but seemed unconcerned.

We immediately went into Marty's room, and Marty grabbed his notebook out of his book bag. As he started to read, Jesika got up and went toward his grandpa's room.

One evil person faces another.

This sounded like one of Jesika's riddles.

"What does it mean?" I asked. What he read next made the hair on the back of my neck stand up. It was written like a scene from a movie.

Mattie's mother was in the canyon. She picked up a branch and hit Mattie on the head. She had gotten so mad because she couldn't convince Mattie to come home. It happened in a split second. She hit Mattie on the temple hard enough to break the skin. She thought that she had killed her.

Suddenly the killer came from behind the tree and said, "NOOOO, she's mine! You've spoiled everything, and now you're gonna join her. You're gonna die tonight!" he said to Mattie's mother.

"I don't think so," her mother said, her voice sounding deranged. She pointed the stick at him. "You're just like me. You can die tonight or you can say, 'job well done,' and let me be on my way. If you come after me, I'll be waiting for you. And I'll give you all the credit, asshole!" she said coldly.

"We'll see each other again," he said.

Mrs. McDuffie replied, "I don't think so," and she headed up the hill with the branch over shoulder. When she got home, she placed it under the trailer through an opening.

Back in the canyon, Mattie moved, and the killer said, "You're alive," and he put the stocking around her neck. He walked behind the tree and through the brush and put the boots and the stockings in the sewer. He was seen by no one else.

"Marty, that's crazy!" I tried to catch my breath as I walked with him to his grandpa's room.

As we walked in, we heard Jesika ask, "Grandpa, are you okay?"

"Hello, are you one of the colored girls? I knew you were here." His voice was weak. "Mattie was hurt by her own mother. You two girls need to be careful. The brothers have been watching you. They will harm you, if you're not careful. Jesika, don't get in their way. You girls will discover another body soon. Tell your uncle this…" Sleep interrupted him.

"Grandpa!" Jesika shook him gently. "Tell my uncle what?"

When Marty's grandpa didn't respond, Jesika walked over to the small Saint Michael statue and picked it up.

"I know you're here too, and I'm not afraid."

Standing at the door with Marty, I asked, "What did he tell you?"

"He said you and I need to be careful. There are two killers, and they're brothers. And then he told me the worst thing you can imagine. Mrs. McDuffie helped kill her own daughter!" She had that distant look on her face as if time was standing still for just a moment. "Sometimes your worst enemies can be your own family," she whispered.

"I forgot to call my mother! Marty, can I use your phone?" An hour had gone by, but it felt like only minutes.

"Sure," he said.

I went into the kitchen to call my mother who picked up before it barely had a chance to ring.

"Marina, what took you so long? I should never have let you go over there! You don't listen!" She was upset.

"Mom, we're alright. There's nothing for you to worry about. Marty's mother is here with us."

"Okay, but I would like for you to be home soon." Her next words told me she had been talking to my uncle. "You're not working on that case, Marina. You're just a little girl, not a detective. And, I'm responsible for Jesika's well-being!" Her voice was loud and full of frustration.

"Mom, please, I know."

"You got Jesika following you around… this is dangerous. You're being stubborn. You're just like your dad!"

Oh, she's mad, I thought. That's what she always said when she was at her wits end with one of us kids.

"I'm sorry I worried you, Mom. We're going to play here and then Marty's mom will drive us home."

We all went back into Marty's room to put the pieces of the puzzle together. I took my notebook out of my sleuth kit.

"Okay, what do we know so far and what do we need to do?"

I wrote across the top of the paper:

Things We Know and Need to Do

Mrs. McD lied about not seeing Mattie that night.

Mattie's dad lied about Mrs. McD's whereabouts. So did her friend, Kathy.

Two killers—brothers.

Mrs. McD. hit Mattie with a branch.

Get evidence from Mrs. McD's trailer.

Give evidence to my uncle.

Mrs. McD. to be questioned—ID's the two brothers.

Brothers arrested for the murder of Mattie.

We hadn't completed the list when we heard Mrs. Jenkins holler, "Oh my God, another girl!"

We jumped up and ran into the living room to see. A girl had been found in Ocean View Park, another part of town, and my uncle was being interviewed. The boy that found her was standing next to my uncle. He had left her in the park by herself so she could finish her beer and cigarette before she went home.

CHAPTER 35

A Second Murdered Girl

"**N**othing bad ever happens around here," he burst into tears. This time, the girl was Black, and she was just sixteen years old.

I wrote in my notebook: *Black girl murdered. Taniya Greenwood. Hung by the neck.*

What I thought next, I didn't write down and listened in hopes it wouldn't confirm my suspicion.

Rodney Larkin, Jr. told the reporter that her mother called his house and said that she had not slept in her bed. He told Taniya's mother not to worry.

"But the minute I hung up the phone, I knew something was wrong."

Rodney went on to say that he called a bunch of Taniya's friends, and they said that they hadn't seen her. So, he went back to the park where he had left her.

"That's where I found her, wearing these pink flip-flops on her feet that I'd never seen her wear before. When I left her, she'd been wearing white Converse sneakers."

He paused as the tears continued to fall.

"I cut her down before calling the cops because I didn't want her parents to see her that way."

I looked at Jesika and saw tears in her eyes.

"This killing is a message for us! Marina, we're too late," she whimpered.

Marty whispered in Jesika's ear, "We're gonna go get that evidence from Mattie's mother's house."

"How? Marina and I have to go home," Jesika snapped back.

"Well, then, I can get the evidence by myself."

"You can't do it alone!" Jesika sounded horrified. "If you get caught, Mrs. McDuffie will murder you too!"

Stepping in to insert some calm, I said, "Marty, Jesika, I *have* to go home. My mom is going back to work in the morning."

"You kids are making too much noise! Marty, take your friends back to your room. I can't hear the news," his mom complained. "Oh, that poor girl!"

We went back to Marty's room to discuss our plans.

"First, we need to call your uncle, Marina," Jesika said.

"I think we should get the evidence first," Marty suggested.

"If we go home now, Jesika, you can ask my mother if I can spend the night at your house," I offered.

"What if she says no?" Jesika countered.

"Then the two of you will hafta go it alone. I know you and Marty can do this…" I said, somewhat disappointed.

"How about this?" Marty offered a new plan, "After everyone goes to bed, we'll all sneak out. And, this time, you'll hafta go through the canyon. It's faster. Jesika, you'll take the lead because your bike has a light on it."

Buying into the new plan, Jesika turned to me and said, "Marty, we'll call you when we leave the house. I'll do an SOS signal in your bedroom window with a flashlight. We'll walk from your house to the trailer park in all black."

We decided we needed to leave and get home as fast as we could. It was already 7:30 p.m., and we didn't want to make my mother any angrier than she already was.

Marty hugged Jesika and told her not to worry.

"We're gonna get the bastards," he promised. There was something different about Marty. An expression of bravery and fearlessness had come over his face.

After all the planning, I concluded that Marty's grandfather was wrong about one thing—we didn't find the second girl.

"I'm glad that we didn't find Taniya Greenwood's body. I don't think I could handle that sight," I said. "We need a big break in this case, and maybe we're getting close."

We hoped that we could recover evidence and give it to the police so that Mattie's mother could at least be further questioned. She could identify the brothers. She might even know where they were hiding. I wondered how much the police knew. My uncle and I hadn't communicated since he had taken us off the case.

My mind was racing with thoughts when all of a sudden, Jesika pressed down on her brakes and her bike skidded to a stop. I almost ran into her.

She almost yelled, "The brothers are twins—identical twins! You know the house that you went to first and you got that uneasy feeling?"

"Yeah, what about it?" I asked.

"One of the twins lives there! Remember your dream about the gate… it was opening and closing? It was a clue! Don't you get it, Marina? Your dream was guiding you!"

"I understand… but you can't ignore his alibi, Jesika."

"I'm not! What if the other twin sat in class for his brother? No one could tell that it wasn't him. His brother could do the murder while the other brother sat in his class, right?"

"Yes, he could. Go on…" I encouraged her.

"What if Mattie's mother thought she had killed her, but she wasn't dead? So, when he saw Mattie move, he finished her off."

"Poor Mattie. It was like she was murdered twice. Her mother is still a monster and needs to be put behind bars," I replied. "And we're gonna put her there!"

"Yeah, all of them belong behind bars!" Jesika agreed. "We're gonna stop them, and St. Michael will be with us all the way!"

She drew her imaginary sword, and I drew mine, and I knew Saint Michael had drawn his for real.

We got to my house and found our mothers sitting in the living room. By the look on their faces, we knew they had been talking about the two of us. We tried to sneak past them, but we weren't quiet enough.

My mother called out, "Marina, we want to talk to the two of you right now!"

I whispered to Jesika, "Don't tell them anything. It will make them worry even more."

"I wasn't gonna," she said quickly.

I smiled, and we walked into the living room together.

"Hi, Mom!"

"Don't you 'hi, mom' me!"

Jesika hugged her mom and sat down beside her, and I sat next to my mother, ready for the tongue-lashing I knew was coming.

"We know what you two have been up to, and you *will not* continue your investigation!"

"Mom, we're not doing anything."

"Be quiet. I'm doing the talking and you *are* going to listen!"

Jesika was nervous and tried her best to change the subject. "Mom, is Dad home?"

"You know your dad isn't home, and he won't be home for another six months."

She'd failed.

"Your uncle called me and told me what the two of you have been doing."

I started to cry, but I wasn't crying because my mother was mad or because I might be in trouble. I was crying because I was so angry. I couldn't believe he had told her anything.

"Mom …" I said and then stopped talking. I knew it wasn't going to do me any good.

"This will be the last time I talk to you about this subject. You understand me?" I couldn't believe this was happening. Understanding the words coming out of her mouth was one thing. Understanding and accepting what she said were two different things. My pause forced her to ask again, with an even sterner tone, "Do you understand me, Marina?"

"Yes, Mama," I said quietly, still whimpering with anger.

"Baby, I love you. I don't want anything to happen to you or Jesika. The person that killed those two girls is devoid of emotion and heartless, Marina. They don't care about human life." Her voice was pleading with me to understand.

It was Jesika's mom's turn to speak, "Jesika, I'm surprised that you would be involved in this at all."

"Why?" Jesika shot back boldly. "Do you think I'm a scaredy-cat, Mama?"

Whoa, girl!

"No, this has nothing to do with bravery. I can't believe you've been walking around that trailer park asking strangers questions as if you're the police." With tears welling in her eyes, she continued, "Anything could happen to the two of you. Do you realize what that killer has done? He has strangled a White girl and hung a Black girl."

"We know, Mom; it may even be our fault." Jesika began to cry.

"No, baby! You are not to blame! This person is evil—a tortured soul," her mother lovingly admonished.

"Like a person in hell without ice water, Mama? Like a person in hell staring at a clock that says, 'tick tock' forever and forever?"

Geez! She doesn't know when to quit! Jesika made me want to laugh, but I held it in.

"Yes, something like that," her mom said flatly.

"Mom, I'm scared. Can Marina spend the night with us?" Jesika ventured.

"If it's alright with her mother…"

My mother hesitated for a moment before she said, "I guess that would be okay."

It worked! I couldn't believe it.

"Mom, can I get my things now? Please don't worry about us. We heard everything you said."

"You two need to stay in the neighborhood," she instructed. "Tomorrow I'm going to work, and your brother will be calling me with a report on your whereabouts."

Jesika's mom added that Pishoung would be keeping an eye on us as well.

Before I went into my room, I grabbed the phone to call Marty.

The phone rang twice, and he picked up.

"Hello, is this Jesika?" he whispered.

"No, Marty, it's Marina," I said with a sarcastic tone. "We won't be at your house until midnight. Can you manage to stay awake?"

"It'll be a piece of cake. It's summer. I never go to bed until 1 or 2 in the morning. Don't worry."

"Okay, I'll flash my flashlight in your living room window three times."

"No need for all that. I'll be waiting outside. My mom will check on Grandpa one last time, and she'll go to sleep. I'll be on my own after that… and my mother could sleep through a fire."

We laughed.

"What's so funny?" Jesika asked.

"I'll tell you later," I whispered, covering the mouthpiece with my hand. "Okay, Marty, we'll see you tonight. Bye."

"Okay, tell me now," Jesika insisted.

"He said his mother could sleep through a fire."

I had a pair of black pedal pushers with a pink bow at the bottom. I pulled the pink bows off.

"Wait, Jesika, I'm gonna get a black T-shirt out of my brother's dresser."

After getting the shirt and stuffing it in my bag, I hollered, "We're leaving now, Mom!"

"Okay, girls, don't stay up too late."

"I'll be over in a few minutes," Jesika's mom called after us.

Jesika had a pair of jeans and a black sweatshirt that had Mighty Mouse on the front of it.

"I'll turn it inside out to hide the colors."

Our plan was to sleep in our clothes, so when it was time to get up, we wouldn't make any noise. I'd replaced my plastic flashlight with my father's metal flashlight.

I hope I don't have to use this.

Jesika found a battery for the light on her bike. We went to get my bike out of my garage, so we could hide both bikes on the side of Jesika's house.

"Why are you trying to hide your bikes?" Sariah's voice made both of us jump.

"Go in the house, Sariah!" Jesika said sternly.

"Make me," she responded. "I'm gonna tell Mommy what you're doing out here."

"Okay, Sariah, what do you want?" I asked.

She spoke up right away, "I want Jesika's blue and white spin top and the five dollars she has hidden in that pink box in her underwear drawer."

"I should tell Mommy you've been snooping again!" Jesika shouted.

"Shhhh. Be quiet …" I hushed them both, concerned that we would be heard.

"Let's see," Jesika bartered, "how about three dollars and no spinning top?"

"Oh, Jesika, just give her the blue and white spinning top too! This is important!"

"No, Marty gave it to me," Jesika whined.

"Who's Marty?" Sariah then began chanting, "Jesika got a boyfriend, Jesika got a boyfriend."

Jesika grabbed Sariah and put her hand over her mouth, and Sariah quickly bit her hand.

"Ouch!" Jesika shouted.

"Enough!" I said. "Sariah, I have three dollars I can give you. Now you'll have six dollars. Is that okay with you?"

"That's even better," she said with a sly grin.

I went back across the street again to get the money.

My brother Lewis came into my room while I was digging it out.

"I heard Mommy talking to you about the dead girls. I know how hard-headed you are," he chuckled, pushing me in my forehead at the same time.

"Stop it!" I grunted. "I'm doing this for Mattie and Taniya Greenwood. Who's gonna stand up for the victims?"

"How about the police, knucklehead? I should tell Dad," he added while handing me his pocket knife. My brother never hugged me. He typically showed his affection by grabbing me around my neck and rubbing his knuckles on the top of my head. This gesture was the closest he ever came to telling me he loved me. I felt it all over when he gave me a tool to protect myself.

Walking back across the street, the block seemed quiet. Jesika was standing in the middle of it, looking up and down the block. Not one single kid in sight.

"It's so quiet, Marina. It's not normal."

"I guess all the parents heard about Taniya Greenwood hanging from the tree. I'm sure some of the parents think that it's the Ku Klux Klan," I responded.

"It's like the bruthas got our neighborhood in a choke hold," Jesika concluded.

We gave Sariah the six dollars and the top to keep her quiet, and then we played Monopoly until it was time to go to bed, dressed in our mostly black clothes. Thinking we might oversleep, we took turns waking each other up every hour.

Right before we went to bed, I heard Mrs. Beckford talking to Pishoung and telling him about the murders and to keep a watchful eye out on us. He said he would.

"That poor Taniya Greenwood. What did she ever do to anyone? Her parents must be going through hell right now. I can't imagine losing one of my children that way. We can't escape it—the hatred—no matter where we go." Her mom sounded like she was choking back tears.

"I'm so sorry," Pishoung said. He said that his commanding officer had read the San Diego Union article to him about the first girl, Mattie.

"I'm afraid, Pishoung," her mom started. "Afraid this is just a reflection of the times we live in. Kennedy has spoken out against segregation and discrimination, and his administration even drafted the initial version of the bill. He even sent Federal Marshals to ensure integration of the University of Mississippi. But time seems to never be on our side. King met with him multiple times on civil rights issues, urging him to sign the bill. Can you believe that our beloved Kennedy has reservations about the legislation? He's worried about political backlash from Southern Democrats, of course. The South won again," she sighed. "King is also fighting to get White government officials in Georgia to allow Blacks the right to vote. There are sit-ins and nonviolent protests where Black people still get killed. I know that he represents hope and change, but the hanging of Taniya Greenwood has only reminded Blacks of the injustices we've faced and how far we've had to go to overcome them. It never ends."

Her words gave way to a moan, and I heard her blow her nose before she continued.

"The FBI's been called in to appease the Blacks residing in Logan Heights. The local authorities are afraid the Negroes will riot, and King gave a speech saying how every Negro has to be evolved to make changes. He said we can no longer stand by and watch the suffering of other Blacks in America. Everyone's always talking about how bad it is in the South, but it isn't any different in the east or the west."

Jesika's mother went on to tell Pishoung that she would never move home.

"I'm from Chattanooga, Tennessee where it was slow and very prejudiced. I couldn't wait to leave. It felt like walking barefoot in knee-deep mud pulling you backwards…" She shared that, as a teenager, she could not walk in through the front door of the restaurant where she worked. She had to enter through the back.

"I also had a father that was so angry, he used religion to confine us, keep us quiet, and stop us from making our own choices. My own mother cries from the memory. Did you know, Pishoung, that it was Nashville, Tennessee, that gave birth to the Ku Klux Klan after the American Civil war?"

"I didn't know. I'm glad you told me. I listen to you," Pishoung said.

"There were White Protestants that hated Blacks, Catholics, and Jews, and there was no telling when they would burn their fiery crosses. It made Blacks afraid to vote for fear they would be visited."

I had never heard Mrs. Beckford express herself in this way, and I listened closely.

"Hitler was an evil madman, and America has its Ku Klux Klan that has opposed the civil rights movement at every turn… to this very day. White America made a stand against Hitler, but they won't take a stand against cloaked and hooded Klansmen. This country has a birth defect, and it's racist. And I don't know if we'll ever live to see its wounds heal."

Jesika's mom said goodnight to Pishoung.

"I'm gonna watch them kids like an eagle," he promised.

Her mother laughed and locked the door behind him.

I woke up Jesika to tell her that her mom had gone to bed, and Pishoung had finally gone to work. Sariah and Jayden were fast asleep in the other twin bed. It was my turn to get some rest.

As I fell asleep, I heard Jesika begin to pray. She was talking to Michael, her superhero.

"I know Taniya and Mattie are with you. Please tell me why people have to be so cruel to each other. Is it free will? All the bad people should be wiped off the face of the earth. I know it is not for me to judge or to say. I'm just so scared,

Michael. Tell me what to do. Should we go? God sent us to do things that we don't want to do. If you're with me, then I will not be afraid."

CHAPTER 36

The Wildebeest

I woke up with Jesika pushing her hand gently into my side.

"It's time, Marina. Let's go."

I grabbed my sleuth kit and put it around my neck. We tiptoed past her mother's door, down the hallway, and through the den to the back door. Slowly, we opened the gate that leads out of the backyard to the side of the house. We picked up our bikes, pushed them to the driveway, jumped on, and pedaled as fast as we could to the end of the block. Then we jumped off our bikes to push them up a small embankment. Once at the top, we got on our bikes again, and rode down the steep hill as slowly as we could. This was never easy as we had to press on the brakes with the right amount of pressure. Too much pressure and you'd find yourself flippin' over your handlebars.

We made it to the bottom of the hill, crossed Market Street, traveled up 54th Street, and made the right turn at Naranja Street. Now in Marty's neighborhood, we noticed his block was quiet enough to hear a pin drop too. We jumped off our bikes and walked them over to the hedges where we could not be seen.

His mother's car was in his driveway, so we got on our knees and crawled to the side of it. Marty was there waiting for us. His entire face was covered in black Halloween paint making his blue eyes standout. We couldn't help but giggle.

"What?" he wondered.

"Nothing," we answered through our giggles.

We crawled around the side of the hedges and stood up when we got to the end of his driveway. I wondered if my friends could hear my own heart beating rapidly in my chest. Marty was leading the way, and we followed. The closer we got to the trailer, the more my stomach began to flip-flop.

"Hurry! Once we get to the trailer park, keep your head low," Marty instructed. "It's curtains if we are seen by anyone in this park. When we reach the McDuffie's trailer, you guys check the front. I'll check the back."

We walked with our knees bent and our heads low along the chain-link fence. Once we got to the trailer, it was more difficult to check the front because of the flower bed. Jesika took one end of the trailer, and I took the other end. There wasn't a hole to be found. All of a sudden, Marty poked his head around the corner.

"I found it," he whispered. "Follow me. It's near the back porch at the bottom. Hold the flashlight down."

I held the flashlight and he put his hand in the hole.

"Ow!" he yelled, waving his hand back and forth. We both gasped when we saw a large mouse trap stuck on two of his fingers. "Get it off! Get it off!"

Jesika put her hand over his mouth, and he began to squirm. The more Jesika tried to pull the trap off, the more he squirmed.

"Marty!" I whispered loudly. "Be quiet! You're gonna wake her up. Be still. Let me get it off."

Too late. The back door opened. It was Mrs. McDuffie.

"I knew I was going to have to deal with you little rugrats. I'm going to break your little necks in two," she growled.

Before I knew it, Mrs. McDuffie had jumped over the porch and grabbed me by the neck and pulled Jesika tight against her with her other arm, covering both her nose and mouth. We were kicking and screaming, but Jesika's screams were muffled by the big, fat hand over her mouth. Soon, Jesika went limp. I knew she had passed out.

Suddenly, Larry showed up out of nowhere and grabbed Mrs. McDuffie around the neck. She let go of both of us and Jesika dropped to the ground.

"Get her, Larry!" I yelled. She was wrestling him like a man. "Come on, Larry! Get her!"

"Punch her in the stomach!" Marty yelled.

It seemed like Mrs. McDuffie was getting the best of Larry. We stood frozen, watching in horror.

Thinking fast, I yelled, "Grab the stick, Marty!"

He did and he handed it to me. I swung that stick around with my entire body and cracked it over her big head. She fell to the ground like a ton of bricks, and we all stopped and looked up at each other.

"That woman fought me like a wildebeest." Larry gasped, out of breath. "Is everybody alright?"

"No, Jesika isn't." I tried shaking her, but she was out cold. Marty walked over to the bird bath to get some water and threw it on Jesika's face.

Slowly coming to, Jesika asked, "Did we get her?"

"We sure did," Marty said. "Can you walk?"

"Yeah," Jesika responded, not sounding very convincing.

"What time is it?" I asked.

Larry looked down at his watch, "It's 2:30."

"We gotta get home," Jesika murmured.

"I'll give you a ride in my dad's truck," Larry offered. "Wait here. I'll be back in two seconds."

"What if she wakes up?" I asked, looking at the big woman on the ground.

"Just hit her in her big, fat head again," Larry instructed with a grin.

When he got back, he picked Jesika up and tossed her over his shoulder like a sack of potatoes and carried her to the truck.

"I can walk, you know," she said, rather embarrassed.

Marty got in the back of the truck still holding his left hand. Larry took him home first and helped him out of the truck.

"Are you okay, little man?" Larry asked.

"No, my hand hurts. I don't think I want to be a homicide detective when I grow up." Marty sounded like he was in pain.

"Don't wake your mom up, man," Larry said.

"I won't. I left my bedroom window open."

Jesika popped her head out the truck window and called after him quietly, "Aren't you going to say goodbye to us?"

"Bye," he grunted without looking back. "I'm tired of being a junior detective like you guys. They ain't gonna give me no stinkin' badges."

Jesika laid back down in the back of the truck and started to giggle uncontrollably.

Larry hopped back in the truck, and we pulled away.

I wanted to ask Marty if he would go to the police station, but I asked Larry instead.

"Sure," he said. "Besides, who would believe this story?"

"Are you keeping the stick as a souvenir?" Larry asked.

"No, it's evidence that we were at the McDuffie's trailer. This stick has Mattie's blood on it. Her mother was hiding it underneath the trailer."

"You mean to tell me that Mattie's mother killed her own daughter?" Before we could answer the question, he continued, "I knew it! But I didn't know for sure. I told your uncle to check her out. I knew there was something wrong with that woman. I need to go back and tie her up, so she doesn't get away." Larry shouted, "We have to go back before she comes to!"

"Larry, we have to get home, or we won't be able to come with you tomorrow to present the evidence. Besides," I said, "we didn't tell our parents, and if they find out, we're in big trouble."

"Okay, okay," he responded. "I'll drop you two off, and then I'll go back and tie her up in her trailer."

He's never gonna be able to get that big woman up the steps and into her trailer by himself, I thought.

He pulled into our neighborhood and cut the lights halfway up the block before stopping in front of Jesika's house.

"Thanks, Larry. If it weren't for you, we might be dead." I sighed, thinking about what was happening when he arrived. "You're gonna hafta tie her up and leave her on the ground."

"Don't you worry, girls. I'll take care of everything. What time do you want to go?" he asked while writing his number on a piece of paper.

"We'll call you tomorrow and let you know," I answered.

"Alright. I'm going back to tie her up."

"Okay, Larry, see you tomorrow," we whispered.

We tiptoed quietly toward the side of the house and disappeared into the backyard, past Jesika's mother's door and into Jesika's room. We didn't have much time to sleep. Anxious to tell my brother, Lewis, what happened, I woke up at 6:00 a.m. and went home.

CHAPTER 37

Undeniable Evidence

Lewis sat and listened attentively while I told him how Larry had saved our lives and that I needed to get the evidence to Uncle Lonny. I asked him to cover for me and Jesika while we talked to Uncle Lonny at the police station. He told me I was crazy and that he didn't feel right lying to our mother. However, since it was for a noble cause, he would.

"Mom wants a report every two hours, but she can't talk on the phone unless there's a serious home emergency. Doctors don't have time for that, so I'll just be leaving a message saying everything is okay. You owe me one," Lewis finished with a punch to my arm. "And I know you're my sister because… girl, you got ... *guts*."

"Wow, a compliment," I answered back a little sarcastically.

"Don't let it go to your head."

He ruffled my hair and walked out.

I called Larry and told him that we could go to the police station at 8:00 a.m. He said he would pick us up at 7:00 a.m. sharp. Now we just had to tell Pishoung so that Jesika could come with me. We ended up telling him the whole story, including the fact that Marty's grandfather was the key to all the inside information.

"He was one that told us Mattie's name, about Mattie's mother, and that we needed to be careful."

Pishoung didn't have a problem believing that Marty's grandpa had visions.

"In our country," he said, "the priestesses are called Babaylans. They are our religious leaders, like a Catholic priest, bishop, or pope. We are very connected to nature—just like you, Jesika." He pinched her playfully on the cheek. "When you use a part of God's creation, a tree for example, you must plant another tree in its place. If there's no attempt to replace the tree, nature will become angry."

"And you don't want nature to become angry because then you could have an earthquake," Jesika finished his thought matter-of-factly.

"Yes, Jesika, you got it… How many times has man taken from the earth and not given back? To the earth, we are like fleas that can be shaken off at any time. Maybe I should come with you to help with the story," he said.

Larry picked us up promptly at 7:00 a.m. He had convinced Marty to come along, so we hopped in the back with Marty while Pishoung got in the front seat.

"Hey, Marty. How's your hand?" Jesika asked.

"It's better," he said sharply.

I could tell Marty still had his attitude.

"Who's this?" Larry asked.

"This is my brother, Pishoung," Jesika answered.

"Yeah, I'm her brother, and I'm going to make sure that the police understand what happened."

Larry looked puzzled. He stared at Jesika and then Pishoung but didn't say anything for a moment.

"I know what happened. I was there, " Larry finally responded.

I marveled at the difference in Larry's voice. He sounded so gentle and nice.

How odd, I thought as I recalled the day we questioned him on his porch and all the names he called us.

Curious, I asked, "Larry, how did you happen to come by last night?"

"Yeah, Larry," Jesika joined in. "How did you happen to arrive in the nick of time?"

"I was in a dead sleep when I heard this voice say, 'Wake up, Larry.' I thought it was my mother waking me up. I looked at my alarm, and it was really early. So, I drifted off to sleep again. The voice spoke again, 'Wake up, Larry.' So, I got up and got dressed, and grabbed my smokes off the dresser. I walked toward the back of the trailer park and was about to light my cigarette when I heard this commotion coming from the back of the McDuffie's trailer. I saw the 450-pound wildebeest had you and Jess by the necks. It ticked me off. I had to help!"

"Thank you for saving the girls from the 450-pound wild-eee-beest," Pishoung said.

The way he pronounced wildebeest made us all laugh.

"Did you go back to tie her up?" Jesika inquired, her tone urgent.

"Yes, I did. But before that, I made a stop at my buddy Robert's house to ask for help," Larry responded, his tone tinged with mystery. "When I revealed that Mrs. McDuffie had killed her own daughter, he agreed to assist me. My heart was pounding in my chest as we reached the trailer, and a sinking feeling came over me. She wasn't there. We combed through the backyard and searched every inch of the space, but it was as if she had vanished into thin air. Jesika," Larry's voice shook as he continued, "I was overwhelmed by an eerie sensation of being watched. It sent shivers down my spine, and you know I'm not easily frightened. That's why Robert and I decided to leave. I thought it would be best to inform your uncle about Harriet's disappearance."

"So, she's missing and probably hiding out." Jesika's words were laced with concern. "Don't you worry, Larry. My uncle is relentless. He'll find her."

When we finally arrived at the downtown precinct, I was nervous and doubted that we would make any headway. We walked through the door and went to the front desk, and it dawned on me we should have called first.

It's too late now.

"We'd like to see Detective Lonny Talbert." I felt my hand trembling as I spoke.

The officer at the desk called, and Uncle Lonny came down right away.

"What brings you all here so early in the morning?" he asked as he led us back to his office.

"You won't believe what we have to tell you, Detective Talbert," Larry started. "Marina has the evidence in her hand."

Uncle Lonny glanced at the stick and kept walking.

"Okay, who wants to go first?" he asked after he took the seat at his desk. "Marina, you got the stick, so why don't you go first…"

"Uncle, this stick…" I knew I needed to choose my words wisely. "This stick has Mattie's blood on it."

"Where did you get the stick?" he asked cautiously.

"From under Mrs. McDuffie's trailer," I answered.

"And how did you know where to find this particular stick?" he pressed.

I took a deep breath and looked at Jesika who nodded and smiled to encourage me.

"Mr. O'Kelly, Marty's grandfather, told us. He has these visions, and he told Marty that Mrs. McDuffie was with Mattie the night she was killed. Her alibi was false. Kathy and Mrs. McDuffie's husband gave false witness."

"Marina, I guess you and Jesika didn't know that you… uh… need… a search warrant to search one's premises. Did you know that? What did I tell you about communication? Go on … "

My hands were still trembling as I continued, "Mr. O'Kelly, Marty's grandfather, told Marty that Mrs. McDuffie wanted Mattie to come home, but Mattie told her mother she wasn't going. Mrs. McDuffie got so mad that she picked up this stick and hit her daughter on the head. It still has her blood on it. Uncle, Mattie's mother thought she had killed her instantly, but she hadn't. Then one of the brothers came from behind the tree and said, 'You ruined everything. She was mine. Now you're going to have to pay for it.' Marty's grandfather says, 'Evil faces evil.' He said that Jesika and I need to be careful because the brother is watching us."

"Did he tell you the brothers' names?" Uncle Lonny looked concerned.

"No, but Jesika and I figured out that the brothers might be twins."

My uncle dropped his head for a moment and then raised it back up.

"Marina, I made a big mistake. I should've told you that detective work is not for children. You and Jesika could have really gotten hurt. I should've never encouraged you. I can't be in two places at one time. I need you and Jesika to go home and just be kids. I want you to promise me. I'm no longer the lead on this case. The FBI has taken over."

I didn't say anything because I didn't know what to say. I knew from another conversation there was something wrong happening with Uncle Lonny and the case, and I felt bad.

"So, what else happened?"

"Mrs. McDuffie told the one brother that he could try and kill her, or he could let her be on her way. She would give him all the credit, and if he came after her, she would be waiting for him. When Mattie suddenly moved, the brother knew she wasn't dead, so he strangled her with the stocking. He crept back up the hill and hid the boots and the stocking in the sewer. Uncle, you have them. Did they find anything on them?"

He didn't answer.

"You interviewed one of the brothers, so you know his name. Those killers put Mattie's flip-flops on Taniya Green's feet. I believe that this stick and the stocking is the only factual evidence that fits this crime scene."

My uncle looked up from his notes and asked, "What gives you that impression?"

"Mattie had on flip-flops. She didn't have boots or stockings on. This evidence is from another crime scene. The boots and the stockings are from another victim—another dead girl—and we haven't found her yet."

"What time did you get to the McDuffies' trailer?"

"Hmm, let's see… We left Jesika's house at midnight." My voice shook a bit.

"How did you get there?"

"On our bikes." I gulped.

My uncle looked toward Marty and noticed he was holding his hand.

"What's your name, young man?" Uncle Lonny's voice was professional.

"Marty Jennings," he replied, squirming a bit.

"Were you with the girls?"

"Yes," Marty responded. "I'm the one that found the evidence. That's how my hand got hurt. There was a small hole at the bottom of McDuffie's trailer. Mrs. McDuffie placed the stick through the hole, hiding it where she thought it wouldn't be found. But we found it. Boy, did we find it! She put the stick in first, and then a large mouse trap. When I put my hand in the hole, the trap snapped on my hand."

Jesika interrupted, "I had to put my hand over his mouth, so he wouldn't give us away. The mouse trap was huge, and his pain was unbearable. Marty started yelling, 'GET IT OFF, GET IT OFF!' Marina told Marty to stop squirming, and she got it off. That's when the porch light came on. Mrs. McDuffie had heard him scream. She came through the back door and jumped over the porch railing. She grabbed Marina, then me. It all happened so fast. We tried to get away, but she was strong. I passed out because she had her hand over my nose and my mouth, and I couldn't breathe. Larry came from out of nowhere and wrestled with the 450-pound wildebeest, but she was getting the best of Larry. Finally, Larry worked his way out of her grip. That's when Marina took the stick and cracked it over her head. Boom! She fell like a ton of bricks," Jesika reported proudly.

"The wildebeest is Mrs. McDuffie, I take it." Uncle Lonny was trying to hide a smile.

"Yes, Uncle," we all laughed. "Larry took Marty home, and he said that he didn't want to be a junior detective anymore."

"I don't blame you, son," Uncle responded to Marty. "And thank you, Larry, for coming to their rescue."

"Don't mention it, sir. I would have done it for anybody," Larry said humbly, then continued, "I'm sorry to inform you that Mrs. McDuffie got away. I went back to her trailer with my friend Robert, and Mrs. McDuffie had disappeared. She was knocked out cold before we left. We searched everywhere for her, Detective Talbert."

"You don't have to worry about Mrs. McDuffie. We will take it from here. The FBI agent is going to come in and interrogate you one by one. I want you to be as honest as you were with me," Uncle Lonny requested.

"Oh, Detective Talbert, are you going to issue a warrant for the arrest of Harriet McDuffie?" Larry asked. "She murdered Mattie. You do know that, right?"

"Yes, Larry, we are going to make the arrest when we find her."

My uncle took the stick from me and said, "You're not gonna be able to keep this from your parents, you know."

"Yes, Uncle. Can we tell them at the right time?" I pleaded.

"If you don't, I will. And, by the way, there is no right time."

More Interrogations

He called the FBI agent, Kyle Lombard, who walked into my uncle's office a few minutes later with a clipboard in his hand. He was very tall and dressed in a black suit, white shirt, black tie, and nice black shoes. The expression on his face went from stern to a nice, warm smile as he introduced himself. He wasn't at all intimidating anymore. He asked Larry to go into Interrogation Room A, and then he asked Marty to go into Interrogation Room B. Jesika went into C, and I went into Room D. It felt weird being on the other side of the two-way mirror. Now we were being watched for how we would respond to the agent's questions. There were two agents in Larry's room and one in Jesika's room. They sent out four detectives, including my uncle, to canvas the trailer park and surrounding neighborhood. They were also told to pick up Mr. McDuffie for questioning, and an All-Points Bulletin was sent out to all the officers in their patrol cars to be on the lookout for Harriet McDuffie. She was to be considered armed and dangerous.

After the agents interrogated Larry, it was my turn next.

How hard can this be? I kept telling myself not to be nervous.

"We heard how brave you and Jesika have been." He smiled. "So, little miss, you're the ringleader of the junior detectives?"

"No …" I said, not sure what to say to him.

"Your name is Marina Massey?" he asked.

"Yes," I answered.

"Do your parents know where you are right now?" he asked.

"No, sir."

"Did you tell them about the incident that occurred early this morning around 2:30 a.m.?"

"No, sir."

"Did you tell your uncle about what happened this morning?"

"Yes, sir."

"Did you tell your uncle about the thing Marty's grandfather said … before today?"

"Yes, I mentioned it, but not before our most recent events, sir." I said nervously. "He asked me how we knew the dead girl's name. It hadn't been released in the news, and I told him that he should talk to Marty's mother."

"Did he take your advice?" the man asked curiously.

"No, I don't think so. I guess he didn't feel it was factual. Some of the information regarding Mattie's murder was even hard for me to believe, sir. Mr. O'Kelly seems like an honest man, and Jesika said he was in-between, so he knows things.

"What do you mean?" he prompted.

"You know, his body is here, and his soul is on the other side. Jesika says it is a slow crossover sometimes. That when the person is on the other side, they can see things. I started to believe him because he described the event so clearly. It was important for us to get the evidence—the murder weapon. So, we made plans to sneak out of the house without our parents' knowledge. But I did tell my brother, Lewis. When we woke up this morning, Jesika told Pishoung what had happened."

"Tell me about the plan to find the murder weapon."

"Do you want me to start from when we found the body?"

"No, I have your uncle's report."

"Well … Marty came over to my house because his grandfather had given him some additional information. He said that he wasn't asleep this time. He wrote down all that his grandfather described to him. First thing he said was, 'One evil person faces another.' He told Marty that Mattie's mother was in the canyon …" I recited every word that Marty's grandpa had told him. I also told him what he had told Jesika while she was standing in his room.

"Is Marty's grandfather terminally ill?" he asked.

"Yes, he's dying of cancer, and he sleeps a lot."

"Why didn't Marty's grandfather tell you about Taniya Greenwood?"

"I don't know," I answered. "Marty's mother, Mrs. Jennings, was watching the six o'clock news and that's how we found out about Taniya. He didn't have to tell us... It was our motivation for finding the murder weapon. We figured that Mattie's mother could identify the brother, but now she's missing."

Agent Lombard wrote some information on his clipboard. I hoped he was coming to some of the same conclusions I had and wondered if he thought the serial killer had a twin.

I bet Uncle is thinking of Nigel Glasgow as a suspect.

"How many interviews have you done?" he continued.

"Four, sir. Larry, Jack, Mrs. McDuffie, and Kathy."

"Oh, one more question," Agent Lombard said. "Why didn't you interview Bethany, Mattie's best friend?"

"I thought about it, but she lived too far away. We would have needed a ride to her house." Besides, I knew my uncle would interview Bethany sooner or later.

"She's here at the station. Would you like to say hello?"

"Yes! I would love to meet her!"

"She's in your uncle's office. Stop by there before you go into the lobby. This concludes the interview. Don't leave town, Miss Massey," he said with a smile. "And one more thing before you go … Would you do me a big favor, Marina?"

"What is it, sir?"

"Go home and be a kid. Please. I'm asking nicely."

"Sure, Detective, it's the only thing I can be." I was sick of hearing everyone say this to me, but I was nice about it. As I exited the interrogation room, I saw two officers escorting Rodney Larkin, Jr. to an interrogation room in handcuffs.

CHAPTER 39

Bethany

I hope the FBI isn't arresting him for Greenwood's murder!

I opened the door to my uncle's office and saw Mattie's best friend, Bethany, waiting for him. He had called her in again so the FBI could ask her some more questions. She had a short plaid skirt with a pretty, white blouse and high go-go boots. Her short, curly, black hair framed her face.

"Hi, Bethany. I like your outfit," I started.

"Thank you." She smiled.

"Are you waiting to talk to Detective Talbert? He's my uncle."

"No, I already spoke to him. I'm actually waiting to speak with Agent Lombard. I told your uncle everything I could think of. Mattie was supposed to come over to my house after she met with Jack. She was going to call me, but she never did. I just figured that she was with him, so I went over to my friend Jewel's house. She and I were watching a movie when I saw the news. They said you found her body on the way home from church, but they didn't release your name. I tried to call her mother, but she never picks up the phone. The killer is still out there somewhere, and sometimes I feel like somebody's watching me. I don't know. Maybe I'm just being paranoid." She yawned. "I haven't had much sleep."

"What was she like?" I asked as my uncle returned, and we both sat down to listen.

"Oh, she was wonderful, smart, and beautiful. We shared our clothes with each other, so it seemed like we had a lot of clothes. She liked looking at models in Vogue, and she was a huge fan of Marilyn Monroe and Elizabeth Taylor. She knew how to sew, so sometimes she would make an outfit for each of us. My parents and brothers loved her. I've got four brothers, and they all thought she was pretty.

"My mother never had anything nice to say about Harriet. I was terrified of her, and I had good reason to be. I remember asking my mother if we could adopt Mattie. She said she wished we could, but my father's job would not pay for more than the five of us we already have."

"What does he do?"

"He works for the City of San Diego in the Transportation Department. He's responsible for operations and the maintenance of streets, sidewalks, and storm drains. His major focus, he says, is on our water quality." She paused and tears filled her eyes. "My family and I buried Mattie at a small funeral last week. It took forever for the medical examiner to release her body."

"No one told us about the funeral." I stood up, a little miffed.

"I'm sorry. What's your name?" she asked.

"My name is Marina Massey. It was me and Jesika Beckford who found the body. I'm sure you saw us on the news."

"Well, yes, but when you're grieving, you don't always think straight. Please accept my apology. We didn't mean to exclude you and Jesika. My mother was upset that the medical examiner was taking so long before allowing us to put her to rest."

"Well, she won't rest until her killer is found." I crossed my arms and plopped back down in the chair.

"What? I don't understand." She fixed her eyes on me.

"Of course, you don't understand. None of you do." I realized I was starting to sound like Jesika. I was angry, and I knew Jesika would be too. "It's okay, Bethany," I said, understanding that it wasn't really her fault. "It was nice to meet you," I said before getting up to leave the room.

CHAPTER 40

Twins and Warnings

They interviewed Jesika and Marty together to speed things up, and I stood in front of the two-way mirror watching.

Agent Lombard walked through the door and said, "Hello."

Jesika folded her hands and sat straight up in her chair. She was ready for the questioning.

"Hello, Agent Lombard." Marty simply waved.

"You two are Jesika Beckford and Marty Jennings, correct?" the agent began.

"Yes, sir, that's us," Jesika answered.

"So, you're Marina's sidekick." He grinned at Jesika.

"No, sir, I'm her partner. We found Mattie McDuffie's body."

"Yes, I heard you fainted and then ran home."

Jesika responded seriously, "I did that because I hadn't seen a dead body before."

"You also found some boots …" he prompted.

"Yes, right before we found Mattie's body. I ran home with the boots on my feet."

"Your friend, Marina, stayed to review the crime scene, then ran to a neighbor's house to call the police. A … Mrs. …"

"Yes, sir, she's a great detective. She is not just my partner, she's also my best friend. In fact, she lives right across the street from me." Just as the words left Jesika's mouth, the door swung open far enough for her to see Rodney Larkin, Jr.

being escorted out of the interrogation room in handcuffs. Her eyes widened in disbelief.

"Hold on a minute!" she exclaimed, her voice loud with determination. Marty placed his hand on her shoulder, as if to assure her it was going to be okay. "Before I answer any more questions, I want to know why you're arresting him. He didn't do anything wrong! We have our rights! You can't just treat him like this!"

Another FBI agent walked into the room with a calm, yet authoritative presence and responded, "You most certainly do, Jesika." He walked to the table and handed Agent Lombard the stick with Mattie's blood on it. "Rodney is simply being interviewed for what he knows. The handcuffs are merely a procedural precaution."

"See, Jesika, no need to worry anymore. Rodney isn't being arrested," Marty reassured.

"Is this the stick you found at Mattie's residence?" Agent Lombard asked.

"Yes, it's the stick that Mrs. McDuffie hid underneath her trailer," Marty said. "That's when the mouse trap snapped on my hand. Larry happened by and saved us from the wildebeest."

"How did you find out about the stick?"

"My grandfather, sir. He told me that the girls needed to be very careful. He said that if the girls got in their way, they would harm them."

"Who's they?"

"The twin killers."

"Do you think they're twins?" he asked. "Marina's uncle interviewed one of them, and he offered an alibi that checked out."

"Yes, sir!" Jesika piped in. "They provide a provable alibi for each other. Marty's grandfather told us about the brothers and the one waiting behind the tree when Mattie's mother showed up. He was upset that Mrs. McDuffie had hit Mattie on the head. He thought that Mrs. McDuffie had deprived him of the opportunity to kill her. They had a confrontation and the killer backed up."

"Why did Mattie's mother hit her own daughter in the head?"

"She's a crazy woman, Agent Lombard!"

"Yeah, she's nuts," Marty agreed.

"Jesika, when you listen to Mr. O'Kelly, why do you suppose he has all this information?"

"Well, he is in the in-between. You know, Agent Lombard, the soul is like a balloon. It can leave the body at any time and come back to the body. It's easy when you are sleeping and dreaming. Mr. O'Kelly is always sleeping, and when he dreams, he can talk to souls on the other side. The string is an invisible cord."

Marty added, "Like an umbilical cord connecting a mother to her baby. Love is a string that keeps some people attached to their bodies when they're near death. What we do in the in-between is entirely up to us."

Agent Lombard was silent as he turned his head and looked at the other agent for a moment.

"Did Mr. O'Kelly tell you about Taniya Greenwood?" He started another line of questioning.

"No, sir, he didn't. The reason Taniya Greenwood got killed was a warning for Jesika and Marina," Marty said.

Jesika put her head down, and Marty put his hand on Jesika's shoulder and consoled her. "It's not your fault."

"No, Jesika. You mustn't blame yourself," Agent Lombard repeated.

Jesika lifted her head and grabbed the Saint Michael medallion around her neck.

"Are you Catholic?" the agent asked.

"Yes, we both are." Marty pulled out his medal and kissed it.

"Alrighty, that's enough questions for today," Agent Lombard sighed. "Would you do me a favor, Jesika?"

"Depends on what it is." Her voice was somber.

"I would like for you to go home and just be a kid. You too, Marty. We can take it from here." The agent said it with a warm smile.

"Agent Lombard, I would like to do that, but my girlfriend wants to be a detective," Marty replied.

Annoyed, Jesika pretended not to hear Marty's declaration and answered for herself, "I can't make any such promise. It's not about me or you. It's about Mattie and Taniya."

The agent shook his head as Jesika and Marty walked out of the room.

I joined them as they walked into the lobby where Pishoung and Larry were asleep. Larry, head propped on Pishoung's shoulder, was snoring with his mouth wide open. What a sight! They were both obviously exhausted. I sat down on one side of them and Jesika sat down on the other with her arms crossed.

"Marina, the cops had Rodney in handcuffs." Jesika's voice was trembling with fury.

"I believe Agent Lombard," Marty gently argued.

"Argh! And Detective Lombard told me and Marty to go home and be kids," Jesika growled.

"Yeah, he told me the same thing. That was his polite way of telling us that we aren't to be involved anymore. I'm tired of them telling us to be kids."

After a moment of silence, I interjected, "Jesika! I spoke to Bethany. She was in my uncle's office. They buried Mattie without telling us."

She stood up, ready to say something, and then sat down.

"There's nothing we can do about that now. Where's she buried?"

"I don't know. I was so mad, I forgot to ask her. I bet she's at Mount Hope Cemetery. We'll go visit her and pay our respects, Jesika. Even if we have to ride our bikes."

Jesika shook Pishoung to wake him.

"What? What? Can't a man get any sleep around here?" He looked around. "What did I do?"

"You didn't do anything, silly," Jesika laughed.

CHAPTER 41

A Crowd Full of Anger and Pain

We all walked outside to a large crowd of angry Black people, and Marina and I immediately looked at each other.

"Oh, sweet Jesus, Saint Michael, we need your help!" I whispered.

Marty and Larry responded in unison at the sight, "Oh shit!"

The crowd had picket signs that read, "Free Rodney Larkin, Jr." His parents and Taniya's parents were at the front of the crowd.

Larry just stood there with his mouth open, trying to take it all in.

Without thinking, Pishoung spoke to the crowd, "I am leaving soon, and you will forgive me if I speak bluntly. The universe grows smaller every day, and the threat of aggression by any group anywhere can no longer be tolerated. There must be security for all, or no one is secure. This does not mean giving up any freedom, except for the freedom to act irresponsibly. Your ancestors knew this when they made laws to govern themselves and appointed the police to enforce them."

"Those are lines right out of 'The Day the Earth Stood Still'!" Jesika whispered to me while he spoke.

He had the crowd in the palm of his hand until he said, "the police to enforce them."

That's when Mr. Larkin, Rodney's father, threw his sign at us and shouted back, "Tell that to those pigs inside."

"Are you trying to get us killed?" Jesika screeched, scared and annoyed.

"Why did you say that, Pishoung?" I asked. "You just made matters worse."

Something needed to be done before the crowd stormed the police station, and we shook our heads as the police started to come out in groups with shields on their faces and tear gas and bayonets in their hands.

"Can I talk to Mr. and Mrs. Larkin?" Jesika asked as she moved toward the crowd. When she reached them, she asked, "Did you know that another girl was killed three weeks ago?"

"Yes, we heard about Mattie McDuffie. She's the White girl that got killed near the trailer park," Mrs. Larkin answered.

"What does that girl have to do with our son? If you harm our son, we will attack you!" Mr. Larkin threatened.

"We're sorry about Mattie, but what about our daughter, Taniya?" Mrs. Greenwood questioned. "Will the police look for our daughter's murderer?"

"No, cause she ain't White!" someone in the crowd yelled out.

The crowd started chanting, "We want justice! We want justice!"

"Right now, the police are investigating Mattie's murder, and they are also looking to find out whether the two murders are connected. My friend's uncle, Lonny Talbert, is a Black detective on the police force. He cares about Taniya Greenwood. He will see that Taniya receives justice. Please, we don't want anyone to get hurt," Jesika implored the crowd.

I walked up and stood next to my friend, and Pishoung, Larry, and Marty stood behind me.

"My uncle is a good man and a good detective. I believe in him," I said. "And he always does what he says he's gonna do."

"When will they release my son?" asked Mr. Larkin.

"They just want to ask him a few questions—nothing more. Mr. and Mrs. Greenwood, they're going to find Taniya's killer. The FBI is involved in this case, and Agent Kyle Lombard is taking the lead. Only thing we can tell you is that there may be other victims out there. Please make sure your children are safe. These killers have no conscience. Rodney Larkin, Jr. is not a suspect." I repeated again, "Rodney is not a suspect."

Agent Lombard came out and calmly asked the Greenwoods and the Larkins to speak with them in his office. Then he asked the officers that were ready to control the angry mob to stand down.

"I want to hear what they have to say," Mr. Larkin told the crowd.

They followed Agent Lombard into the police station as Channels 8, 6, and 10 news teams showed up and walked through the crowd asking questions.

Jesika and I did not want to be interviewed, so we followed the Larkins and the Greenwoods into the police station. His parents appeared surprised to see Rodney sitting in the lobby.

"Oh, my Lord!" Mrs. Larkin blurted. "Are you okay?"

His father hugged him and said, "Let's go home, son."

"You've been through enough, Mr. and Mrs. Larkin," Agent Lombard told them. "You can take your son home now. He's no longer a suspect."

Rodney Larkin, Jr. walked up to Taniya's parents sobbing and told them that he was so sorry for not staying with her.

"It's my fault she was killed."

"It's not your fault, Rodney. We won't let you carry that guilt," Mrs. Greenwood said, embracing him.

The crowd outside was being interviewed by the news teams, all trying to get the first scoop on what had happened.

"Mr. and Mrs. Greenwood, we are doing everything to find your daughter's killer," Agent Lombard said gently.

I could not hold back my own tears, and neither could Jesika.

"That was a close call," Larry said. "I was scared to death. I've never seen so many Black people in one place. Well, we'd better get you two home."

We jumped into the back of Larry's truck. He dropped Marty off first, who again didn't even say goodbye. Then he dropped me, Pishoung, and Jesika at her house. We were back safe and sound before our mothers had noticed we were gone.

CHAPTER 42

Truth Be Told

*I*t was about 10:30 p.m. and I hadn't spoken to my parents yet about what had happened because I'd lied to my mother and wasn't looking forward to her reaction to that fact. I had called Jesika, and she said that Pishoung was going to tell her mother what happened too. She was sure she would get a whoopin'.

"I'm going to pick my own switch. And it better not be a little one."

"My parents aren't going to whip me because they don't believe in whipping, but my mother is going to put me on restriction for sure. I won't be able to go outside and play for a long time. Or have any friends over."

When the doorbell rang, I knew it had to be my uncle.

"I gotta go, Jesika." I said and hung up the phone real fast. I felt sorry for Jesika, but I was also scared that I might be getting my first spanking. My heart was beating a mile a minute when I heard my father open the door and say, "Hey man, what brings you here at this time of the night?"

"I need to speak with you and my sister. It's about Marina and Jesika."

Dad asked my uncle if he wanted anything to drink.

"Just some water."

My mother had already gone to bed because she needed to get up early the next morning, and my father reluctantly woke her up.

Once they had joined my uncle in the living, he
dove right in.

"There's no painless way to tell you two," he said. "I'm
putting twenty-four-hour police protection around your house.
We now have a composite of the twin serial killers."

"Twin serial killers?" my mother gasped.

My uncle continued, "Marina, Jesika, and Marty snuck
out of the house last night and recovered the weapon Mattie's
mother used to strike Mattie on the head. We have even more
evidence now."

"Why would Harriet hit her own daughter in the head?"
My mother was aghast, and I, for one, was thankful she
had focused on that rather than the fact we had snuck out of
the house.

"Well, from what we've been able to gather so far, Harriet
and Mattie argued. Mrs. McDuffie became angry, picked up a
branch, and hit Mattie on the head, knocking her unconscious.
She was hurt, but not dead. That's when one of the twins, who
had been stalking Mattie and Jack, came from behind the tree
and finished her off. Harriet confronted the twin, so the killer
knew she had seen him. Mattie's mother took the bloodied
branch and hid it underneath her trailer and placed a large mouse
trap near it. When Marty stuck his hand in there to retrieve it, the
trap snapped on Marty's hand, and he started screaming. Harriet
came out of the house, jumped over the banister, and grabbed
Jesika, covering her mouth and nose with her hand."

"Oh, no!" Mom interrupted. "Is Jesika alright?"

"She couldn't breathe and passed out, but she's alright,
Sis. The twins killed Taniya Greenwood as a warning. The FBI
and police are working together, but it's pretty clear the twins
killed the two young girls and the cranky old lady." He paused,
and it seemed he was measuring his next words. "And I believe

the girls were getting at the truth too quickly for them. They were toying with the police, switching the victim's shoes and such. They think we're stupid."

"None of this makes any sense. Was it a hate crime?" Mom was flustered.

"They're acting like they'll never be arrested. We have an APB out on them."

"I can't go to work knowing that there may be someone out there that might want to kill my daughter." She sounded terrified.

"Don't worry, Ava. I can stay home with Marina." My stepfather consoled her, and I imagined him putting his arm around her from where I listened from my room.

"Sis, our officers will be right outside the house 24/7. I don't want you to worry. I will be checking on them too. There'll be at least three unmarked squad cars on the block."

I heard my mother crying and angry.

"Since when did the San Diego Police Department give a shit about what happens in our neighborhood?" She paused. "I'm sorry, Lonny. That's not directed toward you."

I ran to her.

"Mom, I'm so sorry for lying to you. I didn't want to. Jesika and I just really care about Mattie and Taniya. We didn't mean to make you worry."

"I know, baby, but you need to do everything your uncle says now. Do you understand? I'm sure the police are grateful for your help, but they don't need it any longer. Hand me the phone so I can call Rita."

My mother took the phone from me and dialed the number.

When Jesika's mom answered, my mom said, "Rita, Russell and I and my brother are coming over. It's about the girls. I don't want to talk over the phone. We'll see you in a moment."

Hanging up the phone, Mom said, "Marina, I want you to come with us. Put your robe on, honey."

We all walked across the street and found Jesika's mother standing at the door. She invited us in, and my mother, father, and uncle sat on the couch. I sat in the chair across from them, and Jesika squeezed into the chair with me.

Jesika was the first one to speak.

"Mom, did Pishoung tell you about what happened?"

"No!" she said, worried filling her voice. "What was he supposed to tell me?"

My uncle told Jesika's mother that we had snuck out of the house around midnight.

"They brought us evidence early this morning. It was the stick that Harriet McDuffie used to assault her daughter …" He went on to give Mrs. Beckford the same information he had given my parents.

"Detective Talbert, what are you doing to keep our daughters safe?" Mrs. Beckford asked.

"We have three unmarked cars monitoring the block," Uncle Lonny tried to assure her.

Tears filled Mrs. Beckford's eyes, her face a mixture of anger, worry, and fear. I could tell she was struggling with what to say or do. Finally, opening her arms, she motioned for Jesika to come to her. Jesika slipped into her mom's embrace.

"I thank God that you're alright," she said, beginning to cry.

My mother said, "They can stay at our house, if it's okay with you."

Turning to look at my mom, she said, "Thank you, Eva, but I have Pishoung to watch over my kids." There was a tone to her voice I'd never heard before.

"But, Rita," my mom gently argued, "Pishoung can't stay up all day."

"Don't you worry about Pishoung, Rita."

"But I really think it would be safer if your children stayed with Russell during the day."

Jesika's mom must blame me for what's happening, I thought.

Jesika must have been thinking the same thing because she suddenly blurted, "It's not Marina's fault, Mom. I have a mind of my own."

"Jesika, this is not the time! Go to your room! Now!" Mrs. Beckford's anger had found its voice. "I wish your father was here. Always in the damn submarine. I don't want to hear another word from you, young lady."

Instead of following her mother's orders, Jesika took a challenging stance.

"I'm always afraid. I'm afraid of the dark!"

Oh no, she's in for it now! That girl doesn't know when to quit.

"Well, Jesika, there's always gonna be nighttime. You're never gonna be able to escape that."

"But I don't want to be afraid of the shadows anymore. I believe that Saint Michael was sent by God to protect Marina and me and everyone. Don't you believe he was with us?"

Her mom hesitated as if she were deep in thought and then took hold of Jesika's hand and pulled her in close again.

"I believe… I do. But I'm also afraid, Jesika. I can't lose you." After another silent moment, she gave in. "Okay, you can stay at Massey's house."

My mother tried to console Jesika's mother while my uncle assured her in a somber tone, "Everything's going to be okay, Mrs. Beckford. We're gonna get to the bottom of this case."

She brushed off his words with, "Jesika and Marina, go and wake up Sariah and Jayden."

With us guiding them, the younger ones stumbled into the living room with their eyes still closed. My mother picked up Jayden while my father picked up Sariah.

"Russell, here's my work number. If anything happens—a break in this case, anything—please give me a call," Jesika's mother implored. "I won't be able to sleep until this case is solved."

"I promise," said my father as we all got up to go back to our house.

Sariah and Jayden slept on the living room couch, and Jesika and I slept in my bed. We didn't go to sleep right away.

"Jesika, you are one of the bravest people I know."

"The only person I'm afraid of is my father."

"It took a lot of guts to say what you said to your mother. My mother was so mad, I didn't dare say a word."

"Well, at least we're together," she responded. "Mattie became our responsibility when we found her body."

"You're right. I couldn't agree with you more."

"I love you, Jesika."

"I love you, Marina."

We high-fived and went to sleep.

CHAPTER 43

Neighborhood Patrol

Jesika's mother came over every night to tuck in Jayden and Sariah, but Jayden kept having nightmares. My parents would find him at the foot of their bed in the morning.

After a few nights, I overheard my mother telling my father that, even though the police were patrolling the neighborhood, she had an uneasy feeling in the pit of her stomach. Her nights were restless, and the lack of sleep was affecting her work at the hospital.

The whole situation was also taking its toll on the neighborhood. Even though our two families were having dinner together every night, my mother never mentioned her discomfort to Rita.

Around 7:30 p.m., the sound of the phone ringing broke the silence.

"Hello, Marina." I heard my uncle's voice when I answered.

"Hi, Uncle. Do you want to speak with Mom?"

He chuckled, "No, I got the right person. I was wondering if you and Jesika would like to grab an ICEE at the 7-Eleven?"

My heart was filled with joy. "Absolutely, Uncle, I would love to. I'll give Jesika a ring right away." And then my curiosity got the best of me. "Any updates on the case?"

"Indeed, there are some developments," he answered in a mysterious tone. "I'll be there in a half hour to share them."

Brimming with anticipation, I hung up hastily, forgetting to say goodbye, and quickly dialed Jesika.

"He'll be here in thirty minutes. You got time," I assured her when she said she wouldn't miss it.

She hung up without saying goodbye and showed up in record breaking time. Even before she crossed the threshold, she was asking questions, "Did he find and arrest the Glasgow twins? Was there another murder?"

"Slow down. You're making me dizzy with all these questions. I don't know, Jesika. I think he is just being nice because we're under police protection. We're stuck on the block."

"Yea, you're probably right."

The doorbell rang.

"You two ready?" Uncle said when we opened the door.

"Yep, we are. I'm getting a strawberry ICEE," I declared.

It was a quiet evening at 7-Eleven, and Uncle grabbed his favorite soda while we picked out our ICEEs. Once we got our treats, we settled back into the car with him. Turning to face us, he disclosed that he had arrested Kathy and Mattie's stepfather on charges of obstruction of justice.

"Did they fingerprint them?" Jesika asked.

"Yep, they did. They were taken into custody and processed. They're waiting for a trial date now." Uncle took a long gulp of his soda and sighed. "Brace yourself, girls. What I'm about to share is far from pleasant and may haunt your dreams, but I believe that you deserve to know the truth."

We stopped slurping and stared at him.

"I found Harriet McDuffie," he announced, his voice thick with mystery.

"You arrested her, Uncle?" I interrupted.

"No, Marina, I found her. Are you sure you want me to continue?" he asked.

"Yes!" we said in unison.

"Please continue. We're not afraid," I spoke for both of us.

"Harriet is dead. The twins got to her before I could make an arrest." He didn't try to hide his disappointment. "I had a gut feeling nagging at me, a relentless whisper in my ear that urged me to search her trailer. I did another sweep of the house, but nothing suggested the possibility of her demise, and I thought she was hiding."

We were all ears, hanging on his every word.

"I decided to go over to the twins' house and have another look around. When I reached their block, I turned off my headlights and parked. Walking up to the back door, I took my gun out of its holster and twisted the knob. The light outside the back door lit up the kitchen, which was dark and quiet."

"Did you think the twins were in the house, Uncle?" I asked.

"Yes, I did. I could almost feel their presence, but I couldn't be certain. I walked into the bare living room and noticed thick wool blankets over the windows. In the hallway bathroom, I pulled back the shower curtain. Empty. I moved toward the smaller bedroom and peered into the closet. Again, nothing. Then, I saw it…" He paused for effect, and we leaned in on cue.

"A bloody handprint on the wall—too small to belong to Harriet. It was likely one of the twins'. I hurried to the larger bedroom where there was so much blood pooled on the floor that I lost my footing and dropped my flashlight."

We laughed at him when said he lost his footing, and he joined in for a moment.

"Thankfully, I held onto my gun. I was convinced that Harriet was in that room. Redirecting my flashlight toward the closet, I saw the silhouette of a person through the small crack. Moving cautiously to prevent another fall, I opened the closet door and found Harriet on the floor, her head resting in her lap, with an ominous note protruding from her mouth."

We gasped.

"What was on the note?" Jesika asked.

"That I can't tell you, girls," he said as he turned on the engine. "At least not yet."

He drove us back to my house, where we thanked him for the ICEEs, hugged him goodbye, and watched him drive away.

Jesika, ever the detective enthusiast, believed that keeping the content of the note a secret was his way of assigning us some thrilling detective homework while we were stuck on the block and had nothing else to do. Meanwhile, I couldn't shake the feeling that whatever was on that note held crucial significance for all of us.

The next four weeks were challenging as we tried to fill our days with something to do. The first week, we played every board game we owned between the two houses, and then we pleaded with my dad to go outside. When he finally gave his consent, it felt like we were getting released from jail.

We often discussed the diabolical message found in Harriet's corpse, placed in her mouth by the twins, and how it could have said anything. We initially considered going to the twins' house to do our own investigations, but decided against it. And we discussed our feelings toward Harriet's murder. Jesika said she felt nothing, and it wasn't for us to judge. Or maybe we just couldn't say out loud that the mean lady had gotten what she deserved.

During the second week, we got to know all the officers on the block. The officer at the dead-end was Harry McCormick, and the one at top of the hill was Sam Tilman. The officer in front of my house was Clark Tisdale. Occasionally, they would switch places, but for the most part, they just sat in their unmarked cars. Sometimes they would play kickball with us. It was hilarious watching them running around the bases. Most of the neighbors were surprised the police were even in our neighborhood, and many of them brought the officers breakfast, lunch, and dinner, or coffee and doughnuts.

The third week, my cousin Elisabeth extended an invitation to join her weekend slumber party. Excitement filled the air as she gathered a group of her girlfriends. However, I quickly realized we didn't have much in common anymore. When I enthusiastically suggested we watch *Moonalisa,* none of them knew who she was. That Saturday, every kid in Emerald Hills gathered at Jesika's den to indulge in a spine-chilling horror feature that aired at 3:00 p.m. on channel 10 KOGO, but I was stuck with Elisabeth who told me that horror movies gave her nightmares. At that point, I was ready to go home.

They didn't want to play outside at night either. All they wanted to do was play with Ken and Barbie and make them kiss. Disgusting. I asked them if they wanted to learn how to play kickball, but they said, "That's for boys!" They wanted to play hopscotch, puzzles, and board games instead. I was bored to death. In the meantime, I knew that Jesika was probably down the street playing tetherball or doing a *Moonalisa* matinee, and I felt jealous and left out.

I called her house, and when she picked up the phone, I asked, "Are you doing a *Moonalisa* matinee?"

"Yes!" she said excitedly. "You'll never guess what's coming on!"

"What?"

"It's *The Tingler.* The preview has been playing all week. It's going to be good."

"Oh, no! I'm going to miss the after-movie discussion."

"It's okay. You'll be here next Saturday." Jesika tried to comfort me.

I tortured myself by asking who was showing up.

"We didn't give out invitations this time because you weren't here. It's gonna be Douglas, Vicky, Iris, Juney, Carlton, and Marty."

"Marty's coming over?" I couldn't believe it.

"Yes, you're going to miss it, but you can watch it with your cousin."

"Yeah, I could, but they have nightmares, so they don't watch scary movies." I sighed.

"Oh. Well, I'm going to Mrs. Davis's church on Sunday. My mother is doing an extra shift at the hospital, so we gotta go over there."

"Well, I'm thinking about coming home tonight," I said.

After we hung up, I realized I really missed my friends and neighborhood. I called my dad, and he came and got me.

CHAPTER 44

Unstoppable, Unappreciated Laughter

The next morning, my mother, father, and I got home from church way before Jesika. I waited on her front porch.

When Mrs. Davis pulled up in her driveway, I ran over to them just in time to hear her say, "I'm going to tell your mother how you two embarrassed me in front of the whole congregation."

"What did they do, Mrs. Davis?" I asked.

"Mind your own business, Marina. This has nothing to do with you."

I couldn't wait to ask them what they did. They were quiet as mice as I followed them back across the street, running to keep up with Mrs. Davis. She was holding their hands and literally jerking their bodies back and forth.

"Wait until I call your mother," she scolded.

"What happened?" I asked again, and they both started laughing.

"What's so funny?"

Sariah's little motor mouth started racing.

"Mrs. Davis invited us to go to church with her. She did it in front of our mother, and so we couldn't say no because you don't say no to adults. We've never been to a Baptist church before and the Sunday school teacher was out with a cold, so we had to sit in the pew with Mrs. Davis. They didn't have holy water and didn't make the sign of the cross. No kneeling and standing, and they didn't speak in Latin or sing in Latin. They have pastors instead of priests, and boy did he get to preaching and jumping up and down! The pastor was throwing his head back and snapping it forward. Marina, you should have seen him! He looked so funny. The choir got to singing and dancing and everyone was fanning themselves. My sister and I have never seen anything like it in our lives."

She could barely talk over her laughter.

"Five big, old, fat women in the pew in front of us fell out onto the floor, one by one. You could see their bloomers! It was hilarious to me and Sariah! We had to put our hands over our mouths to stop laughing!"

I laughed so hard, my belly hurt. I wished I could have been sitting in the pew with Jesika and Sariah. Old ladies lying on the floor with their bloomers showing at church? Hilarious! Jesika laughed until tears welled up in her eyes, and she shook her head at me as she wiped her eyes.

"Marina, we just couldn't hold it. The laughter just came out of us, and it wouldn't stop! Mrs. Davis yanked the both of us out of our seats and right out of the church, but we were still laughing. She spanked us outside the church, and we were still laughing, because it didn't hurt. She is going to tell my mother that we embarrassed her. My mother is going to be so angry with us, we may not get to go again." Breaking into even bigger gales of laughter, she said, "Maybe Mom won't spank us if we tell her Mrs. Davis already did."

"Yeah, and maybe she'll even let us go again."
Sariah smiled.

CHAPTER 45

Good News, Bad News

Monday night, my uncle came over to tell us that they hadn't found the twins yet. "The good news is … we haven't found another body either." Evidently, they'd had a lot of leads come into the station at the beginning, but nothing that turned up anything worthwhile. And now, it seemed the leads had dried up. It was like the Glasgow boys disappeared, and their trail had run cold. The police had canvassed certain areas with no luck.

"Their picture is posted around the city, but no one has called the police station." He paused again, like he knew we would hate his next words as much as he did. "The police chief is pulling the officers from the block. He said they can't afford the manpower anymore."

This news made my mother so angry, she threatened to go down to the police station and give him a piece of her mind.

"I *did* give him a piece of my mind, Sis. I went to his office, certain that he would sympathize with me because he has two daughters of his own. I calmly asked him to reconsider his decision, and he refused. I pushed, and he raised his voice at me and held his ground." He took a deep breath to collect himself before he continued. "The chief is a hard man, Sis. Besides, they're all involved in a domestic homicide case now. I guess some man shot his wife. Only he didn't leave the scene. He called the police himself. No mystery there…"

My uncle went on to say that he had gone over to Marty's house to talk to Mr. O'Kelly.

"Marty answered the door, and I asked him if I could speak to his grandfather. He said he had gone into the hospital, and the doctor told them that his grandfather was in a coma. Marty started talking about his grandfather being in the 'in-between.' He said that Jesika told him about his grandpa being there. And then he said, 'I guess he's on the other side now.' I felt so bad for him. I didn't know what to say to that boy."

My uncle had seen Jesika outside playing hopscotch with Irene, and he asked me to get her. I asked him if I could be the one to tell Jesika about Marty's grandpa, and he said it was okay.

CHAPTER 46

Beyond the In-between

So, I went outside to deliver the news.

"We've got to call Marty," she said immediately, running into her house and dialing his number.

The phone rang and Marty picked up.

"Marty, are you okay?"

"I'm fine, I guess. My grandfather is on the other side."

"I heard. I'm going to say a rosary for him. Saint Michael is with him no matter what, Marty," she assured him.

"Jesika, I don't want him to die." He sounded so sad.

"I know, Marty."

"I want him here with me and my mom." It was obvious he was trying hard not to cry.

"I don't know where a coma is, but he can come back from it, right?" Jesika asked.

"I think he wanted to go," Marty murmured.

"Why do you say that?" she wondered.

"I don't know."

"Marty, can we go and visit him?" Jesika looked up at me, as if asking me to go with her too.

"He can only have immediate family."

"We *are* family." Jesika's voice was firm.

"I know," Marty said.

"Maybe we can sneak in," she suggested. "I can get Pishoung to help us tomorrow."

"Okay. Come and get me, and I'll do what I can to help you and Marina see him."

"Marty, keep your chin up, okay?" Jesika did her best to encourage him.

"Okay, see you tomorrow."

"Why did you tell him that?" I asked. "How are we going to get to Balboa Navy Hospital when we can't even leave the yard?"

"We'll ask Pishoung. He'll take us."

"He's never even met Marty's grandfather," I protested.

"So, that doesn't make any difference! It won't hurt to ask. We'll give him our puppy dog faces," she said, using her best one on me.

With that expression on her face, her head cocked to the side, and two pigtails, she really did look like a puppy dog.

"Pishoung is probably sleeping, and we shouldn't wake him," I said. "Just call Marty back and tell him we can't go! I'm not getting into any more trouble."

"I would do this for you. Pleeeeeease." She gave me the puppy dog look again.

"Oh, alright." I gave in. "You wake him."

Jesika knocked on Pishoung's door.

"What do you two want?" Thankfully, he wasn't asleep.

"Marty's grandfather is in the hospital. He wants us to go with him to see his grandpa."

"Oh, no, that's very bad," he cautioned.

"Pishoung, they don't let little kids that aren't relatives visit," she started.

"I know that," he responded. "So what … are you going to sneak in?"

"Well, we've thought about it and figured maybe you could help us. Please, Pishoung, we'll polish your shoes and press your uniform …" I promised.

"Marty's grandfather's in a coma." Jesika added in a desperate voice.

"Well, in that case, I'll take you. What do we tell your mothers?" And then, answering his own question, he said, "We'll tell them the truth, but not the part about sneaking in. You let me talk to your parents. It'll be okay."

"We'll go call Marty back. He said that visiting hours are between 5:30 and 7:30 p.m."

Marty asked if he could come over early so that we could spin tops. Before he hung up the phone, he thanked Jesika for caring about his grandpa.

That night, our two families got together in Jesika's living room and said the Rosary for Mr. O'Kelly. Pishoung spoke to our parents about visiting Marty's grandpa in the hospital, and my mother mentioned the concern that they wouldn't let us in his room. Pishoung told her he knew a woman in intensive care, a registered nurse named Maryanne.

"She'll help us get in to see him."

CHAPTER 47

Marty's Homerun

The next day, Mrs. Jennings dropped Marty off at my house before she went to work. We played with the tops that Marty brought from home until Douglas came over with his rifles and cap guns. Jesika went home to get hers. After we got tired of falling in the dirt and playing dead, we got a bunch of kids together to play kickball. Fourteen in all. Sariah and Jesika were better than everyone in the neighborhood, but I was becoming a good player, thanks to Irene's tough brother. The pain made me a better dodger and a better thrower. The only way you were going to get me out was if I kicked the ball in the air and you caught it.

Marty was surprised at how good everyone was and appeared a little intimidated in the beginning. He was the only White face on Jesika's team. The first time Marty kicked the ball, I got him out before he could reach first base.

"Oww, Marina that hurt!" he yelled, rubbing his leg.

I remembered that sting all too well.

Jesika hollered, "That's alright, Marty, you'll do better next time."

We were in the fifth inning, and Marty was up at home plate. It was a tie game. Carlton was pitching the ball, and the bases were loaded.

Jesika yelled, "Marty, you can do this! Come on, Marty, bring everyone in."

Carlton was known for his spinner. He threw the ball hard against the ground with his dangerous spin. It was fast, Marty missed the kick.

"Strike one!" Carlton yelled.

The rest of my team started shouting, "Aw, he can't kick the ball!"

Carlton did it again. Strike two.

The look on Marty's face was pure determination. Carlton rolled the ball again even harder. This time, Marty kicked the ball over everyone's head. It went up into the air and landed in Jesika's front yard. Everyone on my team just watched the ball fly. Marty had kicked a grand slam! He brought in everybody on the bases, and then he ran across home plate. Jesika's high-five met his hand in mid-air. The rest of her team surrounded him, each high-fiving him one at a time. They had won!

"Good game," Marty said to Carlton. "Let's play another five innings."

I reminded him that it was getting late and that we needed to clean up and get dressed to go to the hospital. I went into the house, and the rest of the kids went to get their skates and bikes to play taxi. I left Jesika and Marty sitting on my front porch talking to each other, but I could hear them through the window.

He told Jesika he was sorry that he had never talked to her during the school year.

"I don't blame you," she said. "I stay invisible most of the time."

"I thought it was funny how you were always late," he chuckled. "I liked it when you told Mrs. Poppinggoat that you weren't going to spell your name with a C, it was with a K. You kept saying, 'It's Jesika!'" They both laughed. "I also thought it was cool when you went and got your picture out of the trash. I was looking over your shoulder when you were drawing it. The picture of a body with different people at different parts of the body. You titled it 'The World.' Does this mean that we are all one body?" Marty asked.

"I guess so," she said. "And I felt bad when she made you stand in front of class and spit in a bucket until you couldn't spit anymore. Just because you were chewing on a rubber band."

They're cute, I thought as I got ready.

CHAPTER 48

A Special Prayer for Mr. O'Kelly

It was about 6:30 p.m., and it was time for us to go to the hospital. My dad had made us wash up and put on something nice. Even Pishoung was dressed nicely in a fresh navy uniform, and Marty put on clothes that he had brought in a bag. We climbed into Pishoung's car and took off for Balboa Navy Hospital. It didn't take long for us to get there. Pishoung signed himself in, and then Marty, and then us two girls. He told the receptionist that Marty was here to see his grandpa and that he was in intensive care. She said that maybe Marty could go in but the rest of us couldn't because we weren't relatives. Jesika sighed, and Pishoung said that we were planning to wait in the visiting room.

When we got to intensive care, a nurse greeted us.

"He really did know a nurse named Maryanne," Jesika said happily.

Pishoung said that we must be quiet and couldn't stay long.

"Follow me," Maryanne said as she pulled the curtain back. There was Marty's grandpa with tubes going into his nose, and an IV hanging out of his arm.

"Don't be alarmed, kids. It looks a lot worse than it is."

Marty walked up to him and picked up his hand while Pishoung sat down in a chair and lowered his head. I figured he was praying. Jesika and I stood looking but said nothing.

"Grandpa, don't leave me now. Me and mama, we need you," Marty pleaded as he laid his head down on the bed and started to cry.

Jesika and I could not hold back the tears.

"Grandpa," Jesika said. "It's me and Marina. We're here because we need you too. They haven't found the twins yet."

"I don't care about them, and he doesn't care about them." Marty was upset by her comment.

"I know. I'm sorry, Marty," Jesika apologized and started to pray. "Lord, you have made Grandpa perfect even though he is old. We rejoice because you have not taken him away. Lord, I don't know where a coma is, but he stands between life and death. Only you can tell him that now is not his time to die. I know the power of your love and the power of our love for him. Lord, please hear Marty, Pishoung, mine and Marina's prayer. Oh, Lord, and Marty's mother's too. Grant us this petition in the name of the Father, the Son, and the Holy Spirit."

Marty whispered, "Thanks, Jesika."

Maryanne told us it was time to leave, so we kissed Grandpa goodbye. Then we took Marty home, hugged him good-bye, and Jesika told him to keep the faith.

Pishoung asked us if we wanted Chinese food.

"Yeah!" we said at the same time.

We stopped at one of his favorite places.

While we were eating, Pishoung said, "I can tell that Mr. O'Kelly is a strong man." I remembered how his eyes were filled with tears when he looked up.

"He was kind to me and Marina. I did the only thing I could do for him … and that was to pray."

I told Jesika that it was going to work because I felt the "Holy Spirit" through her prayer.

I walked across the street and found my dad at the door.

"Hi, Dad."

"How's Marty's grandpa?" he asked.

"Marty was really upset when he saw him."

"I know it's hard for Marty. There's a possibility he may lose his grandfather, Marina."

"I know, but Jesika said a prayer, and there was something about it. I can't even explain it."

My father quickly responded, "Hmmm. I feel a miracle—a healing miracle."

"Maybe. Dad, I'm full and tired. I'm gonna go to bed. Goodnight."

"Listen, Marina. If Marty's grandfather should happen to take a turn for the worse, just be a good friend to him, okay?"

"Okay, Daddy, that's easy. I like Marty."

"I have to go back to work in the morning. Please stay on the block, Marina. Your brothers will be around to keep an eye on you."

CHAPTER 49

A MiraCle and an Upset

Early the next morning, Marty called Jesika to let her know that his mother had heard from the nurse in intensive care, and she ran over to my house to tell me the good news.

"Marina! Marina!" Jesika yelled. My dad had let her in, and she shook me several times. "You'll never guess what happened!"

"What is it?" I asked, and then said, "I know. Mr. O'Kelly came out of the coma, right?"

"Yes! He's out of the coma. He's awake."

I jumped out of bed and started jumping up and down with her.

"You wanna call Marty?" she asked.

"Yes!" I said. "Then let's call my uncle, okay? I dialed Marty's number, and Marty joyfully told us that they would be picking his grandfather up from the hospital the next day. He said that we could come over to visit him once he got settled in.

I called my uncle next. The phone rang and my cousin Elisabeth answered the phone.

"Hi, Elisabeth."

"Oh. Hi, Marina." Her voice sounded annoyed and sarcastic.

"Can I speak with your father?" I asked.

"Yeah, but my father has been through enough."

"What are you talking about, Elisabeth?"

"The chief has been on his back, and the other officers that work with him are disrespecting him. First, they take him off the case and let the FBI take over. He's getting very little help from the other detective and the other officers. He's literally on his own now. And they want to close the case, and pass it off as unsolved."

"They can't do that! We're so close!" I responded in a panic. "There are two killers out there. And Beth, they … will … kill … again."

"You don't know that for sure," she said.

"Maybe not," I replied. "But maybe together we can solve this case."

"Is that what you're trying to do? That's the whole problem."

I was quiet for a moment, as I was getting her message loud and clear.

"The word around the police station is that he's got two nieces that are better detectives than him. And Jesika's not even his niece."

I gasped.

"Elisabeth, I didn't know."

"Your mother and father know," she retorted.

My heart was pounding, and my best friend read the expression on my face.

"What's she saying to you?" Jesika whispered. I put my hand up because Elisabeth was still talking.

"My mother's upset. She doesn't understand how the two of you got so involved. I heard my parents arguing about you and Jesika. And my parents hardly ever argue."

"I look up to your father. I want to be a detective just like him someday," I said, trying to smooth things over.

"You got way too involved."

"You said that before, Beth."

Now she was making me mad.

"We're just kids, Marina. You should let the grownups do their job."

"I just saw him the other day, and he didn't mention any of this to me."

Jesika grabbed the phone, "You're not her mama, so stop acting like you're her mama!"

Elisabeth hung up on her.

"Why did you do that? You just made matters worse, Jesika."

"Oh, so what? Let her hang up! What was her problem, anyway?" Jesika asked.

"It's a long story, so maybe I can put it in a nutshell. My uncle could lose his job because we haven't found the killers. Elisabeth is blaming us."

"Oh, she's just being moody and jealous."

"No, I think her concerns are genuine. What do we do? Who can we talk to about this?" I wondered.

"We'll go and talk with Mr. O'Kelly when he gets home, but let's give him a couple of days to settle in first.

CHAPTER 50

Thelma and Jesika

"Yeah. Okay. In the meantime, I'll talk with my grandmother. She's a very wise woman. Besides, you haven't met my grandma. You'll like her."

"Marina, we still need to talk with your uncle. He said we need to communicate. So, let's communicate," she said firmly.

This was the first time I felt that the outcome of this case was looking bleak.

"I wish we were older," I said.

"We're old enough," Jesika said. "Is your grandmother at home now?"

"Yeah."

"Let's just ask Pishoung to take us."

"No, I'll ask my dad."

"Dad, can I go over to Grandma's house?"

"I don't know. I don't think that's a clever idea."

"It's been two weeks, Dad. There haven't been any reports on the news."

"Okay, I'll ask Lewis if he'll stay over there with you. Call your grandmother to make sure she doesn't have plans."

"I'll go tell Pishoung where I'm going," Jesika said, "Will it be okay if I let my brother and sister tag along?"

Her mother was at work, and Pishoung was babysitter for the day.

My grandmother was okay with me and my friends coming over, so Father dropped us off and told us to give my grandmother a big hug for him. We rang the doorbell because her door was open, but her screen door was locked.

"Hello Grandma, we're here," I hollered.

"Hello, kids, how are you today?" She looked happy to see us.

"Fine, ma'am," they all said.

"Grandma, this is Jesika, and this is her sister, Sariah, and her little brother, Jayden."

"How old are you, Jayden?"

"I'm three, Grandma."

"Y'all hungry?" my grandmother asked.

Sariah said, "Yes."

"What have you had to eat?"

"Ma'am, we don't have a grandma," Sariah said.

"Oh, everybody has a grandma and a grandpa."

"Well, we never met ours."

"If you want one, baby, you can call me Grandma."

"Okay!" Sariah was overjoyed.

A short time later, my grandmother hollered, "Marina, bring your friends into the dining room."

She had made French Toast, bacon, grits, and some peaches.

"I'm hungry. Can I have seconds, Grandma?" Sariah asked.

"You haven't even had your first plate yet," I scolded. Sariah put her fist up to me.

"Oh, you got a little mean streak in you," Grandma said, chuckling.

Sariah quickly put her fist down. "No, ma'am, I'm just hungry."

"Sariah, mind your manners. You're always hungry," Jesika said.

"It's okay, baby, she can eat to her heart's content."

"Marina, I like your grandma." Sariah stuck her tongue out at me.

"You don't scare me, Sariah," I said, sticking my tongue back out at her.

"Alright, we'll have none of that at the table," Grandma said as she sat down with us. "Marina, would you like to say a blessing?"

"Okay! Bless us, Oh Lord, for this food which we are about to receive from thy bounty. Bless the hands that made this food." I looked toward my grandmother and she smiled. "May it be used to nourish our bodies. Lord, may you nourish our families' souls and our hearts. In the name of the Father and the Son and the Holy Spirit."

"Amen," my grandmother said.

We ate and then went into the back yard. Grandmother had flowers blooming everywhere. She had honeysuckle, so there were hummingbirds that stood in mid-air. Her blessed Mary statue was surrounded by red and white roses. There was an old shed that looked like a tiny house. She said that Grandpa had built it with his own two hands.

Jesika noticed my tree right away and said, "What a magnificent tree! You're so lucky, Marina." She ran up and hugged it, which was impossible because it was so big.

We took turns swinging in the tire swing, and then we tried to climb the tree. It was the kind of tree where the first branch was high up, and we needed a ladder to get to it. Grandma came outside to warn us that it wasn't a good idea. Jayden wanted to swing on the tire, so we helped Sariah put Jayden in the tire. Once Jayden was in the swing, that was our cue to speak with Grandma alone.

"Grandma! Grandma!" We walked through the backdoor, hollering, "Where are you?" She didn't answer back, so we went up the stairs to look for her. As we reached the second floor, we called again, "Grandma! Grandma!"

"I'm in my bedroom," she hollered back.

"What are you doing?"

"I'm looking at some pictures." Her voice was discernibly sad. "This is a picture of my sister, Thelma."

"Grandmother, you never talk about her," I said. "She's pretty."

"I want to see the picture," Jesika said.

When I handed the picture to Jesika, she looked at it and put it to her chest and then sat next to my grandmother.

"She looks like your mother, Marina," Jesika said.

I nodded, but I was paying attention to Grandmother. I recognized that look in her eye. I had seen it so often before. It was sorrowful.

Jesika looked at my grandmother and asked, "What happened to her?"

"She married a boy named Clayton Hamilton Mathews. He had blue eyes and curly brown hair. Thelma didn't like him at first. She said he paid too much attention to his light skin, and he only did it in front of her."

"And that bothered her?" I asked.

"Yes, it did, Marina. She told him often she didn't care about his light skin. She just loved him for who he was. He'd laugh and make a vain comment about his good looks. They say that love is blind."

My grandmother sighed. After a few more wistful looks and sighs, she went on.

"My mother and father didn't like him, so their relationship had to stay a secret. I was the only person that knew on our side of the family, and she swore me to secrecy. My father said Ham's kin was a sharecropper, and being a sharecropper was like still being a slave. My father would make comments about how his skin was so light, he could pass for White. He was sure that they were kin to people that owned the big house in the middle of a plantation."

She sat back and got comfortable in her chair.

"Ham was tired of their relationship being this big secret because he wanted to marry Thelma and move her to South Carolina. He told her he had a brother that owned land there. He couldn't wait to tell our parents, as he believed Thelma was exaggerating their hate and discontent. She tried to tell him otherwise, but he wouldn't listen. He came over early one morning, demanding to talk to my parents. He was drunk. Thelma saw him through the window and went running outside.

"He wanted to stay, so she grabbed him by the hand and took him over to the well and splashed water on his face. He said she was gonna be the mammy to his children, and she told him she wouldn't marry him if he kept saying horrible things. He tried to make it better by telling her she was beautiful, but he said it while licking his lips and smiling."

Grandmother grimaced at the memory.

"I heard what he said to my sister, and it horrified me. He was hiding his true self, and my sister was so in love, she didn't want to see it. He straightened up for her, and they walked into the house together, only to wind up in an ugly confrontation with our daddy and momma. Our parents told him to get out, and my sister just went with him.

"When she came into our room and started to pack, I tried to talk her out of it and told her I felt something bad was going to happen. And she just told me to pray for her."

Grandmother's eyes got misty.

"Listening to my mother moaning with grief, I recalled a conversation we had about Hamilton's mother, Candice. It was a story my mother only told me once, but it was embedded deep in my memory bank.

"Hamilton was a twin, and he and his brother Edward's appearances denied their African heritage. They fell into that particular category of Blacks who rejected their own blood, only to then be rejected by the White blood they aspired to embrace. Their fair complexion granted them the dangerous privilege of passing as White.

"Residing on a vast, expansive thirty acres, the twins lived under the roof of their mother and stepfather. Their mother, with her light skin, had been coerced into marriage with Bowman Reese as a means to conceal the plantation owner's scandalous secret. Rumors whispered that the twins' mother was the mistress of the affluent plantation owner, Templeton Leapold Duncan.

"Candice toiled for years in the kitchen as a cook and a servant, enjoying a privileged life in the grand house. Other servants often witnessed her sitting on Templeton's lap, feeding him fruit, laughter echoing through the halls. Viola, Templeton's wife, became aware of Candice's affection for her husband and expelled her, forbidding her to return.

"Though Bowman always believed he was the twins' father, his pride was shattered when Templeton's jealous wife revealed the truth. He initially dreamt of giving them more opportunities, wanting to spare them from a life of perpetual sharecropping. From then on, their days were spent toiling in the fields, from sunrise to sunset, picking cotton, and tending to the rice crop. Forbidden from secretly learning how to read at Miss Hatty's, the twins' education was abruptly halted.

"The twins became victims of Bowman's relentless labor, toiling in the cotton fields of the Temple Plantation. Bowman would loan them to the other sharecroppers where they suffered abuse and ridicule. Daily, he unleashed his anger upon them and subjected them to relentless beatings.

"Edward and Hamilton hatched a plan to escape the plantation, wary of cowering in the presence of White individuals. Edward would pass for White, achieving success, and subsequently inform his brother to join him. However a condition accompanied their pact—to exact revenge on Bowman for the relentless torture he inflicted upon them.

"Templeton eventually shot Bowman in the back of the head in front of the twins.

"The boys, horrified, grabbed each other, thinking that they would be next. He grabbed the two boys and hugged them around their necks while apologizing to them for what they had witnessed. He promised no one would ever lay a whip on their backside again.

"Edward and Hamilton grew up in a life of privilege and luxury, but they harbored the scars of their previous life." Grandmother cleared the emotion out of her throat, or maybe made room for more.

"I prayed every day to hear from my sister. Finally, six months later, I got a letter from her. She and Hamilton and his brother and his wife had moved to Georgetown, South Carolina. The name of the Plantation was Silver Hills, a two thousand five hundred fifty-seven point seven acre riverfront property.

"She described the beautiful home in detail and told me about his identical twin and how she couldn't tell them apart. She said both men worked hard, and there was nothing to worry about.

"I wrote her back and asked if I could come and visit, but whenever she wrote, she never responded to my request. She wrote a lot about Caroline and Edward's children and the time she got to spend with them, and how she taught them to fish. She seemed happy; however, I was afraid for her. I couldn't shake the feeling.

"It took Thelma a year and three months to respond to my next letter. When she finally did, she shared that she had been frequently left alone, and that Ham's brother visited her when she was alone in the house, which made her feel uncomfortable. Ham kept making excuses for not taking her into town, and his excuses didn't make sense. She suspected that he was ashamed of her and went into town without her. They got into a terrible argument about it. When she went to talk with Caroline about it, she was cold and distant and suggested that people around there didn't like mixed marriages. She told Thelma she should be happy with her surroundings, and if she'd like, she could give Thelma a job in her kitchen.

"She decided to take her horse into town and found Ham and his brother in a brothel. She saw them, but they did not see her as she watched the two of them kiss the women on their laps until she couldn't bear to look at them anymore. She ran out of the brothel and got on her horse and rode fast until she arrived home." Grandmother wiped the lone tear that trickled down her cheek as she finished the story. "I was so worried about her. I wanted to go visit."

I wondered how long I had been holding my breath when Grandmother looked at me and shrugged sadly, but we were both distracted when Jesika, who had been staring off into space like she often did, suddenly passed out.

Her eyes started to roll back in her head, and her body slammed back onto the bed, her legs thrashing about.

Thelma's picture fell on the floor, and I stood and backed away cautiously. I couldn't believe what I was seeing.

My grandmother, however, sat with her back straight, looking at me. Time seemed to stand still between the past and the present.

When I moved to grab Jesika's hand, my grandmother intervened.

"Don't touch her, Marina."

"Grandmother!" I shouted. "What is happening to her?"

"Marina, she'll be okay. I'm here."

That's when Jesika began to speak with a voice that was not her own. I watched her body become still and listened to the voice that was soft and had a sweet tone, like an angel's.

Somehow, I knew she was channeling Thelma.

"In the depth of my despair, I paced anxiously in my kitchen, the weight of my emotions suffocating me. With a trembling hand, I prepared my tea, my mind racing as lightning pierced the darkened sky outside. The ominous atmosphere mirrored my inner turmoil, causing me to startle and spill my tea as a sharp pain seized my lower abdomen. Collapsing to my knees, I cried out, cradling my belly in anguish. The agony intensified, tears flowing uncontrollably as I knew it was too soon! I was seven and a half months pregnant. Struggling to rise, I gripped a nearby chair for support. Just then, Hamilton and Edward stumbled through the door, their presence heightening my distress.

"For a moment, I found my courage to ask Ham why he treated me so poorly—what I had done to deserve such treatment. Ham, in a slurred state, responded with denial, his words muddled and obscure. Edward, barely able to stand, clung to Hamilton, the two of them embodying a beastly savage aura.

"My heart raced as I witnessed their transformed masculinity. Their eyes turned as black as coal, sending shivers down my spine. Ham erupted in anger, pounding on the table, accusing me of being a bad girl, insinuating an illicit relationship with his brother. I protested, my voice quivering with pain and betrayal. I desperately attempted to diffuse the tension, urging Hamilton to promise never to return to the gentlemen's club. But my plea fell on deaf ears, as the truth unraveled before my eyes. Edward revealed our intimate encounter, mocking my innocence. And that's when I realized the depth of their deceit. Overwhelmed with despair, I whispered through my tears, realizing the cruel game Ham played with me and my heart.

"At that moment, I understood that escaping this house alive was impossible. Consumed by the weight of realization, I succumbed to unconsciousness …"

Jesika's face returned to normal, as Thelma's spirit released Jesika's physical body.

Grandmother grabbed Jesika's hands.

"Get up! When you were born, you had a caul on your face. You're special." Then she looked at me and said, "You are intelligent and smart just like your momma and daddy."

When she turned back to Jesika, she continued, "We were meant to meet today. You have always had an eye for seeing. Don't be afraid of this gift, child. When your momma gave birth to you, she thought you had colic. But you didn't. You see and hear people from the other side. You call it the in-between now."

"Yeah. It's where Marty's grandfather has been for a while."

"He won't be able to help you with the case now because he is no longer in-between. He is on this side now. However, he will be able to remember some things."

"You know about Marty's grandfather?" Jesika asked.

"How, Grandmother? How do you know?" I wondered.

"I know he went into a coma because he stopped visiting me in my dreams. Baby, they don't know where people go when they are in a coma. I think it's because of anesthesia. I know he's home because I feel his spirit, and his spirit is happy to be with family."

I didn't know I had a grandmother with an eye for spirits. Nobody talked about that kind of stuff in my house. Jesika asked her if she saw Saint Michael, and she said that she felt the presence of God every day.

"I feel God is present in the mountain, in the rivers and lakes, other people, and even in that big old tree outside."

"Saint Michael is my protector," Jesika said. She pulled out her Saint Michael medal to show it to her. "Marina has one too, and so does Uncle Lonny."

"Yes, baby, I know. I also know you wanna talk with your Uncle Lonny, Marina. You two have been very brave, I must say. You don't have to worry about Elisabeth, Selma, or your uncle. They'll all be just fine."

"Grandma, I called Uncle Lonny, and Elisabeth wouldn't let me talk to him."

"I'll call him now, and the three of you can sit down in the living room and talk. You need to communicate, so that you are all on the same page. He needs you, and you both need him. I saw the two of you on the news, Channel 10. Black people have a lot to be angry about these days, and it doesn't take much. Taniya Greenwood was killed by those twins, and I see those evil souls still moving from one river of life to the next. You two standing together made me proud, and that fellow named Pig-shine."

"Grandma, his name is Pishoung!"

We laughed loudly, and so did she.

"Well, he almost got y'all mauled. You two calmed that crowd down, and I was so proud. No use procrastinating. I'm calling your uncle at the station right now."

It was as if my grandmother knew exactly what time to call Uncle Lonny, who said that he would be over at 5:30 p.m. Grandmother made sure that dinner would be ready.

We played hide-and-seek outside for a long time, but I couldn't stop thinking about what happened to Jesika when she was in Grandmother's room.

CHAPTER 51

Real Talk

My uncle arrived earlier than we expected.

"Hello, Son. Your niece and Jesika are right there in the living room."

"Can't I give my mother a hug first?" he asked, arms open.

"You sure can," she said lovingly.

When he came into the living room and sat in my grandmother's rocking chair, I opened the conversation.

"I tried to call you last night, Uncle, but Elisabeth wouldn't let me talk to you."

"I'm sorry you two had harsh words, Marina. Detective work is hard, and the clues don't always come together as quickly as we want them to. It causes tempers to flare up. Accusations start to fly, and good people sometimes say things they don't mean."

"You're talking about work, aren't you, Uncle?"

"Yes, I am, baby girl. The twins are hiding out there somewhere, and we can't find them. I'm so afraid there are other girls in shallow graves, and it sickens me."

"Uncle Lonny, you told us that dead bodies have a way of showing up," Jesika interjected. "Sadly, this is when we will find them."

"I hope so, Jesika. I hope so."

"I think the twins are hiding, and they've changed their hair color, the way they dress, and their demeanor. No one can recognize them from the drawing, because they don't look like that anymore."

"You're probably right, Jesika. You've just confirmed what I've been thinking about myself."

I knew my uncle was an exemplary employee and thorough. His one mistake was allowing us to help him, and the chief didn't take him seriously anymore. Elisabeth told me that his boss was angry and told Uncle Lonny he was on his own. I looked at it like it was a chance for my uncle to prove himself. No sweat. Black people are good at proving others wrong.

Jesika whispered, "We aren't talking about what we're going to do."

She had grown tired of the chit chat and just wanted to get to the bottom of this case. All of a sudden, she blurted out in typical Jesika fashion, "I'm tired of trying to figure out what is in your adult head!"

Instantly, I knew that she was not thinking about me by the tone of her voice.

How dare she talk to my uncle like that. Is it because of her episode in my grandmother's room?

"Your uncle doesn't really want to work with us," she said.

"Okay, Jesika …" I didn't know what else to say.

"Hold on, Jesika," my uncle interrupted. "This is my career we're talkin' about!" Then he threw his hands up. "Why am I about to argue with a child?"

"Uncle, Jesika is just extremely tired." I tried to smooth things over.

"I'm not tired!" Jesika snapped back. "Yeah, tell that to Taniya, Mattie, and whoever else is out there! We got to do something!" She got up and started pacing the floor. "We're sitting here with our thumbs up our butts!"

Uncle Lonny was quiet for minutes until Grandmother broke the silence by saying, "Please come and eat dinner. It's ready."

During dinner, my uncle mentioned he wanted to go to Marty's house so he could speak to Mr. O'Kelly. He told Jesika and me we could go but to take our time eating.

"We'll take Sariah and Jayden home first," he said.

They all ate at a comfortable speed, but Jesika and I couldn't eat fast enough.

"Does anyone want dessert?" Grandmother asked.

Jayden and Sariah chimed in unison, "Yes."

"Aw, come on, we have police work to do," Jesika pleaded with them.

"Jesika, everything happens in its own time," Grandmother admonished.

Once our bellies were full, we all said goodbye to Grandmother. She told Jesika to get some rest because she'd had a long day.

Pishoung came out to the car to greet us when we pulled into Jesika's driveway.

"Good evening, Detective Talbert. How are you?" he asked.

"Just good," he answered.

"It's going to be a full moon tonight, and it's going to shed a lot of light."

"You think so?"

"Oh, I'm sure of it, Detective. Is everything okay?" Pishoung inquired.

"Yes," Uncle Lonny answered, unconvincingly. "The girls are going to take a ride with me over to Mr. O'Kelly's house to see how he's doing."

"You tell Marty that I'm glad that his grandfather is okay. That was very good news."

"I'll give him the message," Uncle Lonny replied.

"Have a good evening, Detective," Pishoung said with a wave.

CHAPTER 52

A Hole in the Ground

From Jesika's house, we went straight to Marty's. We turned down 54th and made a right onto Naranja Street, passing the twins' house, which was dark and spooky. I thought about Harriet McDuffie and how she had ended up dead in the twins' house.

She wasn't tough enough to take on the twins.

Next we were on Carver Street, Marty's block, and Jesika couldn't wait to get out of the car.

I knew what my grandmother meant by Jesika being different. She could pick up on people's emotions and their energies. It made her a loner at school. It made her talk to God, saints, and angels. It made her close to nature. And it made her love Marty. It also made her talk to my uncle in a tone that was unfamiliar.

I followed my uncle and Jesika to the front door, and she rang the doorbell.

Mrs. Jennings answered the door and looked at Jesika.

"Hello," she said, and then hollered over her shoulder, "Marty, your friends Jesika and Marina are here."

My uncle introduced himself, "Hi. I'm Detective Lonny Talbert."

"Nice to meet you, Detective."

"Would it be okay if I speak with your father for a few minutes? I heard he was in the hospital yesterday. I won't take a lot of his time."

"Yeah, he is eating and talking up a storm. He likes to tell jokes. He'll probably tell you at least one, Detective, before you leave."

"Oh, I love a good joke, Mrs. Jennings."

"I liked it better when he was 'in-between,'" she said, using air quotes. "That's what Marty called it. Children have the strangest name for things."

I followed her and my uncle into the living room.

"Hello, Mr. O'Kelly. How are you this evening?" Uncle Lonny started.

"Oh, I'm just fine, Detective. Hello, Marina. How are you?"

"Fine, Mr. O'Kelly. I'm glad to see you doing much better."

"Where's Jesika?" he asked.

"Oh, she's talking to Marty. She'll be in here in just a minute."

It was rude and embarrassing for me that she didn't come right away.

Maybe she's just mad at my uncle. I hope she doesn't forget her manners.

"Aileen just made the best spaghetti. You should try some. I can't get enough of it. So, you're Detective Talbert. You're the uncle to those pretty little girls, and they've been helping with the case."

"Yes, I …"

Mr. O'Kelly interrupted, "I'm happy to see the girls are alive and well. I think you'd better watch over those two."

"Oh, don't worry about that, sir. Is there anything you can tell me about the twins? They've been eluding us for some time now."

"Since I've been out of the coma, I don't see things like I used to. I vaguely remember seeing images of a hole in the ground in someone's yard."

"Are you sure you can't remember anything?" Uncle Lonny probed.

"Just a hole in the ground, but I can't possibly tell you where that is." Marty's grandfather looked upset that he couldn't offer more.

"Well, thank you, Mr. O'Kelly. I'll let you get back to your dinner. It sure smells and looks good."

"Have some dinner, Detective. Aileen will fix your plate."

"Thank you, but no thank you. We just finished eating at my mom's."

"Well, if you won't have some dinner, then let me tell you an old Irish joke. Two men were sitting next to each other at Murray's Pub in London. After a while, one bloke looks at the other and says, 'I can't help but think from listening to you that you're from Ireland.'

"The other bloke responds proudly, 'Yes, that I am!'

"The first one says, 'So am I! And where in Ireland might you be from?'

"The other bloke answers, 'I'm from Dublin, I am!'

"The first one responds, 'So am I. Mother Mary and Jesus. And what street did you live on in Dublin?'

"The other bloke says, 'A lovely little area it was. I lived on McCleary Street in the old central part of town.'

"The first one says, 'Faith and it's a small world. So, did I! And what school would you have been going to?'

"The other bloke answered, 'Well now, I went to Saint Mary's of course.'

"The first one gets excited and says, 'And so did I. Tell me, what year did you graduate?'

"The other bloke answers, 'Well now, let's see, I graduated in 1943.'

"The first one exclaims, 'The good lord must be smiling down upon us! I can hardly believe our good luck at winding up in the same place tonight. Can you believe it? I graduated from Saint Mary's in 1943 myself!'

"About this same time, Vicky walks up to the bar, sits down, and orders a drink. Brian, the barman, walks over to Vicky shaking his head and mutters, 'It's going to be a long night.'

"Vicky asks, 'Why do you say that, Brian?'

"'The Murphy twins are drunk again!'"

Grandpa and my uncle started laughing their heads off, and so did I.

"Are you sure you won't have dinner, Detective?"

"Oh, no thanks, I just had a big plate of food at my mother's house. But I've got a joke for you, Mr. O'Kelly."

CHAPTER 53

Impersonations of Truth

"**Y**ou do? Then let's hear it. Laughter is good for the soul … especially in your line of work. Come on, let's hear it."

My uncle cleared his throat, and said, "Sting like a bee, and float like a butterfly," in a voice that was not his own.

"I know him," Mr. O'Kelly responded. "It's Cassius Clay. He goes by the name … uh, what's his name? Oh yeah, Muhammad Ali."

It wasn't really a joke as much as an impersonation of Muhammad when he was being interviewed by Michael Parkinson. My uncle told Mr. O'Kelly that he remembered it fondly by its wisdom and humor.

Uncle started his performance, mimicking Muhammad's tone and facial expression. It was remarkable as he sat back in his chair and began to speak and tell the story of a very young Muhammad asking his mother a bunch of questions. This was a side of my uncle that I hadn't seen in a while, and I wished Jesika was in the room to hear him do his impersonation of the well-known boxer who broke from his normally serious personality into being a comedian.

"'Mama,' I asked. 'How is everything White? Jesus is White with blond hair and blue eyes. Why is the Lord's Supper all White men?'"

When I heard my uncle say this, it made me ask the same question. It wasn't necessarily as funny as it was informative. I could tell by the look on Mr. O'Kelly's face that he felt the same way.

Uncle Lonny cleared his throat again and continued as Muhammad:

"I said, 'What happened to all the Black angels when they took the pictures? Oh, I know. If the White folks were in heaven too. And the Black Angels were in the kitchen preparing the milk and honey…I decided to ask my mother if milk and honey was a laxative.'"

Mr. O'Kelly and I laughed loudly at the thought, but Uncle Lonny kept going with his impersonation.

"She said, 'Listen, stop saying that, boy.'

"But I was always curious. And I always wondered, Why did I have to die to go to heaven? Why couldn't I have pretty cars and good money and nice homes now? Why do I have to wait until I die to get milk and honey?

"And I said, 'Mama, I don't want no milk and honey. I like steaks, and milk and honey is a laxative anyway! Do they have a lot of bathrooms in heaven?'

"I always wonder why Miss America was always White? All the beautiful brown women with their beautiful suntans, beautiful shapes, all types of complexions, but she was always White. Mrs. World was always White. Mrs. Universe was always White. White Swan soap, White King soap, White Cloud tissue paper, White Rain hairspray, White Tornado flo-wax. Everything was white.

"And the angel food cake was the white cake. The devil food cake was the chocolate cake…

"And the president lived in the White House. And they got some stuff called White House cigars.

"And Mary has a little lamb, and his feet were white as snow. And Snow White. And everything was white. Santa Claus was white. And everything bad was black. Little ugly duckling was a black duck.

"And the black cat had bad luck. And if I threaten, I'm gonna to blackmail you.

"I said, 'Mama, why can't we call it whitemail? They lie too.'"

My uncle's impersonation made me proud. Not only was he funny, but it also provoked questions of my own. I would not look at the statues in the church the same ever again.

"Well, Detective. That was incredible! Thank you for that." Mr. O'Kelly smiled genuinely.

Uncle Lonny beamed with appreciation for the older White man who understood.

"Grandpa, I'm so glad that you are doing okay now," I said.

"You remember to come and visit an old man." He winked at me.

"I will," I promised.

Jesika finally came into the living room to give Grandpa a kiss goodbye.

"You take care of yourself and your uncle," Grandpa said.

"You take care of *yourself.* I'm glad you're better now. You had us all worried, Grandpa," Jesika responded.

CHAPTER 54

Uncle Lost His Mind

I thought my uncle would drop us off back at home right away. Instead, he stopped in front of the twins' house.

"Why are we stopping here?" I asked.

My uncle looked down at his watch. He looked back over his shoulder and told us that this house was a house of horrors.

Jesika's eyes got really big.

"What do you mean?" she asked. The tone of her voice was that of a frightened little girl. My uncle reached over to his glove compartment, opened it, and pulled out a gun.

"Uncle, are we going into the twin's house?" I asked.

"No, we're gonna search their backyard, and I need you and Marina to help me look."

I'd never seen my uncle so serious. It was almost scary.

I guess he isn't in a funny mood anymore.

"Jesika, I want you to take this gun," he instructed, handing it to her.

"I don't know how to shoot a gun." She stared at it in her hand.

"You just point the gun … and you shoot it."

Jesika was careful not to put her finger on the trigger. She realized at that moment that she could accidently kill one of us, so she held the ring near the trigger, so it was swinging.

"I don't think I could kill anyone, Uncle Lonny."

He snatched the gun out of her hand and gave it to me.

"Can you use this gun if you have to?" he asked.

"I can if you show me how to use it. I've never even held a real gun before—only a play gun," I said.

We looked at each other and instantly had a Vulcan mind melt.

What in the hell has got into him?

"No, Uncle, I can't shoot anyone either. I'm a conscientious objector." I started to cry.

I did not understand my uncle's behavior, and I questioned myself.

How much can we really help my uncle? We can't shoot a gun and don't want to shoot one.

This was the reality that struck both of us.

What good are we?

"We're going in the Glasgows' backyard. Mr. O'Kelly gave me some vital information that we need to follow up on." I guessed he was talking about the hole in the ground. "Are you with me?" he asked and waited for us to nod in agreement. "I'm going in the house to make sure they're not in there. In five minutes, I want you to get out of the car and meet me at the back gate."

We watched my uncle disappear downhill until we couldn't see him anymore.

"I'm scared," Jesika said. "I don't wanna go in the backyard, I don't wanna go near that house. It's spooky."

"And you think I'm not scared?"

We both sat there quietly for a few minutes and then got out of the car as we'd promised. Walking slowly down the hill, we found the gate and entered the backyard. The full moon lit up the backyard while we waited. The grass was overgrown and the weeds were like small skinny trees.

We saw a dark figure come out the back door of the house.

"What if that's not your uncle?" Jesika whispered.

"It's him," I whispered back, recognizing his silhouette.

"The house is clear," he said when he got close.

"Boy, that's a relief," Jesika sighed.

"We're going to divide this backyard into three sections and search it. Marina, you take the south end, and Jesika, you take the north end over there. Be sure to check along the fence. That's very important. We're looking for a hidden hole in the ground."

I looked at the tumbleweeds that were bunched together.

"Uncle, do you have any flashlights?" I asked. "Even with the full moon, it's still hard to see what's on the ground."

"Yes, I have two in the trunk of my car. Hurry up, we can't take all night."

He handed me the keys, and Jesika started to follow me to the car. I knew she was scared and stalling.

"Jesika, you can start looking in your section. Marina will bring you a flashlight."

Jesika didn't respond. She just started walking slowly toward her section. When she looked back at me, the expression on her face screamed, *Please hurry up*.

My uncle went to his section which was closest to the house.

CHAPTER 55

The Hole in the Ground and Its Inhabitant

"I don't see anything over here, Marina," he said when I returned with the flashlights.

"We've covered every inch of this section," Jesika said.

"Okay, let's do my section now," I said.

The first thing we did was check along the fence and then in the middle of the yard. Nothing. We looked again just to be certain and then went over to my uncle to see if he'd had any luck.

"No, nothing is in the yard, but there are two shovels on the side of the house and several buckets … I need to phone home, Marina. Selma is expecting me to be home early, and I don't want her to be worried."

"Okay, Uncle, I'll keep looking," I replied.

"Finish this section, and make sure you search along the outside of the fence, please. I have a feeling that it's on the other side, and it will have a cover of some kind."

"If you're not back when we find it, we'll come and get you," I told him.

"Uncle, are you coming right back?" Jesika asked, still sounding spooked.

"Yes, Jesika, as soon as I finish my phone call."

"Marina, I hope he gets back soon … I hope he gets back. We can't be here all night. And if we find something, it's gonna be bad."

She was holding on to her Saint Michael pendant.

"Isn't it nice that we're working with Uncle, and he trusts us enough to do this job? We're official." I moved the flashlight up and down the yard slowly.

"I don't know about you, but I'm scared, Marina. I've got this bad feeling, and I feel it in the pit of my stomach."

I grabbed her hand, and we exited the gate and started searching along the outside of the fence.

Suddenly, Jesika hollered, "Stop!"

"What's wrong, Jesika!"

She pointed her flashlight toward a rock, and I slowly walked up to it with Jesika behind me.

"It's just a boulder," I murmured.

"Check underneath it," she said.

Sure enough, there was a cement square with a three-inch lip, and the boulder only covered half of it. We pushed the big rock over and it rolled a few inches to reveal a lock on the heavy wooden top.

"Darn!" I started. "We need something to cut off this lock. I know Uncle Lonny has some large, heavy-duty lock cutters in the trunk of his car. Jesika, can you run to his police car and get them? I'll stay here."

Jesika ran at the speed of light and was back in no time. It was going to take both of us to cut this lock, and I wanted to do it before Uncle Lonny found us. I placed the large clipper on the lock, and both of us pressed down with all our might. It felt like we had help from above, and the lock snapped. The wooden door was heavy too, but we managed to open it. I picked up my flashlight so I could see inside the hole.

"Marina, you're not going down there! We need to wait for your uncle. We said we'd go and get him."

"Hand me some rocks, so we can see how far down it goes."
I threw the rock down the shaft, and heard the clink and clang of
rocks against the metal ladder. Then I used the flashlight to see if
I could see the bottom. I couldn't. And I still couldn't figure out
how far it went down.

I started to climb down, and Jesika was horrified.

"What if the twins are down there?"

I paused and stared at her wide eyes.

"I don't think so. They're smart enough to know
we'd eventually find this place. I'm going down. Are you
coming with me?"

As I started to climb down, I could see the gray and
uneven cement plaster on the wall. The sight gave me an
uneasy feeling in the pit of my stomach. Jesika followed,
putting her flashlight in her back pocket.

I dropped my flashlight halfway down, and heard it shatter
when it hit the ground. And when the ladder ran out, I couldn't
feel the ground.

"Jesika, there's no more ladder. Hand me your flashlight.

"Don't drop it!" she said.

I could see the ground, but it wasn't close.

"Jesika we're going to have to hang from the last bar, and
then jump down so we don't get hurt."

"Okay." Anxiety riddled her voice.

I clung to the bar with both hands, my body dangling.
Looking up, I could see Jesika's legs shaking. I let go and hit
the cement floor hard and right next to my flashlight that was
all busted up and scattered.

Jesika was still hanging from the bar when she said, "What's
in the dark is in the light, what's in the light is in the dark."

This was her prayer when she was really scared, and she
repeated it several times before she dropped.

It was pitch black, until we turned on her flashlight. I pointed it down the long hallway—so long that I could not see the end.

Jesika walked behind me.

"Did you hear that?" she asked.

"No. What?" I kept the flashlight pointed ahead of us.

"Do you hear that?" Jesika asked again.

This time I did hear it. It sounded like someone scurrying. We entered a large room and found a blanket on the floor, a table, and a desk. There were steak and chicken bones all over the floor and a bowl of water near a pink blanket.

"Jesika, I think there's a dog down here."

"We better get out of here. Maybe it's hungry," she said. "Marina, it smells down here. Let's go back up."

I heard the noise again, and I pointed the flashlight toward the sound. Something jumped from the table and then to the desk, and I shined my light, trying to catch a glance of it.

"Marina, let's go now!" Jesika yelled. "What is it?" Her voice was shaking. "Come on, let's go!" she yelled again.

It jumped in front of me in plain sight. It was snarling and growling and had fangs. Its hair was matted, and its feet were dirty. When I saw it, I fell backward to the ground, moving back as fast as I could on my hands and feet. My head hit Jesika's lip and busted it. She also fell backward, but she got up and took off running down the hallway. It ran past me and took off after my friend.

"Run, Jesika, run!" I screamed.

I heard Jesika hollering all the way through the narrow hallway. Then all of sudden, I heard Jesika say, "In the name of Jesus. I command you to stop!"

It stopped and a tiny voice said, "I just wanna go home. Please, can you help me get out of here?"

I picked up the flashlight I had dropped and walked toward the end of the hall near the entrance where the little girl stood. Her hair was matted, she smelled, and when she turned around and looked at me, I could see her face was dirty.

"What's your name?" Jesika asked her.

"My name is Rachael. Two men kidnapped me and put me down here."

"Come on, we'll get you out of here." Jesika said, grabbing her hand. "There's a ladder. You can climb up with our help. Here, we'll give you a boost, okay?"

We cupped our hands together and lifted her until she grabbed the ladder and started climbing up. After a few steps, she looked back and asked, "What if they're up there?"

"Don't worry. They're not," Jesika assured her. "Just keep going until you reach the top. Wait there, okay?"

"Okay."

I hurriedly got in a position to give Jesika a boost.

"But how are you going to get out of here, Marina?"

"There's a box in the room. I can use it. Don't worry about me. I'll be up in a minute. Hurry! Go make sure Rachael is okay!"

I gave Jesika a boost, and she climbed up the ladder as fast as she could. When she got to the top, Rachael was looking at the moon, and I could hear them as I pulled the box to the ladder and began my climb.

"It's so big. I feel like I could touch it. It's so pretty," she gushed. She pushed up on her tiptoes and tried to touch it.

My uncle had finally finished his phone call, thanks to Mrs. Mildred Harris, a kind neighbor who let him use the phone. He'd spoken to Selma, then Elisabeth, and then his son. He thanked Mrs. Harris and headed back across the street.

We started back up the hill holding Rachael's hand and met Uncle at the top of it. He froze when he saw us coming and stood silent, his mouth open.

We were grinning from ear to ear.

"This is Rachael. We found her in the hole …

''Rachael … Evans?" my uncle asked.

Rachael Evans was a six-year-old that had gone missing about a year earlier.

CHAPTER 56

News and Gratitude

My uncle got on his radio and called for backup, and one officer showed up right away. It was his friend, Officer Johnston. He also radioed for an ambulance and then ran back over to Mildred's house and called Channel 10 news and told them he had a scoop for them. The EMT's put Rachael in an ambulance, and she asked if we could go with her.

Then Channel 10 news showed up shortly after along with the San Diego Union. The reporter from Channel 10 interviewed my uncle, who told them that if it wasn't for his two nieces, he would have never found Rachael Evans.

"The suspects are still at large, but we have a little girl that would love to see her parents once she's been checked out."

Staring into the camera, the reporter said, "This is the section of the canyon where Mattie McDuffie's body was found, and over here is the house where Harriet McDuffie, Mattie's mother, was brutally murdered. If you'll bear with me for a few minutes, I'll show you where Marina and Jesika found Rachael Evans." The cameraman followed her to the hole in the ground, and she took the flashlight that my uncle had given her and shined it down into the hole. As she did, Officer Johnston emerged from it.

"Oh, Officer," she said, startled, "What does it look like down there?"

"This is what I see." His voice filled with somber intensity. "I think those bastards slept in the cots while Rachael Evans laid on the cold floor. They fed her chicken and steak bones."

"Oh, no, officer," she gasped. The reporter, marred by her profound sadness, frowned. "Truly, it is a miracle this little girl survived this harrowing abyss."

When the reporter returned to the street, we got out of the ambulance and walked over to her.

"They also murdered Taniya Greenwood who was left in Ocean View Park, a Black girl who was just fifteen years old," I said loudly.

The reporter ignored me and showed the composite that my uncle had drawn to the camera.

"If you see these two men, they are identical twins and they are armed and dangerous."

The San Diego Union paper interviewed us and asked how two little girls got so brave.

"Weren't you two afraid to go down in that hole?" the reporter asked.

I answered, "Of course we were afraid, but a good detective never lets fear get in the way. And, it's not just a hole in the ground, it's a fallout shelter."

"How do you know?" the reporter asked.

"Jesika has one in her backyard," I replied.

"You do?" The reporter focused her attention on Jesika.

"Yep, I sure do! We gotta go now," Jesika said. "We're going to the hospital with Rachael."

When we got back in the ambulance, I was still annoyed by the reporter.

"I'm so glad you two are going with me. Will my parents be at the hospital?" Rachael asked.

"Yes, and they can't wait to see you!" I assured her.

The ambulance took off with its siren singing loudly and my uncle riding behind us. When we got to Paradise Valley Hospital, Rachael's parents were waiting with the doctors and nurse that met her outside the emergency doors. News that it was the missing girl from a year ago spread fast. She was taken from the ambulance and put on another bed and wheeled quickly into a room of her own. Her parents followed behind the doctors. Rachael was crying for her mother, so the doctor let her parents stay in the room but told us we had to wait in the waiting room.

Eventually, the doctor asked Rachael's parents to leave so that he could examine her further, so they came out to talk with us in the waiting room.

"How can we ever thank you two?" The father spoke first as they sat down at the table across from us.

"We don't need thanks. We were just doing our job."

Mr. Evans looked puzzled.

"My uncle had a hunch, so we went to check out the twins' backyard," I answered his unspoken question.

"The twins?" Mr. Evans responded. "Who are the twins?"

"They are the serial killers that killed Mattie and Taniya, the Black girl."

"Oh, no!" Mrs. Evans grabbed her husband.

"Yeah, they kept Rachael in their fallout shelter behind their house."

"They could have killed her at any time," Mrs. Evans whispered, and Mr. Evans hugged his wife again.

"By the grace of God, she's alive," he whispered back.

The doctor brought Rachael out in a wheelchair with the IV still in her arm.

"Hello Mr. and Mrs. Evans. I'm Dr. Stuart Meyers. This is one brave and lucky little girl. She's going to be alright," he said with a big smile.

The Evans shook the doctor's hand and thanked him and the emergency team for paying special attention to Rachael.

Then Dr. Meyers and his staff even came over and praised us for finding her. He said he wanted to keep Rachael overnight to monitor her because she was malnourished and severely dehydrated due to a lack of proper foods and fluids. She also had severe muscle weakness.

"We'll be treating all her symptoms while she's here." Dr. Meyers stated. "Will she have protection, Detective Talbert?"

"Yes, doctor, around the clock," my uncle replied.

Dr. Meyers was concerned. "Good! We need her to be safe from those two evil human beings!"

"Don't you worry, doctor," Mr. Evans started. "I'm not leaving her side. If it's okay with you, I'll be sleeping in the chair right next to my baby girl. Her mother is going home later to get some rest."

CHAPTER 57

Saint Michael

Once he'd left, Rachael said, "A beautiful angel came to me and told me that I would be free soon. God sent them to find me, Daddy. I said my prayers every night. I prayed to Our Father." She turned to face me and Jesika. "And I'm sorry I scared you two. I had to act like a dog or they wouldn't feed me. When you guys came down, I thought you were them."

Rachael's mother put her hand over her mouth to muffle her cry. Then she knelt next to Rachael to comfort her.

"You know, Rachael, that angel was Saint Michael," Jesika said.

"Saint Michael is a beautiful angel, and he's got a great sense of humor," Rachael exclaimed. "He made me laugh. I kept his image in my head when I got scared. They threw me scraps and made me sit and do tricks. I'm hungry, Daddy, it's been a long time since I've eaten. I only had water to drink. Can me and my new friends go to Jack in the Box?"

"Rachael, I don't think it is a good idea for you to eat hamburgers right now. They have prepared you some broth," her father said. "The nurse will bring it in a minute."

Her mother was finding it hard to hold back her tears as she responded, "When you get better, honey. For now, Daddy will go and get Jack in the Box burgers for your new friends. Let's get you showered. I brought you the prettiest pajamas." Her mother was smiling through her tears.

"Girls, I need to speak with Rachael and her parents. Do you mind sitting at the other table in the corner?"

"Uncle, Mr. Evans went to get Jack in the Box for us."

"Okay, I have a few questions to ask you, Mrs. Evans. Can you fill me in on what happened the day Rachael went missing?"

"It should all be in the missing person report we filed with the police department. Please, can I just spend some time with my daughter without all the questions? Please, Detective."

"Okay, Mrs. Evans, this can happen at a later date. I understand." My uncle's voice was full of compassion.

"Nice detective work, girls," he whispered to us.

I was elated! It was the first time he had said "excellent job" to us.

"I can't wait to tell Marty and Grandpa and Pishoung what happened!" Jesika said. "And I can't wait to tell my mother. I don't think our parents are going to be so happy with your uncle … or us."

"Maybe they didn't watch the news," I replied.

When we saw Rachael again, we couldn't believe our eyes. Her mother had dressed her in pretty pajamas and combed her hair the best she could. It was still kind of matted in the back.

We ate our hamburgers, fries, and chocolate shakes together while Rachael delicately sipped her broth and politely declined to answer Uncle's questions about her captivity.

"I apologize, Detective Talbert, but I am unable to speak with my mouth full. It is not polite."

CHAPTER 58

Mothers and Daughters

An hour later, my uncle parked in front of my house and went with Jesika to speak with her mother first. I followed them inside. Her mother was sitting in the living room with a beer in her hand.

"Detective Talbert, I just saw my baby on channel 10. She and Marina were the breaking news… Hello, Marina."

"Hello, Mrs. Beckford. How are you this evening?" I asked, already knowing the answer.

"Not good," she replied.

I wanted to defend Jesika, but Mrs. Beckford was looking pretty scary-mad with that beer in her hand. I dared not.

"Detective, tell me why my child was in the serial killers' backyard… I'm waiting for an answer," Jesika's mother demanded.

"Mrs. Beckford, at no time were the girls put in any danger," my uncle responded nervously. "They helped me search for holes in the ground."

"Mom," Jesika tried to interrupt.

"Jesika, go to your room!" she said sharply.

"I never get to talk!" Jesika stomped off, and I followed her.

"Marina, you better go back out there with your uncle. He's no match for my mother. She's had two beers, and she's pissed. He's gonna get cussed out! If you go back out there, she might hold back her tongue. My dad says she can't drink more than two beers before she's drunk."

"Okay," I said. "I'll see you tomorrow."

"I don't think so. I'm gonna be grounded for sure."

I felt bad for Jesika as I walked back into the living room. Her mother was still sitting in the chair, working on her third beer.

"Marina, your uncle went to your house. You better get home." As I headed for the door, she suddenly stopped me. "Wait! I want to know one thing, Marina. Why did you go in that hole? Don't you know that you and Jesika could have been killed? Then where would I be, and where would your mother be?"

"Mr. O'Kelly said there was a hole in the ground in the twins' backyard, and Uncle Lonny decided to investigate, and—"

Mrs. Beckford cut me off, "Yeah, yeah, I know all about the hole in the ground."

"He said to make sure we checked along the fence on the other side," I said, lowering my voice. "We wanted to help him, and we did. Jesika had a bad feeling, and I felt something was down there. I'm sorry, Mrs. Beckford." I apologized, not really understanding why I was sorry.

"You see this doesn't make sense to me, Marina. Jesika follows you around like a little lost puppy dog. She doesn't listen to me anymore."

"Mrs. Beckford, Jesika is not lost, and she doesn't follow me. She's my partner. That little girl had been down in that hole for an entire year, getting fed steak and chicken bones with only a little bit of meat on them. The twins treated her like a dog for their amusement."

"Marina, I don't want to hear anymore."

"Rachael Evans said that an angel told her that she would be saved, and Jesika said that angel was Saint Michael. Jesika is the bravest person I know. She feels things. My grandmother says she is sensitive. That's the reason we went down there. Jesika trusted me, and I trusted her."

"Your mother is waiting, little girl," Mrs. Beckford said with a flick of her hand.

I pulled out my Saint Michael pendant and showed it to her and left.

"Jesika!" I heard her mother yell as I shut the door. "Get out here. Right now!"

I stood quietly, waiting to hear what was going to happen.

"What, Mama?" I heard Jesika say. "Do I have to get my own switch?"

"No, baby. I was just scared. Please don't go down any more holes in the ground."

"Mom, I think it was a bomb shelter, only better than ours."

"You are not off the hook yet, young lady. If your father was here, he would give you a good spanking."

"Okay, Mama, I won't."

"Your friend, Marina, is too grown and too smart for her own good. Do you want to be a detective when you grow up?" her mother asked.

"No, Mama," Jesika replied.

"I'm just so glad you're okay," her mother said as she held Jesika close.

I walked across the street and into my house and found my mother talking to my uncle. She didn't look mad, but I could tell she wasn't happy either as she insisted that he didn't involve me and Jesika in anything anymore.

"Sis, I know you think I'm being negligent. The girls were okay, trust me."

"What you can do for me, Lonny, is catch those two murdering bastards, so they can't harm anyone else. Goodnight, Lonny."

My mother doesn't cuss, so we both knew then she was angry.

Uncle Lonny left without saying anything to me, but he'd already said enough. He'd taught us a valuable lesson that night—what you needed to be a good detective—on the way home. He'd said that we had heart and called us heroes and finished with, "There are two kinds of people: those that stand still and do nothing, and those who won't let fear stop them."

I got dressed for bed and thought about calling Jesika, but I was afraid her mother would answer the phone.

I hope her mother didn't put her on restriction.

I got on my knees and prayed to Our Father and then went to bed thinking about trust.

The word trust was often said out loud, but no one seemed to have any. Jesika's mother didn't trust me, and my mother didn't trust my uncle. Jesika had the ultimate trust in God and in angels. We were learning to trust our own judgment.

CHAPTER 59

Heroes and Attention

I got up the next day, hoping it would be a normal day. *It sure would be nice to just play.*

But it seemed like every kid on the block came over to ask us questions about Rachael Evans. Bonnie and Sherrie came over to my house and rang my doorbell three times. My brothers had gone to a party the night before, and Billy answered the door half asleep, and he wasn't happy.

"What do you want?" he growled and then hollered, "Marina! It's for you!"

Bonnie and Sherry's mother had baked me and Jesika cupcakes that said "Hero" on them, and they couldn't wait to give them to us.

Jesika told me that her doorbell rang at 8 a.m. It was Irene, Douglas, Carlton, Carl, Vicky, Thomas, Jerod, and Juney. She said that they had so many questions she couldn't wait to come over and get away from them.

With so many kids hanging around, I tried to get them to play a game of kickball, but no one wanted to play. Marty even came over to ask if we would sign autographs for his friends on his block. He had brought a polaroid camera and took several pictures of us. Even though it didn't really feel right to us, we signed them for Marty.

A reporter phoned. Dad took her number and information and said he would call back. He then hollered for Jesika and me to come into the house.

"Marina and Jesika, come home, please!" My dad's voice drifted from the direction of our house, and we headed back.

When we arrived, he told us that a reporter from a Black newspaper called *The Viewpoint* phoned and asked if she could interview us.

"I'm gonna call your mother at the hospital to see if it would be okay for you to do an interview with *The Viewpoint*. What do you think about that? I'm proud of you two brave girls. The world needs heroes like you two."

"Dad, I don't feel like a hero," I sighed.

"But you are."

"I don't feel like a hero either, Mr. Massey. I don't like all this attention," Jesika said.

Marty walked in the house with our pictures and showed them to my dad.

"These are some nice pictures, Marty. What are you gonna do with them?"

"I'm gonna give a few of them to some friends in my neighborhood, and then keep the rest. Mr. Massey, did you look at the *San Diego Union*? The girls are on the cover."

"No, I haven't," he said. "I'll get the paper out of the yard."

Sure enough. Our pictures were on the cover with Rachael. Rachael didn't look like herself. She was filthy from head to toe.

"Oh, no!" Jesika said. "Our lives will never be the same."

"I forgot what I was doing," my father said. "Let me call your mother."

He dialed the hospital and happened to catch my mom on her morning break. She agreed to let us do the interview as long as she was with us.

My father called the reporter back and set the interview up for 6:30 p.m.

That afternoon, I thought about what Rachael had told us on the way to the hospital. She said that at one point, she had gotten really sick in the shelter, so they had brought in a mattress for her to sleep on. They fed her chicken noodle soup until she got better. But after she got better, they took away the mattress, and she had to be on the cold cement floor again. They told her she could keep the pink blanket, because they didn't want their little doggy to die.

I felt sick to my stomach.

As I thought about the reporter, I realized I didn't want to talk about the house of horrors. Sometimes all the current events would resonate in my mind to the point of fear. I was good at not showing it. I'd just take a deep breath and say the Hail Mary till my fear dissipated. This was another one of those times.

I thought about the update Uncle Lonny had given me. He'd left Officer Johnston at the house of horrors investigating the fallout shelter. He had found a small door behind the desk in the room where they kept Rachael Evans, and he'd opened the door and crawled through a secret tunnel. At the end, there was a door that opened underneath Nigel Glasgow's bed. He couldn't open the door all the way because the bed was blocking it. They had dug a tunnel big enough for them to fit in and cemented it to make it easy to crawl through.

Uncle Lonny told us that he'd mentioned a desire to call in a profiler to get some psychological insight into these two killers, but he wasn't sure the chief would support it. He even admitted that he believed the chief wanted him to fail, but Officer Johnston had assured him that he had officers that wanted to help with the case. They had heard about the Evans girl over the radio. He suggested they have these officers canvas the neighborhood to get some background on the twins. Who their parents were, what schools they went to, their friends, and whether they killed small animals. All the typical stuff.

CHAPTER 60

Our New Friend

We got the surprise of a lifetime when Rachael and her parents came to visit. They had been downtown and decided to come by and meet our parents, and we watched and listened from my bedroom window as they began chatting with my father.

When my mother pulled into the driveway, she got out of her car and immediately greeted Rachael. "Well, hello there!" she said, bending down to her level. "You must be Rachael Evans!"

"Yes, are you Marina's mother?"

"Yes, I am. Jesika's mother isn't home yet," Mom said, glancing quickly across the street.

Rachael smiled and said, "Your daughter and your niece saved me."

My mother couldn't hold back her tears. She picked up the little Evans girl and hugged her so tight. My friends that were still hanging out in the yard started clapping and cheering.

"Can you put me down?" Rachael asked. "I came over to play with Marina and Jesika."

"Oh sure, baby. Marina, Jesika!" my mother hollered. "Please come in, Mr. and Mrs. Evans."

They followed my mother into the house.

"Your home is lovely ... I want to tell you, Mrs. Massey, those two girls are something special. We just wanted to meet the parents of such brave girls."

"Well, I think children have pure spirits and believe, and sometimes as adults we get amnesia when it comes to believing. They remind us that we need to have faith in something bigger than ourselves… I'm sorry if I'm not making much sense."

Jesika and I came running into the living room. "Hey, Rachael!"

"I heard you have a tree house. Can I see it?" Rachael asked.

All the kids in the neighborhood followed us into the backyard.

"All y'all can't fit in the treehouse," Jesika said.

Marty walked up to Rachael and asked if he could take a picture of the three of us.

Jesika said, "Only if it's alright with Rachael."

"It's okay. Can I have it?" she asked.

"Yes, you can," he said.

Rachael climbed up first, and we climbed up after her, and then we just played Barbies until it was time for our interview with *The Viewpoint* reporter.

Jesika's mother came over and met Mr. and Mrs. Evans, and she cried too.

"I know you're grieving, even though you found Rachael," she said.

"We never gave up hope," Mr. Evans responded.

"The Good Lord must have been watching over all y'all. I have some thoughts I'd like to share, if that's okay with you."

"Please, we need all the help we can get right now," Mrs. Evans nodded.

My mother escorted the adults out to the patio and served them some lemonade.

Jesika's mother took Mrs. Evans' hands and began speaking, "You're bound to question fate and God, wondering why this happened to your family, your child …"

"Yes. We've had many sleepless nights trying to figure it out. I've spent months mapping out every possible sequence, trying to determine how it might have happened. It was just so fast. One minute she was there, and the next minute she wasn't. There was no comfort. I couldn't even pray," she said. "My husband had to pray enough for the both of us. I just had to put it in the heart and hands of Jesus."

My father was standing at the sliding glass door and offered Mr. Evans a beer.

Mrs. Evans burst into tears and said, "Can you give me something stronger?"

My mother fixed her a whiskey sour. She took a good strong sip, commented that it was good, and then continued.

"Can you imagine how hard it is to not think about her being down in that hole?"

"No, I can't … What's your first name?" Rita asked.

"It's Barbara."

"Barbara, the challenge that you and your husband face is that … there is no answer. Focus on your baby. She is going to need your undivided attention and love to get through this. Peace won't come overnight. But believe me, it will come. She's young, and her memories of this year will fade away."

"I'm sure you're right, Rita," she said, taking another big sip of her whiskey sour.

She looked around and noticed all the kids in the yard. Sariah and Jayden had come over and climbed up.

"Hi Rachael," Sariah said. "We saw you on television with Marina and Jesika. What happened to your hair?"

"My mommy cut it," Rachael said.

"Your haircut is cute," Jayden said, giving her a quick hug. "I brought my Barbies too. Can I play with you? Barbie looks nice in a black cocktail dress and long gloves. I love my Barbie's bouffant hairdo, and her eyes have such long lashes. I dress her just like my mommy. My mommy's beautiful."

Rachael smiled back at Jayden and said, "You should play with Ken."

Sariah looked down from the treehouse and asked, "Why are all those kids just standing around?"

"I don't know," Jesika said. "I wish they would go home."

Marty spoke up, "I think they just wanna play with Rachael too. We need to find something that we can all do together. How about a game of kickball?"

"Nah. We play that all the time. Let's play dragon tail derby," Jesika suggested.

"What's that?" Marty asked.

"You get your bike, and the other kids hang onto it to form the tail. Everyone, you'll need skates or a skateboard. We'll show you."

"That sounds dangerous!" Marty exclaimed.

"Marty, if you fall, you can hurt yourself really bad," I said. "That's what makes it so much fun. Do you want to play, Rachael?"

"Yes, but Marty and I don't have skates."

"I'm sure one of those kids down there has a pair of skates that can fit you."

Sariah said that she had a pair of old skates that would fit Rachael.

"I'll go get my bike," Jesika said, taking charge. "Marina, you get yours."

Marty yelled down, "We're gonna play dragon tail!"

We climbed down and all the kids ran home to get their skates. Jesika picked all the kids that were going to hang onto her bike, and I picked all the kids that were going to hang onto mine. Jesika had Irene, Douglas, Carlton, Tommy, Lacie, Sacha and Mary. I had Gerald, Mark, Vicky, Deidra Bladelock, Dianne the militant, and Rachael at the end. I put Rachael at the end because if one person fell, she could just let go.

I took a few moments to explain the rules to our newcomers.

"Okay, we pedal as fast as we can to the end of the street. The first team that arrives without anyone falling is the winner. If anyone falls, you lose. We start at the very top of the hill, so we can go really, really fast." I paused, looking at Rachael and then spoke to my team. "Okay, everybody, try not to fall because we have Rachael onboard. Rachael, if anyone on our team falls, just let go so you don't get hurt."

Jesika yelled out, "We got this! Eat our dust, Marina!"

I yelled back, "On your mark, get set, go!"

I wasn't about to let Jesika beat me. I had Rachael on my team. I was faster than a locomotive, faster than a speeding bullet. I could leap a mountain in a single bound.

We were halfway down the street when someone yelled, "Slow down, Marina. Rachael is losing her grip! Slow down, Marina. Rachael is falling!" I pressed gently on my brakes and Diana the Militant grabbed Rachael's hand before she fell. It was close, but we won!

"Wow, that was so much fun. Let's do it again!" Rachael cried out, jumping up and down. This time, Jesika wanted Rachael on her dragon tail.

Diana took Rachael's hand to help her back up to the stop of the hill. Turning to the older girl, Rachael said, "Thank you for helping me stay on the dragon tail."

"You're welcome."

"Why do they call you Diana the Militant?"

"Because my father is a member of the Black Power Party that protects our people against police brutality. We hold meetings at our house every Wednesday. A few people from this neighborhood come to our meetings, but most are from Los Angeles and the Bay area. When I hand out flyers in the neighborhood, I wear my beret and a black leather coat. That's how I got the name. We fight for equal rights for Black people. Freedom to walk down the street without harassment," Diana said as she put her fist in the air.

"I had my freedom taken from me for a whole year," Rachael exclaimed, trying to impress her new friend.

"I saw the news, and I wanted to meet you. I'm sorry that happened to you."

"Marina! Jesika! Time to come in!"

Ugh.

The reporter for *The Viewpoint* had arrived.

Jesika told my dad that she didn't really want to talk about it anymore, and I felt the same.

"Just answer a few questions, girls," he said, opening the front door and ushering us in.

We wanted Rachael to have fun on our block and felt like this interview was interrupting our fun.

CHAPTER 61

An Interview Turns Religious

Fortunately, the reporter was nice. Cecile asked about Taniya, Mattie, and Harriet, and about us being Black Catholic. These were the perfect questions to take our minds back to the murders, our passion to solve the case, and now our desire to find the killers.

We told her we were coming home from church when we found Mattie's body and thought that she wanted us to find her killer.

"So, does that mean that you believe the spirit of a person can speak to you?"

"Jesika likes to pontificate on this kind of thing," I said, "Religion is her favorite subject."

I got up to go outside and leave Jesika to finish the interview. My dad gave me that look, so I sat back down.

"Yes!" Jesika said. "Spirits can communicate with you in your dreams. They also can show themselves to you, but I told God that I didn't want to see anybody. I ain't seen anybody either, but I feel their presence."

Then Jesika said that Taniya was in heaven with Mattie, and she wasn't feeling any more pain on the other side. She shared that we were truly sorry about Taniya Greenwood, and that we felt like it was our fault at first.

"Why did you feel it was your fault?" Cecile asked.

"We figured the Glasgow brothers knew we were on their tail, so they hung her as a warning for me and Marina to stop trying to solve the case or else the same thing would happen to us. But I feel different now, because I feel Taniya Greenwood's presence around me all the time."

"Jesika, how do you feel about being a Black Catholic?" Cecile asked.

"I've been a Catholic all my life. I don't know anything else."

Cecile laughed.

"And, well, I feel like Black people are the chosen ones, just like the Jews. Black people suffer persecution just because of the color of our skin. In Catholic school, we are taught to love one another, as Jesus Christ would, all while being called names like darky, blacky, and nigger on the playground. Being called a nigger makes you sad, and then it makes you angry."

Cecile empathized, "Yeah. I know the feeling …"

Realizing the focus was all on her, Jesika said, "Marina and I know different things. She's the one with the mind of a detective."

"Yes, I've heard that you are a great detective for your age. How old are you, Marina?"

"I'll be thirteen on December first."

"Jesika, how old are you?"

"I'll be thirteen in October."

We ended the interview by saying that we were happy to celebrate the life of Rachael Evans. Marty gave her a picture of the three of us for her paper, and Jesika said that we wouldn't stop looking until we found the Glasgow brothers.

Cecile then began interviewing my Uncle Lonny who willingly gave her all the latest details on the investigation.

Back outside, Jesika and I joined the other kids and played until we were called in for dinner.

My dad had made steaks and chicken on the grill. Mrs. Evans joined my mother and Rita in the kitchen. Together, they made shrimp fried rice and potato salad.

As we all said goodnight to the Evans family, Rachael said, "Mom, I love the kids on Bollenbacher Street!" and then asked if she could come over and play again. Mrs. Evans assured her that we would all be getting together real soon.

I slept that night with a smile on my face.

CHAPTER 62

Summer's End

*I*t was my turn to tell the class a little bit about myself. I had come prepared with pictures I had drawn of my house, my grandmother's house, my tree, and my best friend, Jesika. I told them about Chicago, that my mother was a doctor and my father a high school teacher. I told them I was going to be a detective when I grew up. I even showed them my Nancy Drew kit.

One student interrupted me and asked if I was the girl on the television and in the paper. I said I was. I hadn't planned on talking about it, but it seemed as if I couldn't get away from it no matter how hard I tried. Everyone on the playground wanted to be my friend. My teacher even talked about how brave we were and compared me to a saint.

I thought to myself, *I'm no saint.* I felt like Jesika did: I wasn't bad, but I wasn't good either.

Moonalisa had become a tradition at Jesika's house on Saturdays. Her mother made the popcorn and put it in brown bags for us. We had seen a host of movies like *The Tingler, The Blob, The Thing, The Incredible Shrinking Man, Fifty Foot Woman, Frankenstein, Frankenstein Meets the Wolf Man, The Mummy, Dracula, Invasion of the Body Snatchers, The Fly, The Creature from the Black Lagoon,* and *The House of Wax. The Tingler* had the actor Vincent Price in it, and everyone knew who he was.

Jesika and I had given out personalized, scary invitations to this Saturday afternoon's event, because there were too many kids the last time. Mrs. Beckford didn't want the whole block in her den again. Our friends showed up an hour early so we could discuss what character was the scariest. Sariah sat on the floor with the boys, and Jayden sat on the couch with me and Jesika and the rest of the girls.

Jesika started, "I think Dracula is the scariest, because he gave me nightmares. I always end up running in slow motion." She got off the couch to show us. Her movements were perfectly in sync raising her eyes and pushing her head slowly back. Her legs and arms moving with less than normal speed was just plain creepy. We all laughed so hard.

Irene took over the conversation.

"You're just a big old scaredy-cat!" she said. "Frankenstein is funny, clumsy, and a big buffoon, and you could outrun him."

"Yeah!" Douglas chimed in. "The Mummy was wrapped in enough toilet paper to wipe everybody's butt and mine." Everyone laughed. "And … Dracula, maybe you should be a little scared of him because he can hypnotize you and turn you into a bat."

"The worst part about Dracula is that he can drain all your blood out of you," Irene added.

Putting my two cents in, I said, "All you need for Dracula is garlic, a cross, and a stake."

"Okay, it's time for the show to start," someone said.

Jesika's mom passed out the popcorn and candy. She even closed the drapes and covered them with an extra sheet so that the room would be dark. The feature for this Saturday would be… *Them.*

Jesika's brother whispered mysteriously, "When they found the little girl in the middle of the desert, *Them…* had ate her parents."

Everyone said "Shhh!" at the same time because no one knew who Them was yet. What I loved most about the *Moonalisa Movie Matinee* was being with all my friends and the hilarious discussions before and afterward.

CHAPTER 63

Unanswered Questions about Thelma

Jesika was trying to get a handle on her grades, and I tried to help her. Her father was home, and she couldn't play much. In fact, she got put on restriction a lot. Whenever I came over and she was cleaning up without being told, I knew something was up. With every report card, she got at least two Fs, normally in math and geography. She'd call me on the phone, and she would say, "I can't give my report card to my mom or my dad. Maybe I can stall for two weeks."

I called her up after finishing my own homework on a Wednesday. She was in her room looking at a *Reader Magazine*. It was the only time I'd heard of her reading for leisure.

I wanted to ask her a question that had been gnawing at me since we went to visit my grandmother: What happened after she passed out? She obviously didn't want to talk about it because she usually told me everything.

My curiosity got the best of me and I finally just blurted out, "Jesika, what happened to you in my grandmother's room?"

"I guess Thelma's spirit entered my body. It was like watching a movie, only I wasn't myself. I could hear and feel everything that was going on."

"Did you know that you were kicking and you had your own hands around your neck?" I asked.

"Yes, but I can't explain it … It wasn't me. Let's not talk about it anymore, Marina. I'll dream about it again."

I asked her why she never said anything, and she said Saint Michael had told her not to fear her gift.

"Do you recall what happened after she grabbed her stomach?"

"Argh! You're determined to make me talk about it, aren't you? Okay, this is what I recall." Jesika tilted her head back and closed her eyes. "No one outside of their small house heard Thelma screaming. No one was going to come to her rescue. Edward grabbed Thelma's face and told her he wasn't going to let her go. Thelma jerked her head from his hands and told him she didn't want to be with him and begged him not to harm the baby. He said they wouldn't but then his wife entered the room and Thelma knew what was going to happen and screamed.

"Thelma woke up as they were cutting her baby from her stomach. Her screams … I heard them for several days after. I couldn't get the sound out of my head. Edward and Ham had planned this all along. Caroline was barren and couldn't have children, so Edward and Caroline claimed Thelma's baby as their own. The two little girls Thelma thought were theirs were actually Caroline's sisters."

"Does my grandmother know this? " I asked.

"Yes," Jesika replied. "You know your grandmother has the gift as well. She has always known the reason for her sister's demise. She just never told her parents the truth about Thelma's death. It was too painful. Her mother and father received a letter informing them that their daughter had died due to a miscarriage. The twins told the sheriff the same thing. The sheriff never questioned it because she was Black. They simply buried Thelma and then mailed the letter to her parents. Your grandmother's father would die grieving over his daughter's death. Marina, it's all too terrible for your grandmother to talk about. The agony on Thelma's face, the torture in her eyes, and all the blood. It's not something you want to tell someone, you know. Your grandmother may not have mentioned this horrible tragedy. I have had dreams about monsters, Dracula, the Mummy, and Frankenstein, but nothing could prepare me for what Ham let his twin brother do to Thelma."

''Okay, Jesika, I understand.'' However, it made me wonder if Thelma's spirit was at peace. I thought I might ask my mother if she knew about her Aunt Thelma.

"Why don't you …" she paused, " … ask your mother about your grandmother's sister?"

"I don't know how to ask her. She's never even mentioned that Grandmother had a sister."

"Like I said, maybe she knows something about it." After one of those long faraway looks, Jesika grunted and growled. "Your grandmother said that what I have is a gift. If this is a gift, then you can have it."

Then she abruptly changed the subject.

"Remember when we were in the Glasgow twins' backyard? I was standing over by the window searching my area. When I looked up, I saw a shadow man in the window. I froze from fright, just staring. Its stare was piercing."

"Who was it? One of the Glasgow twins?" I inquired.

"It wasn't the Glasgow twin. It was Edward."

"How do you know?" I gasped.

"I just know," she said in a sharp tone. "My body began to shake. A hand touched my shoulder, and I felt an immediate sense of peace. Then I heard an eerie swoosh and the shadow in the window faded away."

We both sat quietly for a while. In that quietness, I thought, *Jesika's gift is not anything I want.* Somehow, her vision was haunting her, and this was unsettling to me. She had said that Thelma's spirit was not at peace because she wanted to know what happened to her baby.

"Oh, I forgot to tell you," Jesika said, breaking our silence with her motor mouth. "A girl named Cynthia hit me in the face with a dodgeball."

"Ow! I bet that hurt."

"It sure did, it hurt like hell! It was an accident, but it made me so angry that I ran up to her, drew my hand back, and slapped her to the ground."

"Oh, man! Why did you do that? I know you got yourself in trouble!"

"Yup, Sister Cortiles was the playground monitor. She dragged me across the playground by my ear. I had to sit on the bench underneath the stairs going up to the second floor until recess was over. Saint Michael cheered me up."

"How'd he do that?"

"He pretended to kick her in her butt. Just imagine him moving like they do in Laurel and Hardy movies."

She told me that she laughed so hard, it got the attention of all the kids on the playground, and that's when they started calling her names.

"You know you're the only one that can see him, right?" I asked.

At that moment, I knew it was Saint Michael, her protector, that had touched her shoulder in Glasgow's backyard.

"I know," she said, as if it was no big deal, "and a bird was stuck in the hands of the Saint Rita statue. The bird was flapping its wings back and forth trying to get out of her grip.

Blood began to run down the statue's hands. I thought all Saint Rita had to do was open her hand and the bird's foot would be free. Did it happen? Nope. Instead, Sister Catherine got a long pole and tried to dislodge it, and that poor thing lost its left foot in the process. Did you know Saint Rita is the patron saint of abuse victims and bad marriages? Her body has never turned to dust. She looks just like she did when she was alive."

I realized my friend had a fascination with death.

CHAPTER 64

A Disturbing Face in the Crowd

Jesika's father got orders to ship out and would be leaving in a month. Nobody knew where he was going because it was top secret. He told their mother that he would be back before Christmas. Jesika called me on the phone and said this was good news for her. She liked it when he was away for a long time.

"Now it's going to be just me, my mom, and sister and brother. He won't be here to look at my next report card."

"Why don't you just try to get better grades?" I wondered.

"I do try," she insisted. I think she probably did. She got an A in religion, a B in English, a B in reading, an A in writing, a D in geography, a B in music, and an A in art. History was her favorite subject, and she got a C. Overall, I didn't think her report card was that bad. She just couldn't seem to do well in arithmetic. She always got an F. I had witnessed her just putting any answer down on her math homework assignments. When I asked her why, she told me that in second grade, her father had backhanded her across the face because of a subtraction problem. She said that she and arithmetic were never right after that.

By November, I had been chosen by my teacher to be a part of our school spelling bee. Each teacher picked two students out of their class to participate. We didn't compete nationally. It was just something our school did every year to promote healthy competition among the students at Saint Joseph. You had to be in the fourth grade to participate.

You would have thought I had won a million dollars. I couldn't wait to get home from school to tell my mother and father and, of course, Jesika. The competition would be held on a Saturday in the auditorium, and parents and friends could be invited.

I invited my parents, my brothers, and Jesika's family to attend. Boy, was I nervous, but it's always nice to have people cheer you on. I had a week to prepare. Jesika coached me after school, and my father coached me at night.

Our spelling bee rules were simple. If you got the word wrong, then you didn't get a chance to spell another word. There were eight kids on both sides, for a total of sixteen kids. They left empty seats at the front, so that you could sit down with the audience if you spelled the word wrong.

That would be so embarrassing.

It was Saturday and the spelling bee started at 2:30 p.m. If you were late, you were automatically disqualified. My father drove me and my brothers, along with Jesika and Pishoung. My mother rode with Rita, Sariah, and Jayden.

All the contestants were on the stage, and we faced each other, lined up in a row. The microphone was between us on the podium.

When Sister Agnes called our name, we had to walk up to the podium and speak into the microphone facing the audience. Rows two through five were designated for families.

My friend, Nancy, was the first to go to the podium. She spelled the word *gladiolus*. The other team member, a sixth grader, spelled *sacrilegious*. Next, it was my turn, and I had to spell *albumen*.

I got it right, and my brothers embarrassed me by hollering. To make matters worse, they had their uniforms on.

Eventually, it was down to just me and Sarah.

I had to spell *sanitarium,* and I breathed a sigh of relief when I got it right. That's when I noticed Jesika repeatedly turning her head to look toward the back of the auditorium. Before I knew it, they were calling my name again. I spelled *meticulosity*. Sarah spelled *reticulitis*. I spelled *luxuriant*. We went back and forth for what felt like an hour. Finally, Sarah had to spell the word *indict* and spelled it i-n-d-i-t-e. It was now up to me to spell it correctly. I did and won!

We shook hands to show good sportsmanship. I got a huge trophy, and my picture was taken with Sister Mary Catherine, my family, and friends.

CHAPTER 65

Celebrations and Confirmations

On the way home, Jesika called me a gladiator. She called the last few minutes of the spelling bee a spelling battle and said she had her fingers crossed the entire time.

When we got home, Jesika's mother invited us over for dinner to celebrate my win. She cooked hamburgers and hot dogs on the grill, and we ate outside. She complimented me on my spelling skills and thanked me for helping Jesika with her arithmetic from time to time.

My mother said, "Gluttony is so hard to master. I really want one of those juicy, cheese hamburgers, Rita," while she ate the big salad Rita had prepared for them.

"So, do what everyone else does, Eva, and put your dressing on the side of your salad. Then when I serve it to you, pour the dressing all over your salad, and then …" she said, laughing, "your salad will be just as fattening as that juicy hamburger."

My father reminded them he was not on any diet, "So put plenty of french fries on my plate, along with two juicy cheeseburgers!"

After we ate, Jesika and I went down to the fallout shelter and talked about what happened during the spelling bee.

We both started talking at the same time.

"You go first," I said.

"I don't know, but I got this uneasy feeling when I was in the auditorium. And then it hit me! It was the same feeling I got before we went into the hole where we found Rachael. I kept looking back, but I couldn't see who it was. There were too many people blocking my view. It felt like an icy chill all of a sudden. I tried to shake it off. Your father asked me if I was cold, I said 'Yes,' and he gave me his jacket. The chill finally did leave, but I think it was because the person left."

"Yeah, I saw this man standing in the back, waving. At first I thought he was waving at Nancy, but he seemed to be looking dead in my eyes. I almost started to wave back, and then stopped myself," I said.

"Do you think it could have been one of the twins?" she asked.

"Yes, I think so. He had red hair, he was young, and he was smiling at me. When I took my attention off him to spell a word, he disappeared."

"I felt him, and you saw him." Jesika put her head in her hands. "This isn't good, Marina. I think we need to call your uncle right away."

"I don't know, Jesika," I protested.

"What do you mean, you don't know?"

"I just wanna be a normal kid." I sighed.

"I wanna be normal too!"

And we both laughed, remembering how much we had hated those words during the summer.

"Are you afraid of what they might do to us, Marina?"

"Yes, Jesika, I am," I admitted.

"I don't think we have any choice but to tell your uncle. But I really don't want my mama to know."

"I agree. It certainly wouldn't help the situation to tell our parents. They'd just confine us to the house."

CHAPTER 66

Asking for Help

When Jesika and I went to school on Monday, I told my father that I had to stay after school, and afterward, I would take a taxi over to the police station. He gave me money for a taxi and said to have my uncle bring me home. There was nothing unusual about this because my father would often stay after school to help students who needed tutoring. Sister Agnes would call me a yellow cab, make sure I got in the car, and then I'd tell the cab driver the street address.

"Is everything okay, Marina?" He must have picked up on something.

With a quick smile and a hug, I let him know that everything was fine.

When I arrived at the police station, my uncle wasn't there. He was following up on a lead. Someone in Encanto had thought they saw one of the twins. It turned out that the man he saw had a twin brother, but they were Mexican and short with deep brown hair and a lot of tattoos. When my uncle came back, I was sitting in his office doing my homework.

"What brings you here … a ride home?"

"Yes, I do need a ride home, but I have something urgent to tell you."

My uncle sat down in his chair and motioned for me to continue.

"I was in the school's spelling bee contest."

"I'm sorry I couldn't be there. Did you win?" he asked.

"Yes, I did! I even got a trophy."

269

"Congratulations, baby girl," he said. "Now what is it that you want to tell me?"

"I think one of Glasgow's brothers showed up at my spelling bee. I was spelling a word when I saw a man in the back of the auditorium waving at me. At first, I thought that he was waving at Nancy, but he kept looking directly at me. I started to wave back, but then I realized I didn't know him. Then I see Jesika turning her head to look to the back of the auditorium. She did it several times. Later, when I spoke to her about it, she said that she felt a cold chill come over her twice during the spelling bee. My dad gave her his jacket to keep her warm. Uncle, I saw him, and Jesika felt his presence."

"Can you describe what he looks like?" Uncle Lonny leaned forward and picked up his pen.

"Yes, he had red hair with red eyebrows and a red beard. He had on a white shirt with a black tie and black pants. He looked as if he could be the parent of a kid at my school."

My uncle opened his file cabinet and pulled out the composite.

"Does he look like this?"

"Yes, but he needs a beard." I pulled out a red pencil out of my book bag, and drew a red beard on him, and colored his eyebrows red.

"Marina, you might be here for a while, so make yourself comfortable."

He called Johnston on the phone and told Johnston that he may have a lead.

"Let's put an APB out on Nigel Glasgow fitting this description."

"Done," Office Johnston said.

"Man, he had the nerve to show up at my niece's spelling bee. Marina, where's Jesika right now?"

"She's probably walking home from school."

"Damn, I told her mother that she needed to get a ride home every day until this is solved."

"Pishoung picks her up when he can. She doesn't always take the shortcut through the canyon. Sometimes she walks the long way home." Fear bubbled up in me. "Uncle, can we leave right now? I'm really worried."

"Me too. Johnston, I want to be sure she makes it home safely."

We left to see if we could find Jesika.

Uncle took Market Street so that he could hit Euclid, hoping we might see her walking if we drove her route home.

I was frantic inside, but I didn't let on.

"There she is, Uncle. Stop!"

He pulled over to the curb, and we watched her cross Market Street at the light. Seeing my uncle's car, she made her way to us and stuck her head in the window.

"What are you guys doing here?"

"Get in," I said. "I told Uncle what happened at my spelling bee. We were worried about you walking home alone, so we came looking for you. Uncle put an APB out on Nigel Glasgow."

"You did!" she said excitedly as she jumped in the back seat and sat back with her arms folded. "You're too late for that. They've changed the way they look by now. If they had red hair, they'd have green hair now."

"Don't be silly," I said.

"Well, they don't have red hair anymore. There's nothing we can do about it …"

My uncle looked back at her and said, "Tell your mother that I don't want you walking home alone anymore. You and your sister need to be picked up every day after school. By the way, where is Sariah?" he asked.

"She's at home sick with Pishoung. She's got a cold."

"Is your father home?"

"Yes, but he is on base right now. You can talk to Pishoung if you need to. He's probably sleeping, but he won't mind."

My uncle followed Jesika and me into the house, and Jesika knocked on Pishoung's door.

"What is it?" Pishoung asked sleepily.

"Detective Talbert would like to speak to you about something," Jesika hollered through the door.

"Okay, I'll be there in one moment."

After a bit, he joined us in the living room.

"Hello, Detective Talbert. What's going on?"

"Jesika and Sariah need to be picked up from school every day. One of the Glasgow brothers was at Marina's spelling bee."

"Okay, don't you worry about them. I'll set my alarm clock and be there as soon as they get out of school. Thank you, Uncle Detective," Pishoung said nervously.

"Thank you, Pishoung."

"Jesika, you make sure and you and your sister wait for me after school," Pishoung said to her again.

CHAPTER 67

Mr. Beckford's Temper

*I*t wasn't more than a few days later when I knocked on Jesika's door, but no one answered. I was wondering if I should go around to the side of the house, or just go home, when I heard Jayden yelling, "I sorry, I won't wet the bed anymore!"

I heard screaming next, and it sounded like Jayden, so I ran around to the side and into the backyard.

Jesika and Sariah were standing at the sliding glass door yelling, "Stop! Daddy! Stop! Please stop!"

Irene and her sister and brother were laughing as they watched from their fence. I didn't see anything funny. Mr. Beckford had stripped Jayden's clothes from his body and was spraying him with the hose. Then he started beating him while he was wet.

I ran up to him, yelling at the top of my lungs, "STOP BEATING HIM! HE'S JUST A LITTLE BOY, MR. BECKFORD! PLEASE STOP!!!!!!!"

Jesika and Sariah tried to grab the belt, but it hit Jesika across the face. She dropped to her knees and grabbed her face, still crying, "Please stop, Daddy! He won't wet the bed anymore, we promise."

Mr. Beckford had bit down on his own lip so hard, it was bleeding. He looked at me and said, "Marina, go home …"

"He's only four, Mr. Beckford! How could you do that to him?" I looked at Jesika and ran out of their backyard. I could still hear Irene and her siblings laughing.

Mrs. Beckford had just gotten out of her car, and I bumped into her so hard, I almost knocked her over.

"What is it, Marina?" she asked.

"What is it?" I was crying so hard, I couldn't catch my breath, and I couldn't talk. Finally, "Let me go!" erupted out of me and she let me go.

When I got to my house, I ran into my room and slammed the door.

I stayed in my room because I didn't know what to do. At some point, my mother slipped quietly into my room, sat against my pillow, and held me in her arms. She said that she was sorry for what I had witnessed.

"There are just some things that I can't shelter you from, Marina, when it comes to someone else's family."

"He should be locked up," I said. "Jayden is just a little boy, Mommy."

"Yes, and you're just a little girl, and you have seen things that most children don't ever see. You have experienced more than you should in a year's time. Rita will do something about her husband. The girls told me what made him stop beating Jayden."

"What's that, Mom?"

"You yelled, 'Who beat you like that?' Baby, his parents beat him like that, and his grandparents beat his parents like that, and his great-grandparents beat his grandparents like that … all the way back to the days of slavery."

She paused, and the weight of her words rested on both of us.

Then my mother said, "I believe all your ancestors were behind you when you yelled. They were screaming through you." I had never heard my mother talk like that before. She reminded me of my grandmother.

"Even Jesika's ancestors," I said.

"Yes, all the ancestors." She was still talking as I drifted off to sleep in her arms.

I could barely hear her when my grandmother's voice entered my ears.

"It will be a long time before the perils of time are erased from our memory. Our scars are deep and the circumstances tragic. One by one, group by group, we will rise from our own brokenness."

When I went to visit the next day, Jesika told me what happened after I left. Her mother had walked in the house and saw Jayden stripped of his clothes, Sariah crying and trying to dry him off, and Jesika hugging his head while he cried. Then she ran into the backyard and started beating Mr. Beckford with her hands. He pushed her down on the grass, and then he left.

She put Jayden, who had been beaten down to the white flesh, in the tub.

"We watched my mother bathe him, telling him how sorry she was, and that Daddy would never hurt him like that again. She held him in the chair in the living room all night."

I asked Jesika why he beat him like that, and she told me it was because he hated Jayden. She went and got a picture of Jayden sitting next to him at a picnic.

"Look at the expression on my father's face," she said. Only Jesika would have picked up on the expression. "It says, 'You can't be my son.'" She paused and stared past me, then added, "He was trying to beat the sissy out of him that morning." She said it wasn't the first time he had beaten him like that.

CHAPTER 68

The Twins' Profile

The following weekend would change our lives for the better. We had no idea what would transpire. My uncle was still chasing the Glasgow brothers, who were like ghosts. I had spent two days during the week over at my uncle's house, so Elisabeth and I got a chance to talk and make up. She told me her father had surprisingly shared some information with her. I could tell that made her happy. She came across his file on the twins and read their psychological profile in detail, and she'd made some notes so she could read them to me.

Both twins went to Saint Rita's until their parents took them out in the third grade to homeschool them. Sister Cotildist said the boys may have been possessed. She said, "They never talked to other kids, and they had their own language that made my skin crawl. The other kids in the classroom were afraid of them."

Father Giles said he felt they needed a psychological evaluation, not an exorcism. No one in the neighborhood remembers their parents dying or even moving away.

"I wish I hadn't read it. That's what I get for being nosey."

"They are psychopaths," I said. "That serious mental illness is beyond crazy. My mother told me that they don't feel things and only care about themselves."

"Yes, that sums it up. It's all in their file," Beth said.

She asked me if I wanted to read it, but I said, "No, thank you."

CHAPTER 69

Why Do Bad Things Happen?

Jesika's father had left on another top-secret mission to spy on a Russian ship from some coastline. She said that he would often talk about his missions at the dinner table, and she thought his stories were interesting, but when she went to repeat them, she couldn't remember all the details. I told her maybe it was because she wasn't really listening. When I asked if her sister and brother were okay, she said they were and that her mother was still angry and glad he was gone.

I spent the night at her house Friday night, and we had a *Moonalisa* party the next day. All the same kids were there. Jesika's mom had to go to work, so Pishoung made Jiffy Pop popcorn in a paper bag just like her mom had, and he put the blanket over the drapes to make the room dark. There was one thing different, though. He watched the movie with us. The featured film was *The Birds* by Alfred Hitchcock. Most of us liked the movie for its drama, but we didn't like it because he didn't give a reason for the birds to attack.

"When Melanie is in the diner talking to her father on the phone about the deadly birds in Bodega Bay, the man in the diner yells out, 'It's … the … end … of … the … world,' I said to my friends. "Why is it always the end of the world when something strange happens?"

The only kids that would attempt to answer that question were Douglas and Jesika.

Jesika answered first. "If you went outside right now and a bunch of birds started to peck you in your head, you would think it just might be the end of the world. That stuff never happens."

"Yeah," Douglas added, "a mother bird will sometimes protect its nest if you get too close to it." Then he said something ridiculous. "But what if it was a bunch of stinky buzzards or a big, nasty bird? You'd run for your life! And when the seagulls swoop down and knock over the guy at a gas pump and gas was pouring out of the hose, I knew a big explosion was coming! I like explosions!"

"You forgot about the man that threw the match down," I said.

"Oh, yeah," Douglas said.

Jesika said the birds attacked because they didn't like the lovebirds.

Irene said it was because of Mitch's jealous mother. "She just didn't want to see her son happy, so the birds attacked."

"So, they attack everybody," I said. "Why didn't they attack her?"

"Some birds don't get along with other birds in the wild. That's why Melanie got pecked in the head on the boat," Douglas responded.

Jayden said he wouldn't fall down like the girl in the movie. He would run like Superman.

Vicky said she was surprised that they didn't attack when they were walking to the car at the end of the movie, and they almost killed Melanie in the room.

"If it hadn't been for Mitch pulling her out of the room, she would have been shredded beef."

Sariah said she liked Mitch's ex-girlfriend, the teacher, played by Suzanne Pleshette, better than Melanie.

"Melanie should've been found with her eyeballs plucked out."

Tommy said he would've gotten his BB gun and picked the birds off one by one.

"Ah, sit down," Carlton piped in. "There ain't no damn reason. It was just a stupid ass movie!"

"It's not polite to say ass, young man. Watch your mouth in front of young ladies," Pishoung scolded. "Did you know this movie was inspired from real-life events? But don't let me interrupt. Please continue. Figure it out."

Our conversation about *The Birds* ended, and we all went outside. Jesika's Uncle Travis was coming over to pick up Jesika so she could get her hair done at 5:30 p.m. I was going with her because her Aunt Clara was going to do my hair too. I liked Aunt Clara. She didn't seem anything like Jesika had described her to me when we first met.

It was about 3:55 p.m. and we had nothing to do, so we decided to wait it out in the tree house.

"I'm glad we're going over to my Aunt Clara's house to have my hair done. She's gentle. My mother knows I'm tender-headed, but she acts like she doesn't care sometimes. She always says, 'This is what it takes to be beautiful.' I don't care about being beautiful or pretty."

I'd witnessed some of these exchanges, so I knew it was true. Her mother would say, "If you don't stay still, you're gonna make me burn your ear." Jesika would try to stay still for a moment and then go back to crying, "My legs, my legs. You're hurting my legs, Mama."

I decided to ask why her legs were hurting.

Sariah answered first, "Because she got nappy hair," and then walked out the door saying, "Jesika's got Zing Bop, Zing Bops."

She made me glad that I had brothers.

Jesika changed the subject by saying she didn't really like the movie.

"Yeah, neither did I… How come Sariah's not getting her hair done?"

"Because my mother washed and pressed her hair last week. She gets all kinds of things in her hair, and she sweats a lot… So, when do you want to go see Mattie?"

"It would be nice to go now, but we would just get in trouble. Besides, we don't have enough time," I said.

"We gotta go and see her, Marina. We gotta say our goodbyes."

"We can do it tomorrow. We'll go after church and ride our bikes."

"No one's gonna let us ride our bikes to church. Have you forgotten what your uncle said about going anywhere by ourselves?"

"If we go to church, I'll ask my dad. He won't mind."

We were still in the treehouse at 5:30 p.m. when Sariah climbed up the ladder and told us that Uncle Travis was at the house already. We walked into the house, and he was sitting at the dining room table talking to Jesika's mother.

"Are you two ready to go?" he asked.

"Yep! Thanks for picking us up, Uncle Travis."

"No problem!"

"Tell Clara to call me," Jesika's mother hollered as we walked toward the door. "I have some juicy gossip about a mutual friend of ours."

"That's all you two do is gossip. Don't you ever get tired of talking about other people?"

Jesika's mom didn't answer.

"Don't grow up to be like your mother," he admonished Jesika with a smile.

"I'm gonna be exactly like Mother," she shot back.

CHAPTER 70

Another Dead Girl

The fiery sun sank below the horizon, casting its final desperate rays across the sky, and a chill wind howled as we got into Uncle Travis's car.

"Did you hear that?" I asked Jesika.

"Hear what?"

"Never mind," I responded quickly.

I thought to myself, *What is this feeling?*

I shuddered with anticipation and dread. In the midst of this haunting moment, I felt an appreciation for Jesika's personality as she broke into an animated tale about her mom's beauty and easily distracted me from the stirrings of my overwhelm.

"Once when my mom was the playground monitor for a week, the other kids didn't believe she was my mom. They said things like, 'She's too pretty to be *your* mom.' To prove them wrong, I walked up to my mother and proudly asked if I could jump in while she turned the rope, which I did with perfect timing. Mom exclaimed, 'Now jump out, baby, and jump back in again. Let's show them how it's done!'" She smiled proudly and then paused, her face drooping. "You know, I would look just like my mother if it weren't for my father's wide nose."

I complimented her nose and then asked which actress she thought would best describe her mother.

"Elizabeth Taylor," she answered without hesitation.

Then she asked me the same question. I mentioned Barbara Stanwyck, whom I had only seen once on magazine covers at the grocery stores.

Our conversation was interrupted by Uncle Travis, who said he needed to make a quick stop at the liquor store. Bored with sitting in the car, Jesika ran inside to get a coke. When she came back, she said her uncle was in an intense conversation with the store clerk.

"We may be here for a while. My aunt is gonna cuss him out good."

CHAPTER 71

Face-to-face with Evil

Suddenly, we heard a scream, and four teenagers ran past us with horror-filled eyes, warning us about a body near an abandoned car on the dirt road. I urged them to call the police, but they just kept on running. So, Jesika and I went to check it out.

As we approached the abandoned car, we saw the body of a girl who had been dead for a long time.

Jesika was the first to point out that Taniya Greenwood's Converse sneakers had been placed on the dead girl's feet at the end of her yellow and green legs.

Aha! The Glasgow twins' signature!

We knew we had to call the police, so we headed back to the liquor store to use the phone and to get Uncle Travis.

"This must be the girl that owned the go-go boots," I surmised.

"How can you tell?" Jesika asked.

"Looking at her outfit. I can see she paid attention to detail … and the sneakers, well, they just don't go."

"Another girl," Jesika said. "This feels and smells like those stinking twins."

As we walked down the hill rapidly, I heard footsteps behind us. Before I could turn back to see who was following us, we were both suddenly grabbed from behind just before we reached the liquor store. With a hand over our mouths, they forced us up some stairs and into an apartment.

Jesika, being Jesika, bravely spoke out against them, but I tried to calm her down. I figured we didn't need to make matters worse.

The twins tied us up and stuffed their vile socks in our mouths.

My eyes wandered around their apartment, which reeked of malevolence. The air grew thick with tension and their insidious desire to kill us.

"I bet you're Nigel," I said, spitting the sock out of my mouth at the twin standing in front of me.

"W-r-o-n-g!" he said loudly. "I'm Fidel." He looked over at Jesika and taunted, "I bet you're Jesika. You two thought you were so smart, didn't you? Look where you are now. We were always three steps ahead of you and Detective Talbert, that baboon."

"Yeah, what a box of rocks," the other twin chimed in.

With seething anger, Jesika spat out her sock and yelled, "If I wasn't tied up in these ropes, I would make you eat your words, you cowards!"

"Little girl, little girl, you'd better be quiet or I'll have my brother break both your necks."

"What happened to you to make you so mean? I don't think Nigel is as mean as you are, Fidel." I tried to get them talking.

"He always does whatever I tell him to do, even when we were little," Fidel agreed.

"We had our own language," Nigel added with a laugh, "and it scared our mother. She thought we were possessed, so she locked us in the closet. Stupid woman."

"You two psychopaths are going to be locked up for life when our uncle gets here. St. Michael is already here, and I'm not scared of you two devils!"

There she goes, shooting her mouth off again. I groaned inwardly. *Where are you, Michael?*

I didn't know how we were going to get ourselves out of this one. Perplexed, my mind began to close in on me. This was unimaginable madness, and I began to cry.

Fidel responded to my tears, "You wanted to investigate. Now, you're here! What are you crying for?"

"Yeah, you need your mama's nipple?" Nigel's words dripped with venomous intensity. Their souls echoed a thousand tortured souls put together.

Suddenly, Nigel started laughing hysterically. I thought about Rachael, and I knew that they had something worse for us. They didn't like us enough to turn us into their pets.

"We warned your uncle you girls would be next," Fidel said.

"What are you talking about?" I asked.

"The note we left in Harriet's mouth…" said Nigel, still laughing.

I heard Uncle Travis calling our names, and Fidel said sharply, "If you cry out, I will slit your throat without batting an eye."

We remained quiet.

Turning to Nigel, he said, "Go get what is needed to take care of their bodies." He grabbed my chin and looked in my eyes, "*Your* bodies will never be found."

Our fate hung in the balance, tethered between life and death. I prayed that Uncle Travis would be worried enough to call my Uncle Lonny.

Nigel left and, through the window, I heard his audacity to speak to Jesika's uncle when he passed him on the street.

Fidel went into a bedroom.

"What do you think he is doing there?" Jesika whispered.

"I don't know…"

"Marina, we've gotta untie these ropes somehow and escape." After a few moments, her eyes lit up, "I've got my uncle's lighter in my pocket."

I shot her a suspicious look.

"I wasn't trying to steal it," she said frantically.

"Never mind, I'm glad you did. We gotta do this fast." We started to act simultaneously to move our chairs close together, and I managed to get the lighter out of her pocket. "I might burn you, Jesika."

"Don't worry about that. Just concentrate on the ropes," she braved.

I placed the lighter underneath her hand and flipped it. I could smell her flesh and the ropes, but Jesika didn't make a sound. Suddenly, her ropes were free from around her wrist.

"Hurry," I whispered. "When he comes out of the room, you gotta hit him with all your might. If you don't, we won't get another chance."

I tried my best to make my ropes appear to be tied.

Jesika picked up the small metal dining room chair and stood just beyond the door, far enough so he would not see her right away. Ten minutes went by, and he didn't make a sound.

"Maybe he's asleep. I'll make some noise."

I started moving the chair so it would scrape across the floor, but he didn't wake up.

"Marina, just scream as loud as you can!"

I did, and Fidel burst into the room.

I heard Jesika say, "Michael, we're in battle." And wham! She hit him with all her might. Then I jumped up and hit him again with my chair.

In the meantime, Jesika's uncle had called the police, and my uncle was quickly dispatched to the area. It was dark by the time he arrived at the liquor store, and Jesika's uncle was standing outside.

"I can't find them anywhere," he said. "Man, I've asked a couple of the other businesses, but no one has seen them."

The cashier told my Uncle Lonny about the two men that lived upstairs. He said they never talk to him but would come in the store and buy potato chips and soda. He would try to strike up a conversation with them, but they ignored him.

So, my uncle drew his gun and walked up the stairs, and with the weight of his body, forced the locked door open. We were standing there with Fidel lying on the floor. Jesika had hit him in his head, and I'd hit him in the back.

"Uncle!' I shouted. "The other twin will be back any moment. What do we do?"

He told us to sit back in the chairs and pretend like nothing had happened. He tied up Fidel and put him back in the bedroom.

"I want to get this bastard. I don't want him to escape."

"It's okay, Uncle. We're not afraid."

We sat back down in the chairs and waited. My uncle closed the curtain, so he could not be seen. It seemed like forever before the other twin walked into the apartment, holding a large bucket with a top on it.

"PUT THE BUCKET DOWN SLOWLY!" my uncle demanded, pointing his gun. "If you make any sudden moves, I'll blow your head off!"

Instead of doing what he had been instructed to do, Nigel threw the large bucket at my uncle. Uncle dodged it and fired his gun, striking Nigel in his shoulder.

The bucket bounced and the lid popped off, and a nasty smelling chemical began pouring out onto the floor. Jesika and I jumped onto the couch to avoid the liquid.

The acid was just about to reach Nigel's face when my Uncle lifted his body from the floor and began handcuffing him.

"You're under arrest for the murders of Mattie McDuffie, Harriet McDuffie, and Taniya Greenwood, the abduction of Rachael Evans, and the kidnapping of my nieces, Marina and Jesika."

Letting go of Nigel, who collapsed on the couch choking from fumes, my uncle told us to stand up on the couch and jump to him to avoid the acid. One at a time, we jumped into his arms, and he put us outside the door.

As Jesika and I walked down the stairs, I noticed the burn marks on her wrist and hands had already started to blister.

"I'm so sorry … so sorry for burning you."

My body started shaking, and the tears began to flow.

"It's okay, Marina," Jesika said. "We made it through."

CHAPTER 72

The True Hero

"**O**h, shit!" we said together in reaction to the scene we encountered at the bottom of the stairway. Every police officer and car had filled the parking lot. They stood vigilant, their fingers tightly gripping their rifles, ready to defend against any sudden move.

Cameras from multiple news channels were fixed on the scene, capturing every moment of the unfolding drama. My uncle came out of the apartment with one hand holding a handkerchief over his mouth and the other holding a handcuffed Nigel. He signaled Officers Tilman and Tisdale to retrieve Fidel.

"He's handcuffed to the bed. Be careful! There's acid on the floor in the living room. Cover your mouths."

They both gave Uncle Lonny a "good job" pat on the back as they passed him and quickly climbed the stairs. Minutes later, they brought Fidel out of the apartment and put him in the back of the squad car with his brother.

Amie Reynold, a familiar Channel 10 reporter, approached us with her microphone poised to capture our words. The world seemed to watch with bated breath, eager to hear our harrowing tale of survival straight from us.

"Tell us, how did you stumble upon the nightmare? What happened here?" She started with Uncle Travis.

Jesika's uncle's eyes filled with the mixture of pain and determination, and he spoke with a voice that resonated with the weight of the moment.

"We were passing by on our way to find solace in the liquor store," he replied, his voice tinged with raw emotion.

"Little did we know that evil was lurking in the apartment upstairs, waiting to strike."

Jesika, her gaze unwavering, continued the tale, "When we saw those terrified teenagers running down the hill, screaming about a dead body, we just couldn't idly stand by and do nothing. We had to confront the darkness head-on," she declared, her voice ringing with resolve.

My mind was still reeling with fear, but I added, "We mustered all our courage and went to check it out. And there, behind the abandoned car, lay her lifeless body. It was a haunting reminder of those boys' twisted madness roaming our streets and terrifying our neighborhood."

Amie nodded. Her face displayed a mixture of shock and admiration as she asked her next question, "And then, you were captured by these sinister men? Can you describe the horror you endured?"

Jesika's voice quivered slightly as she recounted the chilling moment.

"They ambushed us, overpowering us with brute force. Their malicious intentions were clear as they tied us up with rope and silenced us by stuffing their dirty socks in our mouths. We managed to spit them out," she finished with a bit of triumph.

I regained my composure and continued to give my account of the ordeal.

"We refused to give in to the darkness that surrounded us. Jesika had her uncle's lighter in her pocket, and it held the tiny flicker of hope we needed in our desperate situation. With unwavering perseverance, we set ourselves free from the clutches of our captors."

A sense of awe washed over the gathering crowd as they listened intently to our tale. The magnitude of our bravery and resilience began to vibrate, spreading like wildfire through the community.

Suddenly, our interview was interrupted by the sound of screeching tires. Dr. Caruso, the medical examiner, arrived on the scene. He surveyed the unfolding chaos.

"I see Detective Talbert has finally caught the culprits. Girls," he said looking directly at us, "where is the dead body?"

"It's on the dirt road up the hill, near the abandoned car," I answered, pointing.

"Do you want to come with me?"

"Nope," we answered at the same time. "We're going home to be kids."

"The weight of the world is no longer on your shoulders," he smiled. "You never faltered."

Uncle Lonny, overcome with relief, embraced us.

"You two are truly heroes," he said, his voice filled with pride and gratitude. "You fought against unimaginable odds and emerged victorious."

"Ahh, Uncle you're the true hero, and your bravery will be remembered forever."

Together, we pushed our way through the crowd and got into the back of my uncle's car. He put his siren on for us, like we were the stars of the Independence Day Parade.

As we passed the apprehended Glasgow brothers sitting in the back of another squad car, we put our thumbs in our ears, twisting them back and forth, distorting our faces, and sticking out our tongues.

The scene played out before the live camera crews, and a collective sigh of relief echoed through the streets of San Diego, mingling with the distant sound of the siren.

Stay Tuned

Marina and Jesika have more mysteries
to solve, and more to do in the crazy
world they're growing up in.

Continue the adventure with them at:
www.BollenbacherMysteries.com

About
Jessica D. Reddick

Raised in a devout Catholic home on Bollenbacher Street in San Diego, California, Jessica D. Reddick came of age during a precarious time in history. Nuclear bomb drills at school, the public assassination of a beloved president, and the promise of the civil rights movement formed the collective backdrop against which she developed her friendships, spirituality, and sense of meaning and purpose.

In addition to being a devoted spiritual seeker, mother of two wonderful children, and G-ma to two beautiful grandchildren, Jessica has developed two creative passions that she pursues full-time in her retirement.

A gifted self-taught musical composer, Jessica weaves together harmonies that transcend genres. Jazz, blues, dance, hiphop, and the enchanting melodies of the exotic middle east are effortlessly alchemized into masterpieces that resonate with the souls of her listeners.

Bollenbacher Street Mysteries was born of Jessica's inspiration to share some of the most precious and challenging moments of her youth while imparting hard-earned lessons in faith and friendship. She believes that by embracing diverse perspectives, we can transcend the limitations of our own upbringing, forgive, and appreciate the rich tapestry of humanity and belief that exists around the world, recognizing the inherent value in each individual's quest.

Acknowledgments

I express my heartfelt gratitude for Marina, my childhood friend whose loving spirit accompanied me as I wrote this book.

I extend my thanks to powerful women who consistently provide strength in my life: Tiffany, my daughter, and my friends Queenae, Johanna, and Jeannetta.

A special acknowledgment goes to Valorie, who encourages me to persist in my journey.

Thank you to the team at Saved By Story Publishing. I really appreciate all the encouragement and hard work you've put in to make this book powerful, beautiful, and ready for its readers.

Warm appreciation also to my parents, Willy and Rita, for always encouraging me in all my endeavors throughout life.

To my siblings, Sherry and Keith, thank you for providing plenty of material to write about. My brother Eric, for your support.

And, last but not least, to all the kids who grew up on Bollenbacher Street, thank you for being the inspiration behind the story.

www.ingramcontent.com/pod-product-compliance
Lightning Source LLC
Chambersburg PA
CBHW021037310726

48969CB00006B/1694